THE BIRD THAT

b

Grace Mattioli

Library of Congress Cataloging-in-publication Data
Mattioli, Grace, 1965-
The Bird that Sang in Color/ Grace Mattioli
p. cm.
1.Families-fiction 2. New Jersey-fiction 3. Italian-Americans-fiction 4. Self-actualization-fiction
I. Title   PS3556.R352   813.54

Cover art by Vincent Mattioli

Dedication

For my sister, Annamae, who was the best example I've known of how to live

What pictures will you have of yourself by the end of your life? By pictures, I mean drawings, not photographs. A photograph is easy. A drawing is earned. I began contemplating this question only in recent years, but once I started, I couldn't stop, and these days, I'm always seeing my life in pictures. For this, I thank my brother, Vincent. He taught me how to untie my hands so that I could be free to draw. He taught me to draw my own pictures instead of copying somebody else's. He taught me to use markers because colorful pictures are better than those that blend into the background. And with his unintentional guidance, I made some really great drawings in the style of his own art that hangs on my walls. I look up at it and remember a long-ago time, when he and I sat in his old room in our old house listening to albums. It was before I devised the great plan that would become my life. A time before Frank, my children, my grandchildren. Before I went to college and before I taught in college. It was when I could see the world for what it is and my brother in all humble greatness.

CHAPTER ONE: 1970

THE GOLDEN GARDEN BIRD OF PEACE were the words painted on the wall in Vincent's room. I thought Dad would have painted over them because he couldn't stand all that "hippie crap." Beside the words hung a bunch of paintings he made. He painted trees, mountains, rivers, flowers, and people with real-life expressions that made them more than just pictures. They were alive, and they told stories.

Some of his paintings were abstract, my favorite being one that looked like a kaleidoscope with no beginning and no end and colors that bounced off the canvas like a beautiful neon sign sparkling against a black sky. I could stare at it all day. I went between staring at it and the album cover before me—*Let It Be* by the Beatles. Vincent sat by the record player, dressed in his usual Levi's, T-shirt, and Converse high-tops, bent towards the revolving album, listening intently, his head of black curly hair moving back and forth, his right foot tapping the hardwood floor, keeping rhythm to the Fab Four.

Finally, he turned his head away from the stereo and said to me, "I can't believe this is it." His face was serious and gloomy, and I didn't know what he was talking about, but I pretended that I did because I'd never let my cool down around Vincent. It was because of him that I knew so much about rock and roll, which made me pretty sure that I was the coolest eighth-grade girl in the whole town and possibly in the whole state of New Jersey.

"I know," I said seriously.

"I mean, I just never thought the Beatles would break up." He shook his head with disappointment.

"So, this is their last album, then?"

"Well, yeah," he said, like I should have known better.

"Hey, check this out, Donna." With the speed of a light switch flicking on, he turned into an entirely different person, no longer sad and gloomy but light and happy. He showed me a drawing he made of an old lady sitting on a chair with half of her body missing, and it looked as if the missing half was on the other side of an invisible door. She wore a mysterious smile as if she knew some extraordinary truth.

"Where's the other half of her body?" I said.

"I don't know," he said, grinning. "You tell me."

"Wow." I sat there, trying to wrap my head around this while listening to the song playing. Just as I was about to figure something out about the picture, and just as I was really getting into the song, he took the needle off, turned the album over, and put the needle on the first song on the other side, a tendency he had that bothered the hell out of our brother, Carmen.

He scratched his head and looked up, his eyes penetrating the ceiling, deep in thought. He resembled Mom with his olive skin, Roman nose, and black curls, and was the only one of us who got her curly hair. The rest of us had straight hair. Mine was super long—to the bottom of my back—and I wore it parted in the middle and was certain that I was wearing it that way long before it was the style.

Vincent was also taller than the rest of us at over six feet. Dad said he took after his own dad in stature. I never knew Grandpa Tucci because he died before I was born, but I was told he was called "Lanky" because he was tall and skinny. I was pretty thin myself and had a bottomless pit. People would say that all my eating would catch up with me one day, but that never stopped me from eating ice cream every day after school. Breyers butter almond was my favorite.

Vincent listened to the music with pure attention, like there was nothing else in the world as George sang *I, me, mine, I, me, mine, I, me, mine.* He was probably trying to figure out what the song was about or how he could play it on his guitar. His acoustic guitar sat in the corner of his room. He had the smallest room in the house, but it seemed like the biggest because it was its own self-contained universe. I felt like I could be on the other side of the world without ever leaving his room.

His paintings and drawings covered the walls. A bunch of leather-bound cases of albums colored red and black and bone sat on the floor between a stereo and a wooden desk with piles of books and sketchbooks on top. Comic books, pens, and paintbrushes were scattered on the floor like seashells on the sand.

I shared a room with my younger sister, Nancy, and she insisted on having the room be as pink as possible. She was the youngest, so she always got her way. On top of making our room a sickening pink paradise, she had a doll collection with faces that really creeped me out, and she started pushing over my beloved books on our shelves to make room for her dolls. A doll named Lucinda with blond hair and a blue satin dress was shoved up against two of my favorites— *Animal Farm* and *To Kill a Mockingbird.*

"Check this out, Donna," Vincent said, emerging from his music-listening trance. He took a skinny metal whistle out of a plastic case. "Got it at the music store in town."

"Neat. Some kind of flute?" I said.

"A pennywhistle." He had a big smile that stretched from one side of his face to the other. "Or sometimes called a tin whistle."

"I wish I could play an instrument," I said. "Just one." I was the only one in our family that didn't play an instrument. Mom wanted me to learn ballet instead because she said I had a dancer's body. I liked it all right and stayed with it until my teacher put me on toe, and the wooden shoes imprisoned my feet and made them ache hours after class ended.

"Have it."

"Really?!"

"Sure." He started fishing in one of his desk drawers for something.

"Thanks, Vincent." No response. He just kept on with his searching. I looked at the tin instrument wondering how I'd learn to play it, when he poked his head up and gave me an instructional songbook for it. I went through it seeing musical notation for simple songs like "Twinkle Twinkle Little Star." It was all new territory for me, but I knew I could learn it and thought I could go anywhere from there. I saw myself playing with Vincent as he strummed the guitar, playing on the street for money, playing in a small orchestra of other penny whistlers. Just then, Mom called out from the kitchen.

"Dinner's ready!" I didn't care that my fantasy was interrupted because I was starving. Vincent was always up for eating and was the biggest eater I knew. He seemed especially hungry because he was walking to the kitchen really fast. Even when he walked fast, he looked cool. He walked with a bounce in his step, his head bobbing back and forth like he was keeping beat to a song that only he could hear. I tried to walk like him once, but I ended up looking like some kind of uncoordinated monkey. I walked like Dad who moved fast and forward-leaning, like he was continually running late for something.

The kitchen smelled of garlic and fish. It was Friday, and Mom always cooked fish on Fridays. A big flat bowl with hand-painted flowers was filled with spaghetti, calamari and gravy—more commonly known as tomato sauce. My older sister, Gloria was setting the large wooden table that sat in the center of the kitchen. She wore her hair tucked neatly behind her ears and a black-and-tan argyle vest that fit snug on her shapely body. Her face had the usual serious, troubled look on it like something was wrong. Anthony—the oldest in the family—was away at college, and Nancy was at a sleepover, so the table was set for only six.

Mom was at the sink, getting a salad together. Above the sink was a long window that looked out onto our backyard, its ledge covered with little ladybug statues, which Mom loved because they meant good luck. She wore a red-and-white apron over a straight skirt and boots and took long, swift strides around the kitchen. Watching her get dinner together was like watching a performance. She'd put on her apron instead of a costume. The music played: the chopping of vegetables, the clanging of metal spoons against pots, and the sweet sound of pouring. She'd dance around, gathering ingredients, sautéing, stirring, occasionally turning towards us—the audience—to say something or laugh with us so that we'd feel a part of the show. She presented her perfect meals like works of art, displaying them on the table, and we'd applaud by eating— grabbing, twirling, chewing—until we couldn't fit anymore in.

Dad was opening up one of his bottles of homemade wine. I had a sip once, and it went down my throat like an angry snake. He leaned on the table like he needed it to support him with his eyes half-shut and his black-and-gray hair falling forward in his face. In his tiredness, he didn't speak, but even when he was quiet, he was loud, and whenever he walked into a room, everybody knew it, even if he didn't say a word.

"Carmen, come and eat!" Mom called out.

In seconds, Carmen appeared in a foyer off the kitchen, flannel shirt, jeans, hair smashed against one side of his head. He yawned and stretched like he just woke from a nap. Everybody took their places and started grabbing stuff. Everybody except Dad that is, who was always less concerned with food and more concerned with whatever he was drinking. I went for the salad as soon as Mom put it on the table for fear of not getting any because Gloria always hogged it.

"Wanna shoot a game of pool after dinner?" Vincent said to Carmen as he took a giant-size bite of his bread. We just got this really nice pool table in our basement, which Dad claimed Minnesota Fats once played on.

"Sure," Carmen said, as he sprinkled Parmesan cheese on his spaghetti.

"Can you do me a favor while you're down there?" Dad said to Carmen, as he held his hands up in the air like he was holding an invisible beach ball. "Do something with that drum set. I want it out of here."

"I'm gonna learn to play, Dad," Carmen said.

"You've been saying that for six months now," Mom said. "And how'd you get that thing anyway?"

"I traded Kenny some comic books," Carmen said.

"That's it?" Mom said as she ate her salad.

"Well, they were some really valuable comic books," Carmen said.

"You told me his parents didn't want it there," Gloria said. She then turned to Mom and asked her if she could go to her friend's house after dinner. Mom said she could go as long as she was home by nine.

"Why don't you ask your father?" Dad said to Gloria. "I guess the only thing I'm good for is paying all the bills." He then turned to Carmen and said, "You have to get that out of here. You can't be playing drums in here. Why do you want to bother the neighbors like that anyway?" He was one to talk about disturbing the neighbors. At least once a week, he'd drink too much and go on a screaming rampage over nothing. Sometimes, he'd scream so loud that one of the neighbors would call the cops, and then the cops would come in our house and start calming him down, saying "C'mon, Cosimo, take it easy."

"Oops," Vincent said as he knocked over his glass of water on the table.

"Why don't you watch what you're doing?!" Dad said to Vincent.

"I didn't get them to disturb the neighbors," Carmen said to Dad. "I got them to play."

"Yeah, he should play the drums," Vincent said in a matter-of-fact tone as he cleaned up the spill with his napkin. "He's gotta play the drums. He has natural rhythm." He put a huge forkful of spaghetti in his mouth.

"You know who has natural rhythm, don't you?" Dad said, like he was well aware of the answer. I sure was. "Your father." He twirled spaghetti on the side of his plate. "I played trumpet for over twenty-five years." His stories always seemed to change, with the numbers always getting bigger. Last time I heard this story, it was almost twenty years, and the time before that, it was fifteen years. But even when he talked nonsense, he sounded smart and authoritative because his voice was so deep and sturdy.

"You know who else has natural rhythm?" Carmen said. "Grandma. She's always saying she could have been an opera star, so you and Grandma have a lot in common." He was talking about Mom's mom, who Dad couldn't stand. Dad would call Grandma a grandstander. She didn't think much of him either. I'm not sure why they didn't get along because they were a lot alike. Carmen was always trying to get Dad's goat, and for some reason, he always got away with it, maybe because Dad got a kick out of him.

"Don't get wise," Dad said to Carmen, smirking.

"Ah shit," I said, getting up from the table and running towards the sink. I spilled gravy on my plaid bell-bottoms, and they were my favorite pair of pants.

"Watch your mouth!" Mom and Dad said at the same time. I said it under my breath, so I didn't think they could hear. Besides, I thought that the possibility of ruining my favorite pants was worth a curse word or two, and besides that, we all cursed, except Carmen. Dad was the worst—expletives rolled off his tongue like raindrops sliding down a sidewalk curb. I rubbed the stain with hot water and dish liquid and was relieved that it came out.

"Did you ever hear Grandma sing?" Gloria said with a sardonic smile. She then started to sing some wordless song like a hysterical opera star.

"Enough," Mom said. "Who stole my napkin?" Mom and Carmen played a game at dinner in which one sneakily stole the other one's napkin. They sat right next to each other, so it was easy to play.

"And anyway, he's got an instrument—the violin," Dad said to Vincent, who stared calmly into the space in front of him, chewing his food.

"He needs more than one instrument," Vincent said. His voice was deep like Dad's but not a fraction as serious and stern.

"Ah," Dad said, waving his arm in the air. "He needs to study his books, so he can make something out of himself. Maybe he'll want to become a lawyer like Anthony does. Now, he has a good head on his shoulders."

Vincent stopped eating and looked down with sad eyes. I knew what he was thinking. I could read everybody in our family, especially him. He was thinking about what Dad said about Anthony having a good head on his shoulders and about Carmen studying his books, so he could make something out of himself. Dad always spoke a weird language. How did a person make something out of himself? What he meant by that is that Carmen would be successful if he studied hard in high school and took up something in college like business, so he could get into something like real estate, which is what Dad did or even better, pre-law, like Anthony was studying.

But Vincent didn't want to do any such thing. He wanted to go to art school. Dad said it would be a waste of time and money and that if he wanted to go so bad, he could, but that he wouldn't pay a penny. Carmen said he wanted to go just because some girl he liked was going, but I knew he was wrong. He wanted to go because he loved to make art. I wanted him to go because he was the best artist I knew.

Just as I was trying to think of something to say to change the topic, Vincent got up and said he didn't feel so good and wasn't hungry. I knew that was bullshit because he never lost his appetite.

"Why did you say that, Dad?" I said after Vincent left. "You know how he wants to go to art school."

"Don't talk back to your father," he said as automatic as a machine gun firing. I didn't think I was talking back because he didn't say anything to me first. "And what does one thing have to do with the other anyway?" he continued. I couldn't answer the question because he told me not to talk back, so I was glad when Mom explained the connection to him.

"He's too sensitive, Gilda. How's he going to get anywhere in life?" Dad said to Mom. "And let me tell you something. My father used to say in Italian 'Those who hate you make you laugh. Those who love you make you cry.'" I knew this one by heart. It was his favorite thing to say that his dad used to say in Italian.

"It's the same with you studying piano in college," Dad said to Mom. "You should have studied history." He turned to the rest of us and said, "She won the award in the whole state of Ohio in some big history competition. It was her parents that thought she should study music."

"Maybe Vince should study acting," Carmen said, scraping the rest of his plate clean. "Remember he acted in that Shakespeare play?"

"Ah," Dad said, waving his hand in disgust. "Acting, art, music. It's all the same."

"Why did your parents think you should study piano?" I asked Mom.

"Because Grandma loved music," Mom said, standing up. Grandma, after all, named Mom Gilda (with a soft *G*) after a character in a famous opera. She then added, "They were from the old country."

Dad still had that look that said that Mom's parents were stupid for making her study music instead of history, so I asked him what was wrong with studying music and art because he seemed to have something against that sort of thing.

"Ah," he said, getting up from the table. "You're too young to understand. Ask me that when you're old enough to know something about the world." Then, he looked in Mom's direction and said, "My parents were from the old country too, but they knew better." With that, he left the kitchen and headed into the living room, where he sat for the rest of the night, in his same old chair under the painting of the pope, drinking, smoking, and listening to Frank Sinatra on the radio.

Saturday morning was cleaning time and Mom turned on an album and sang and danced to "Blame it on the Bosa Nova" as she dusted. We all had our own designated duties, mine being the bathrooms. I know most people would find cleaning bathrooms gross, but I found the job strangely gratifying, and I was really good at it. So good in fact that after finishing with them, I'd even make excuses to walk by them just, so I could admire my fine work.

We had two bathrooms—a green one and a yellow one, which was attached to Mom and Dad's room, where Nancy sat painting her nails, making careful little strokes with the tiny brush, like she was painting the wings of a fly. As I got closer to her, I saw that she was using my copy of *Catcher in the Rye* to paint them on!

"You're going to get nail polish on my book!" I grabbed the book from under her hand, which made the red paint smear on the top of her thumb.

"Look what you did!" She looked up at me with mean eyes stabbing through her poker straight bangs, her evil stare clashing frantically with her pastel flowered bathrobe.

"Well, you shouldn't have been using my book to paint your nails on, so serves you right." I walked out with my book and my head held high.

"Pretty girls paint their nails!" she shouted, so I could hear her as I walked down the long hallway, past a big, wooden crucifix with Jesus nailed to it and blood dripping down. "That's why you'll never be as pretty as me!" She was always saying that kind of shit. I'd just let it roll off my back like fine grain sand.

I grabbed a sweater from my closet and went outside. The sun was a small white ball floating behind clouds that hung heavy in the balmy air. I walked through Mrs. Capelli's yard to go to my friend Mary Ellen's house and found her lying outside in a hammock that her dad put up in their backyard. He tied it to two trees that just happened to be close enough to each other, so that it fit perfectly.

"Hey," I said, flopping down across from her in the hammock. She moved over and said hi without looking up from her copy of *Teen Beat*.

I stared up at the tree branches, that were covered with green leaves, and over at the cherry trees that grew in their garden, remembering the time, years ago, Mary Ellen and I picked and ate white cherries from one of them. I wondered if there were any doughnuts in her house because her mom would get them on Saturday mornings. She looked up from her magazine and started telling me about this guy named Joey who she liked.

"So, I heard Joey's going to give me his ring," she said, making a toothless smile, her hazel eyes shining against her freckled face.

"Oh neat." I tried to seem interested, but my words fell flat on the air. "Do you like him?"

"What do you think?" She put the magazine down long enough to give me one of those *isn't-it-*

obvious looks. "He's only like the cutest guy in class, and he wears the coolest clothes in the world." She went to public school, where people got to wear regular clothes. I'd been stuck in my blue plaid Catholic school uniform since first grade. Next year, in high school, it would be even worse—a gray plaid skirt with a maroon polyester blazer or a vest for the warmer weather.

"Cool," I said.

"Do you want to go inside and play pinball?" she said. That's right, they had a pinball machine in their house.

"Sure," I agreed happily, anxious to see if a box of doughnuts was sitting on her kitchen counter.

Every Saturday night, Mom and Dad went out to dinner at some fancy, old tavern where they served lobster and crab, and a brass band played the kind of songs that their generation liked to dance to. Mom would put on a nice dress over one of her lacy, luxurious slips and make herself up in front of her long, brown dresser that was crammed with perfume, makeup, jewelry, and a black-and-white portrait of herself that was taken when she was sixteen and in her older sister's wedding. Her beautiful soft face was framed with black wavy curls, and she looked as serene as a swan. I sat on the green velvet chair in their room watching her get ready.

"What are you going to do tonight?" she asked me as she put on lipstick.

"I have a lot of homework to do," I said, kind of sulky.

"Honey, it's Saturday night."

"I know but—"

"Order a pizza from Bruno's," she said, giving me a ten-dollar bill. Then, she whispered in my ear, "Don't tell your father."

"Thanks, Mom," I said, slipping the money in my back pocket.

As soon as they left, I went to tell everyone that I had pizza money, and we quarreled over what to order before deciding to get one pie with pepperoni and the other with mushrooms. Gloria said she'd pick it up, and Nancy said she'd go with her. Vincent told me and Carmen that we had to hear the new Jethro Tull album, so we all went into his room, and Carmen and I looked at the album cover while Vincent turned it on. It was called *Benefit* and Vincent said it was one of the best things he ever heard in his life.

"I like *Stand Up*," Carmen said, not taking his stare off the album cover. "I think that's their best."

"You're wrong," Vincent said. "Plus, you haven't even heard this one yet."

"I'm hearing it now and I like it, but I think *Stand Up* is better," Carmen said. Vincent just shook his head like Carmen didn't know any better. I didn't feel like getting caught up in their difference, so I didn't say anything and just listened to the album. I loved it right away. It took me out of myself and let me forget where I was and even who I was, one song seamlessly slipping into the next. A perfect album. I was sure Vincent was right, but I still didn't get involved.

The next morning, we all piled into Mom's car to go to church. I prayed that the sermon wouldn't go on as long as usual, but my prayers went unanswered. I hung on to the sweet thought of doughnuts that I was determined to get to before Nancy poked a bunch of them trying to figure out what was inside. There was a lot to do at mass—sit, stand, kneel, genuflect, listen, sing, pray, line up to get communion, get communion, walk back from communion to kneel some more, then stand, sit, pray, sing, make the sign of the cross a bunch of times, make little crosses on our forehead, lips, and chest with our right thumbs. But even with all that, the mass dragged on, and the hard-wooden benches were about as comfortable as cement.

Mom looked like she was in her glory as she sang "Make Me a Channel of Your Peace." She was a model Catholic: at church every Sunday, even when she was sick; she wouldn't be caught dead without the golden medallion of Mary she got when she was a young girl; and every summer we'd take a trip up to Quebec, so she could crawl up the stone steps of Sainte-Anne-de-Beaupré on her knees. We'd drive up listening to 8-track tapes, sleeping in the car while Mom or Dad drove, stopping for picnics at rest stops along the way. We'd stay at this three-story hotel in Montreal that had a pool and a restaurant where we'd sneak out for late-night tuna fish sandwiches. We'd walk the cobblestone streets, eat cheese fondue in some quaint old restaurant, watch the royal policemen in bright red uniforms line up and move like giant toy soldiers.

I glanced at Vincent to see him listening to the priest as if he were talking about something really interesting. I tried to pay attention, but the priest spoke in a monotone voice that made the sermon extra boring. I caught something about money. The church needed money. That I got.

I decided to make the time pass by thinking about how I could help Vincent with his art school ambition. I knew that I couldn't get through to Dad. Most of the time, I couldn't even talk to him because he'd accuse me of talking back. Vincent sure couldn't talk to Dad. A great wall lived between them. I'd have to talk to Mom about talking to Dad, although he didn't really listen to her either. He didn't really listen to anybody. But still, she was my best hope.

Mass finally ended, and we all piled back into Mom's car and drove home. On the way home, we stopped at the market and then at the bakery for doughnuts. The bakery was in the heart of town, a small building with walls made of glass, so people could look in and see all the pies and cakes when they walked by. After the bakery, we went home and pulled into our long driveway to see Dad outside washing his white Cadillac, which glistened in the sun with streaks of iridescence.

"How come Dad never goes to church?" Gloria said.

"He said he doesn't have to go because he's old," Nancy said.

"I thought that was when most people started going to church," Carmen said. "I always see old people at church."

"Say elderly," Mom said. "Not old people."

We all got out of the car, greeted Dad as we walked by him, and went inside through the back door, which opened into the kitchen. Everybody went off to their bedrooms to change out of their church clothes, but I stayed in the kitchen with Mom, so I could talk to her in private.

"Hey, Mom," I said. "Do you think you can talk to Dad about letting Vincent go to art school? I know how bad he wants to go, and he's like the best artist I know and—"

"All right, Donna." She looked at me with unhopeful eyes. "I'll talk to him, but I can't make any promises."

"I really appreciate it, Mom."

She smiled gratefully and put a pot of coffee on. I left to change my clothes and went back in the kitchen to find Nancy sticking her fingers in what looked like a jelly doughnut, which I fortunately didn't give a shit about. I grabbed the only chocolate cream one before she could get her hands on it, and as I bit into it, Gloria and Carmen came in and both said to me at the same time, "You got the best one." After I finished, I went to Vincent's room and suggested that we go for a walk because I thought it would be best to be out of the house while Mom and Dad talked.

We stopped by the kitchen so that he could grab a couple poked doughnuts, and we went outside, where the air was still and smelled of hyacinths. We passed by our brick flower box where all our tulips bloomed—pink, purple, yellow, and red. When we got to the end of the driveway, I stared at our camel brick ranch house, long and flat as if it was stretched by a gigantic machine to get it that way. The yard in front of the house consisted of a small field of freshly mown grass and a couple trees that turned white in the spring and orange in the fall. It was pretty big compared to the other yards in the neighborhood but still not big enough to shield the neighbors from the noise and commotion that came from our house.

The neighbors on all three sides of us were always complaining about something. Mr. Demayo in the back complained that our dogs barked too loud and too much. (We had two sweet beagles that Dad would take hunting.) Mrs. Capelli on the right side complained that our basketball always bounced too close to her side-window, and Mrs. Luca to the left side of us complained that Carmen, whose window faced their backyard, played his music too loud, and of course, all three of them complained when Dad was on one of his yelling streaks.

As we walked down the street, I hoped that someone in my class would drive by and see me walking with my cool, big brother. Vincent stared at the sky, and I looked at the houses. We passed by my favorite one on the street made of gray stone with white trim and a turret. It sat proud in the middle of the block, the closest thing to a mansion in our little town and belonged to Mr. Galetta, some really wealthy guy—a lawyer or a doctor or something like that. He took his family on all these vacations to places like Paris and the Virgin Islands.

"What do you think of that house?" I ask Vincent as we pass it by.

"Huh? What?"

"That house," I said, pointing back at the house.

"Oh yeah, it's all right. I like that one on the corner of Maple and Fourth. That old red house."

"You mean the house with the chipped paint? The one that looks like it's about to fall down?"

"Yeah, that one." He didn't care about defending his weird answer.

"You're kidding, right?"

"No, that's a real good house."

"That's crazy, Vincent."

He hunched over and laughed, hiding the lower part of his face behind his hand.

The houses went on for a few blocks, and then the downtown began on the same street. Downtown had everything you needed, or at least that's what Dad always said. A grocery store, a pharmacy, a stationery store, a bank and of course, our beloved bakery. Vincent said he wanted to stop by the only clothing store in town, called Melinski's, to see if they had any new Levi's.

We entered the store that smelled of fabric and cardboard, a long, narrow place crowded with clothes stacked high in piles on tables and in shelves. It was lit with fluorescent lights that buzzed on and off like dying bees. I buried my head in some shirts in the girl's section, and when I looked up and around the store, I couldn't see Vincent anywhere, so I went outside and to find him sitting on a bus stop bench and said, "Hey, why didn't you tell me you were leaving?"

"Huh?" he said, "Oh sorry." I could tell he had something on his mind and assumed it must be art school. I wondered how it was going with Mom and Dad at home and hoped that Dad was staying calm and seeing the light. Before I could think about it anymore, Vincent was up from the bench and walking down the street, so I followed. We walked to the end of the main street and crossed the railroad tracks before turning back to go home.

As soon as we got in the door, I heard Dad yelling from his and Mom's room, "What's he going to do with an art degree?! Wipe his—"

"Cosimo! It's Sunday!" Mom said. Then, I heard one of them close the door to their bedroom, and from that point on, I could barely make out what they were saying, although Dad's voice occasionally rose up to blast through the closed door and the two rooms between the kitchen, where we were, and their bedroom.

"I got news for you," he said. "When I was his age, I was already a success. A self-made one too. He'll never be a success. He's too lazy for one thing." Vincent heard this but didn't seem fazed.

After this comment, Dad's voice sunk again, so I just imagined him continuing to make his point and saying things like "It never ends" and "Let me tell you something" while Mom pleaded despairingly. Eventually Dad shouted, "Well, maybe he should just pack his bags and move out, then!"

At that, Vincent left the room with an angry stare that was such a rarity for him that he looked like he was wearing a mask. I was tempted to go and follow him, but I stayed put and let him have his space. I felt pretty sure that he wasn't taking Dad's advice and packing his bags because he didn't have any place to go, and I didn't think he even had any bags or any proper suitcases that is. Dad came into the kitchen, huffing and puffing, taking furious footsteps right by me, like I was invisible. He got in his car, slammed the door shut, and zoomed down the driveway. Mom came in the kitchen shortly after, looking tired and defeated and said, "Well, I tried," and then lit a cigarette.

"Thanks, Mom. I really appreciate it, and I know Vincent does too."

"Why do you think art school is such a great idea anyway?" Unlike Dad, Mom thought I was capable of thoughts and opinions, even though I was just a kid.

"He's a great artist. And he wants to study art."

"People don't always know what's good for them. I'm not so sure I'm crazy about my son being a starving artist either."

"But Vincent's really good."

"A lot of them are really good." She paused and looked up at the ceiling and said, "Sometimes what you want to do isn't what you should do." She went downstairs in the basement, probably to do laundry.

I thought she had a point with the whole starving artist thing. I imagined Vincent really skinny, dressed in rags and living on the street, like I saw people do in Philadelphia. It made me so sad when I saw these people living like rats. Envisioning my own brother as one of them made me want to cry. I kept trying to get that cool, big brother image back in my head, but the sad starving one kept pushing the cool one out. I wanted to be angry at the starving Vincent for pushing the cool Vincent out, but I felt so sorry for him.

I heard his footsteps coming towards the kitchen, slow and heavy, as if he was carrying something big. Sure enough, he was. He appeared in the doorway with his dresser in his arms.

"What's going on?!" I said. "Are you leaving and taking your dresser with you? How are you going to carry that all the way to wherever you're going? You don't drive, and even if you did, you can't drive Mom's or Dad's cars. Where are you going anyway?"

"I'm moving my stuff out to the porch," he said with a deadpan face.

"Why?!" I said, and then without giving him a chance to answer, screamed, "That's crazy! That makes no sense! How is that going to do anything?!"

He didn't respond. He just kept moving his stuff outside on our front porch. Did I mention that our house was on a really busy street with constant traffic and trucks—big Mack trucks?! That made the whole thing even more insane. But he moved all his stuff onto the porch and started living out there like it was completely normal.

He lived there for a whole week surprising me by how long he could last outside, not so much because of all the noise and because it got chilly at night but because there was no outlet for him to plug his stereo into. But once he made his mind up about something, he stuck with it. Even if we didn't have a covered porch, he would have probably stayed out there all week, unbothered by getting soaked in the April showers.

People drove by doing double takes, and Mom said this would cause an accident and that then Vincent would be sorry. I was sure that the bizarre act would make Dad crazed with anger, but he wasn't for some reason. In fact, he even seemed amused. Mom made Vincent come in for dinner every night, and he just sat there and made everyone uncomfortable. Everyone, except Dad that is, who acted like he couldn't care less about his silent protest.

I went to visit him out on the porch every day he was out there, but it wasn't the same as visiting him in his room where we'd play albums, and I could look at his paintings. He did crack his guitar out a bunch and spent the rest of his time reading and painting. He seemed oblivious to all the traffic and rubbernecking of the people driving by. In a way, he seemed to like it out there and might have even preferred it to being inside.

CHAPTER TWO: 1973

"You gotta hear this album," Vincent said, holding up an album cover by one of his favorite bands—The Incredible String Band. It had a bunch of people standing beneath a tree, dressed in Renaissance-era clothing.

He was home from college for Thanksgiving break. He looked like an entirely different person than he did only three years ago, with his hair being the most obvious difference. It was huge with big black wavy curls and frizz that grew out instead of down. Mom started growing hers too, and she said she wasn't going to cut it until he cut his, but I thought she'd give in. He got skinny and dressed in overalls and work boots, and I couldn't decide if he looked like Goofy or a hippie from *Hee Haw*.

We sat in his room, which also looked completely different. He took all his stuff with him when he went to college. That was a sad day for me. Mom wouldn't let me come with them because there was no room for me in the car. I kept coming out to the car with more stuff for him to take to stall their departure.

"You forgot to bring tea bags with you," I'd said, running out to the car. Mom had the motor running. I'd opened one of the backseat doors and put the tea box inside one of the boxes that was full of his stuff.

"We have to go now, Donna," Mom had said to me, sounding annoyed. "You know, I still have to come all the way back tonight."

"All right," I'd said. "Bye, Mom. Bye, Vincent. Don't forget to write!"

He'd waved and made a smile that looked strained, almost painful, and I could tell he was nervous. I'd watched the yellow-and-brown station wagon go down the driveway and the road until it disappeared. Then, I went into his room and just stared at his paintings and tried to keep myself from crying. Carmen didn't want to move into it because he'd liked his own room better, so I'd asked Dad if I could, but he'd said I couldn't because he'd wanted to use it for his home office while Vincent was at college.

"He can stay here when he comes home for breaks," Dad had said to me. "When he's away, the space will be my home office." Within a week, he'd taken all Vincent's paintings down and painted over the letters on his wall. I'd wished I could have stopped him, but I was at school when it happened. I'd come home one day, and it was all done. He'd put the paintings in a dark corner of our basement that stank of mold. I'd rescued them and crammed them into my closet.

Vincent's room became a barren space that smelled of fresh paint—a bright white that looked like the color of a hospital room. All of him was gone, and I couldn't spend any time there without getting depressed. I was so mad at Dad that one day, when he wasn't home, I'd scratched his *Nights in Italy* album with my nails. I thought I'd feel good about it, but I'd felt nothing but guilt for destroying one of the few things that seemed to give him joy.

I looked on top of Vincent's desk to see a textbook entitled *Plato's Republic,* which must have been related to his major—philosophy. I asked him why he chose that as a major, and he said, "I just want to find out what it's all about."

"I don't get it."

"I get to study these old-time philosophers who wrote about what it's all about. Life, that is." He went on naming a bunch of them and said Aristotle was his favorite.

"Why?"

"He had a lot to say about a lot of things, like happiness. He thought it should be like the main goal in life." Philosophy sounded really interesting, and I would have considered majoring in it, but my heart was set on majoring in English. I loved literature and wanted to teach it in college one day.

"Check this out, Donna." He took out a stringed instrument I never saw before and said it was called a dulcimer. It was wooden, oblong-shaped with curves on either side and a fretboard down the middle.

"Oh, that's beautiful. How do you play it?"

"With some of them you have to hammer the strings with this little hammer thing, but some of them, like this one, you just strum while you play the chords." He set it on his lap and began playing along to the album.

"Why do you hold it so weird?" I said, once the song finished.

"This is just the way to hold it."

He continued to play, and I longed to look up at his old paintings that used to hang on his walls, but I couldn't, so my eyes wandered to the floor, where there was a pile of books with a deck of tarot cards on top. Mom was also into tarot cards, but she said she just read them for fun and didn't take them seriously. I picked them up, and beneath them, there was a notebook open to a page with Vincent's handwriting on it. Even his handwriting was artistic, like calligraphy minus the curves and frills.

I looked at it closer and saw the words "dream journal" at the top of the page. The first dream was dated October 20, 1973—about a month ago. It said he was going down some hallway running from something, when he ran into a girl named Lizzy, who told him something, but he didn't know what. Then, he turned into a giraffe. I turned the page to see a dream that happened ten days later. It read: "Last night I dreamt that I was astral projecting, and it was really crazy because I could almost feel my soul leaving my body, so I wasn't sure if I was astral projecting or dreaming."

"Hey, who's Lizzy and what's this about astral projection?" I spoke over the music.

"Huh?" He stopped playing and looked over at me.

"Who's Lizzy, and what's astral projection?"

"Lizzy's a girl at college, and astral projection is just something I've been learning how to do. It's like when you leave your body and go somewhere." He scratched his head and said, "You know if there's any more turkey left?"

"I think it's all gone," I said. "Gloria and Nancy polished off a lot of it. Gloria said there's no fat in it, and if they eat nothing but turkey, they won't gain any weight. So, how do you leave your body?"

"You have to will it, and you have to practice, and if you're doing it right, your spirit just leaves your body and goes somewhere, so it's like traveling but better because you don't even have to leave your room. Plus, you can travel through time. I see all kinds of cool stuff. Last week, I saw Joan of Arc."

"Oh yeah, sure," I said in obvious disbelief.

"No really, I did. She rode a big horse and carried a sword, like she was about to go off fighting one of her battles."

"How do you do it?" I wasn't sure I believed in it but wanted to try to do it anyway. He gave me step-by-step instructions with all this enthusiasm, like he'd been waiting for somebody to ask him this question his whole life.

That night, I lay in bed, trying to astral project according to Vincent's instructions. I blocked out the sound of Nancy sleeping and of Carmen moving around in his room, which was on the other side of the wall. I focused on my breathing in and out, holding my hand over my stomach to help me concentrate. I reached the state between sleep and wakefulness that I was supposed to be in to complete the process, but as hard as I tried to stay awake, I couldn't.

I fell dead asleep and woke the next morning feeling disappointed in myself. But when I heard the sound of Vincent playing the fiddle, I hopped right out of bed, put my clothes on, and went in the kitchen to find him playing with Mom keeping beat to the music as she made coffee. He was hunched over the fiddle, tapping his big work boot on the yellow vinyl floor. I watched his fingers dance around the fretboard so fast and precise and became mesmerized.

"That one's called 'Irish Washer Woman,'" he said when he finished playing.

"I love it," I said, adjusting my eyes to the bright kitchen lights. "Play another."

"After we eat," Mom said as she poured pancake batter on the griddle. The air smelled of coffee, and the table had six plates on it with forks beside each one. Gloria, Carmen, and Nancy staggered in and took their usual places, all leaning over on the table as if still waking up. Mom put a big plate of pancakes down on the table, and Vincent grabbed one off the top and took a bite out of it, consisting of almost half of the entire cake.

"Where's the butter?" Gloria said in the fake New York accent that she developed this past year when she went away to college somewhere right outside Manhattan.

"It's in the refrigerator," Carmen said, mocking her, with an accent that made him sound like a mobster. I laughed, and Gloria gave me and Carmen the stink eye.

"What?" I said to Gloria, trying to stifle my laughter. "You have to admit it's funny." She rolled her eyes with an air of superiority and said to me, "Keep it up, and I won't take you for a driving lesson." I was learning to drive with Mom, but I wanted to give her a break so asked Gloria to take me and she agreed.

"All right, sorry," I said to her.

"Can I come?" Nancy said to Gloria, pouring syrup on her pancakes.

"Why?" I said before Gloria had a chance to answer her. I was sure she'd be a total distraction and make me more of a nervous wreck than I already was behind the wheel.

"Because I'm going to be learning to drive soon too," Nancy said, spilling syrup on her baby-blue nightshirt.

"You're only fourteen!" I said.

"I want to get a jump on things," she said, cleaning the syrup with a napkin.

"Yeah, you can come as long as you keep quiet," Gloria said in a domineering voice.

"Okay, thanks," Nancy said.

"Hey, Vince, how come you didn't learn to drive yet?" Nancy said to Vincent. He shrugged, put his hands up in the air, and made a hapless expression that said he didn't know and didn't really care.

"You should learn to drive, Vince," Carmen said, buttering his second pancake. "Then, you won't have to hitchhike and ride the bus or your bike everywhere."

"You really should," I said to Vincent. "Why don't you come on the driving lesson with us?"

"Oh c'mon, it's a fucking driving lesson, not a party," Gloria said.

"Hey, watch your mouth," Mom said in between sips of coffee.

"I'm sorry," Gloria said. "I'm just used to being at college."

"That's no excuse," Carmen said with this ultra-serious expression, intended to be funny.

My pancakes were fluffy and sweet and went perfect with the coffee that I was finally old enough to drink. As soon as I took my last sip, the kitchen was invaded with the sound of Dad's car zooming up the driveway and coming to a halt. Right after the slamming car door sounded, Vincent said he was going to rake leaves in the yard and scrammed. We three girls headed into the bathroom to get ready, taking turns in the shower, on the toilet, and at the sink like we were playing a kind of musical chairs. Gloria rushed us while Nancy whined about being rushed.

Nancy and I got dressed in our room and headed out to the station wagon to meet Gloria who was waiting by the car. She gave me the keys and said, "Here," and I stared confusion at her and said, "Mom never lets me drive out of the driveway. She always waits until we get to the parking lot at the tennis courts." Gloria said that if I was too scared to drive to the tennis courts, she'd drive there, like she was challenging me. I never backed down from a challenge, so I took the keys and got in the driver seat.

I turned the ignition and drove down the driveway really slow. Gloria said I was sitting up too far, and I looked like I was trying to put my head through the windshield, and Nancy laughed. I got to the end of the driveway, where cars zoomed by from both directions, and I silently panicked, flipping my head back and forth like I was watching a tennis match in fast motion. I didn't know if I could do it, and I was tempted to ask Gloria to switch seats, but then I imagined her being really smug, and my determination to get out of the driveway on my own grew. There was finally a break in traffic, so I could make my turn. I made it all the way to the tennis courts, and once there, driving in the parking lot was a breeze. Gloria had so much confidence in me that she even talked about non-driving stuff for a minute.

"The other night, I saw Dad picking his teeth," she said, preparing us to be grossed out. "And he picked out a big piece of something, and he looked at it like he's examining it, and then he ate it!"

"Ewww," Nancy and I said in harmony.

When we got back from the driving lesson, I felt closer to Gloria than I ever felt in my life. I thanked her, and she said, "Uh-huh," instead of you're welcome, and soon, she was back to her same old-self, with her heavy footsteps coming down the hallway so hard that they sounded like her feet might go through the floor, pounding on the bathroom door while I was in there.

"You're not stinking it up in there, are you?!" she screamed, so the whole house could hear.

"Go use the other bathroom!" I screamed back. "What do you want me to do anyway?! Go shit outside!" I'd say anything to make her go away, even if it meant being crude as hell. I guess it worked too because when I got out of the bathroom, she was nowhere to be found.

I went into the kitchen to drink a glass of water and headed into my room to study for a chemistry test. I sat on my bed and started reading, and after about thirty minutes, I looked at the pages I read to see that just about every word was highlighted, which meant that I wasn't comprehending a damned thing. I've never been scientifically inclined, but besides that, my mind kept drifting to what Vincent said about happiness yesterday.

I wondered if Aristotle gave any instructions on how people could obtain happiness or about what they needed to be happy. Mr. Galetta's house flashed immediately into my mind with an image of Dad's

Cadillac following close behind. I knew that I needed a well-paying job to get any of that stuff. When I told Dad that I wanted to be a college professor, he said that he hoped I'd marry rich because teaching in college wouldn't pay much. So, I decided that I'd marry rich. The expression about it being just as easy to fall in love with a rich man as a poor man played in my head.

Of course, we'd have to have children. We'd have three or better yet, four. I closed my eyes and saw myself as an adult woman, sitting in the backyard of my lovely house, with trees that turn orange in the fall and flower pink in the spring. I could see my husband clipping a rose from one of our many rose bushes, giving it to me, and telling me how much he loved me. I saw our children running through sprinklers and eating popsicles. At first my future life looked beautifully out of focus like some kind of a painting I was seeing from a great distance, but the longer I stared into it, the more distinct and clear it became until I could almost smell the roses.

That night, Vincent, Carmen and I stayed up late watching *To Sir, with Love* on the late movie, and the next morning, I couldn't get out of bed. Eventually, Mom came in, fully dressed in purple slacks with a matching blazer, turned on the light, took the blankets off my bed, and told me to get up and get ready for church. I got up, washed up, and threw on my denim skirt and a white cable knit sweater. I was brushing my hair in the mirror when Nancy ran in, opened her drawers, and started going through them like a frenzied monkey.

"We're only going to church," I said to her as she sent her clothes flying aimlessly through the air. "Why do you give a shit about how you look?"

"None of your business," she said, not looking up at me. I knew it must have been about a boy. She grabbed a black and red dress with a wide, white collar out of the closet and started changing. As I walked out, she screamed, "Close the door!" as if I wasn't going to.

I dragged through church and nearly fell asleep during Father Sacco's boring sermon. On the way home, Vincent and Carmen got into an argument about what made a pizza good. Vincent said it was the sauce, and

Carmen said it was the crust and the cheese. When we pulled into the driveway, Carmen was done talking about pizza, but Vincent couldn't let it go.

"Give it up already," I said to him.

"Anybody can throw cheese on some lousy crust," he said, holding his hands up in the air as if he were doing a lazy cheer. "Now the sauce is where the real art comes in."

We all went inside, and I went in my room to change. I was only in there for about fifteen minutes, and when I came out, Dad and Vincent were at it. They faced each other, Dad in his fighting stance, his body bursting with the rage of a caged lion.

"Hey, I'm doing the best I can," Vincent said defensively.

"That's why you'll never be anything but a flub!" Dad shouted at him.

"You're fucked-up," Vincent said, making me stiff with fright at how Dad would respond. I froze, and for a second, I felt like I was watching a horror movie on a faraway screen, and then all of a sudden and without warning, I was fully in it.

"What did you say?!" Dad said as he picked up a steak knife that was on the cutting board. Vincent had the good sense to get the hell out of the kitchen and sped out the front door. I raced into Mom's room, where she was doing yoga and told her to come quick, and together we ran outside to see Dad chasing Vincent in our front yard with a knife.

"Cosimo! Please!" Mom yelled as she stood on the lawn in her navy-blue leotard. But Dad paid no attention to her, and soon Vincent was running down the street, followed by Dad, followed by me and Mom. I felt stares of curiosity and shock from the people driving by, but I couldn't care less.

After about a block, we caught up to Dad, and Mom stood in front of him, holding her arms out wide, so it was tough for him to get past her while Vincent ran until he was out of sight. She was fearless that way, and she'd do whatever she could to protect one of us. Dad stopped suddenly like he realized, in that very second, what he was doing. The three of us turned around, and went back home, and Mom convinced Dad to go out to the bar down the street that was owned by one of his friends.

"You can relax there, Cosimo," she said to him. He didn't respond, just looked down and took a lot of deep and mighty sighs. I could tell that, in his own way, he regretted his actions and figured he'd just go have a bunch of drinks, so he could forget about what he did.

As soon as we got home, Dad got in his car and left. Vincent must have been spying on our house from a neighbor's yard because right after Dad took off, he came home and told Mom that he'd just hitchhike back to college. She said she wouldn't have it and that she'd drive him back. As soon as she said this, I hurried to tell Gloria, Carmen, and Nancy, and we all scrambled to get our stuff together. We raced to Mom's car and waited for her and Vincent to come out.

When they got there, Mom looked at us all leaning against her car and said, "You all want to come?" like she hoped otherwise. We all nodded yes like there couldn't be any other way, and we piled into the car like bank robbers and drove off down the driveway, with the car kicking up bunches of dead leaves that Vincent raked earlier, making them fly through the air like crippled birds.

Inside the car was all seriousness and silence. Vincent was in a bad mood from fighting with Dad, Mom was tired, and the rest of us just felt lucky enough to be out of the house, so we kept our mouths shut. Outside, a gray sky loomed and everything looked dead and motionless. Mom drove fast like she just wanted to get the trip over with, down the highway and over the Walt Whitman Bridge that overlooked factories, smoke stacks, and the Philadelphia skyline. Next, she was onto the treacherous Schuylkill Expressway and through the charming Mainline with cute little towns that ran right into each other.

We pulled into the entrance of the college, and I marveled at the old buildings made of gray and brown stone, big like castles. Trees were covered in fall leaves, and students walked in all directions with book bags, fast and swift like flies. We reached Vincent's dorm, and Mom handed him some money and told him to spend it on food and not albums or comic books. She let him out of the car and drove away.

We left him standing alone, with sad, lost eyes. I never saw him that way before. From the back window, I waved to him, and he waved back, but it was a weak, half-hearted wave, and that same look remained in his eyes, like he was drowning in a great sea of pain. I could feel his pain through the steel encapsulation of the car and through the distance that grew as we drove on.

About halfway back, Nancy broke the silence and said, "What happened?"

"Dad and Vincent," Gloria said, like no more words were needed. Then, she talked about all the events that led up to the scene I walked into. Vincent started talking about one of his LSD trips, and Dad told him not to talk about that kind of thing in his house. Vincent said something like Dad couldn't understand that kind of thing, and Dad thought he was calling him stupid. Dad said that Vincent couldn't shine his shoes and that he'd always be a flunky, and Vincent said Dad should check himself into a mental hospital. Then, Dad told him he'd never amount to anything.

"I know Vincent should know better than to talk about that kind of stuff to Dad, but still, why's Dad always got to be such a jerk?" I said.

"He doesn't mean to be that way," Mom said. She always had a lot of understanding for Dad because she said his childhood was so difficult. His dad left him and his sister, my Aunt Cecilia when they were kids, and then his mom killed herself. Then, he and Aunt Cecilia had to go live with his uncle and his crazy wife. Mom said they were really mean to him and his sister, and they made them do all the work in the house and yard, kind of like indentured servants.

I kept seeing Vincent with those same sad, lost eyes and kept pushing that awful vision out of my mind, but it just kept returning, each time with what seemed to be a renewed sense of purpose. I was afraid that I'd never be able to stop seeing him like that, or worse yet, that he'd stay that way for the rest of his life. I shook my head and looked out the car window at the red-leaved trees and promised myself that I'd never let that happen. I knew how much he wanted to be happy or else he wouldn't have been going on about Aristotle. I just thought he needed some help and direction in getting to that place, and who'd be better to help him than me? Mom always said that I could do anything I put my mind to.

CHAPTER THREE: 1976

My roommate, Randi and I drove home from college for winter break, gleefully singing to every song on the radio like morning birds on a perfect spring day. I felt a relief that approached ecstasy to be done with the past semester because it was especially tough between my course load and breaking up with this guy in the midst of finals. His name was Scott, and he was tall and stiff like a breadstick, and whenever I'd say something funny, he just looked at me with an expression of profound misunderstanding. I could never be with somebody who didn't get my sense of humor. But despite these obstacles, I made the Dean's List with my crowning achievement being a paper I wrote for my Modern American Novel class: "Imagery, Symbolism and Allegory in the Stories of Flannery O'Connor." I don't think I'd ever been so proud of anything!

"What's your exit, Don?" Randi asked. Her hair was black silk against her skin that glowed in the winter sunlight drifting in and out of the car. She wasn't joking when she asked about my exit, but that particular question was a big joke at college. I heard it the entire first semester of my freshman year. Every time I'd tell

somebody I was from Jersey, they'd say "What exit?"
The first twenty times, it was kind of funny; then it had
just got old, and I couldn't even laugh out of courtesy.

"Twenty-eight," I said, looking outside at the
old, gray snow by the side of the highway.

I met Randi the first day I got to college, and
thank God for that, because Mom and Dad dropped me
off like they were dropping off a hitchhiker. In truth,
Mom wanted to stay with me longer, but Dad was in a
big hurry to get back, and he was the one driving. He
was fed up because I packed so much crap, which
included two huge speakers and an orange crate full of
albums. I packed as if I'd never be going home again,
and I went home the very next weekend.

After we'd unloaded everything in my dorm
room—a dark rectangular space of pure functionality—I
went out to the car with Mom. Dad was sitting in the
driver seat with the motor running. I'd looked at Mom
as if to say "Please don't go," and she gave me a quick
hug and said, "Toughen up," and then she got in the car
and they drove off. I'd watched them drive away until I
couldn't see their car anymore. I must have looked so
pathetic, in my lace-trim prairie dress (I'd wanted to
look good for my first day of college) with that look on
my face of restrained tears, my hair down and falling

into my face, sweat glistening in the hazy sun. I knew
Mom was doing her tough-love thing, but she couldn't
have picked a worse time. I was hurt and wanted to cry.
But I didn't.

Instead, I went up to my room to find this long-
haired girl with cutoffs and Dr. Scholl's standing on her
bed while putting up a *Dark Side of the Moon* poster
beside one of a cartoon-frog sitting at a yellow desk
with the words above him, "I'm so happy, I could shit." I
knew, in that second, we'd be great friends.

"Hey," she'd said in a deep, raspy voice as soon
as I came in. "I'm Randi."

"Hi," I replied. A smile came to my face, and I'd
forgotten how lonely and scared I'd felt. "I'm Donna."

"Wanna go to the cafeteria and get some
lunch?" she'd asked, hopping off the bed.

"Sure thing," I'd said. I'd felt awkward around
her because she was so self-assured, and at first, I'd
thought she must be a sophomore or even a junior, but
she was a mere freshman, just like me.

We'd walked down the hallway, which was
bright and dreary at the same time with fluorescent
lighting, carpet the color of split pea soup, and gray
paneled ceilings with some panels being so loose they
looked like they might fall at any second. Some guy with

big glasses was moving in across the hall, and Randi greeted him saying, "How's it going?" like she knew him.

"Where're you from?" I'd said, trying to keep up with her.

"Jersey," she'd said. I'd never heard New Jersey called Jersey before that.

"Me too," I'd said, trying to act cool and confident. "What's your major?"

"Not sure yet," she'd said as we walked out the door and past the other students moving in, most with their parents and some, presumably the older ones, just on their own. "Something in liberal arts. You?"

"English," I'd said.

"Cool." I'd loved the way she talked without using a lot of unnecessary words—right to the point. We'd gone in the cafeteria where I'd felt overwhelmed by all the people and noise and everything everywhere, but I'd followed Randi, who seemed like she'd been there before because she knew where everything was—the place where we got our meal tickets, the drinks, the line for the hot food, the salad bar, the plates, utensils, and trays. The bright lights and loud, continuous noise made me feel dizzy until we sat down and started eating. We got cheese sandwiches, green salads, and iced teas, and we ate while we'd talked and stared at the sea of people coming through the doors.

She got her own car in her sophomore year, and she always gave me a lift home, and I paid for gas, so it worked out well and sure beat taking the bus. Before I knew it, she was pulling into my driveway, and we were saying bye to each other.

"Come over after Christmas, and we'll go ice skating if the lake by my house is frozen," she said as I got out of the car.

"Sounds like a plan. Are you sure you can't come in for some coffee and cookies? I'm sure there's lots of great Christmas cookies inside."

"I wish I could, but I told my Mom I'd be home by seven."

"Well, bye then and Merry Christmas!"

"Merry Christmas!" she said as she started backing up.

I got through the door and took my coat off, despite being cold, because I had to show off my new brown, corduroy gaucho outfit, even if it was only the family seeing it. It was so refreshing to be back in Mom's sparkling clean house instead of my gross dorm room, where cleaning had been reduced to me or Randi occasionally picking up a dust bunny. I heard Nancy scrambling about in our room and went in to find her feathering her hair. When she saw me, she put down the curling iron and gave me a hug, with this new-found respect she developed for me since I went away to college.

"Hey, Nance," I said. "How's it going?"

"Good," she said. She was decked out in a denim jumper, platforms, and about a pound of makeup with blue eye shadow that could be seen from a far.

"Going to a dance?" I asked.

"Yeah, if I knew you were coming home, I would have planned to stay home."

"We'll hang out tomorrow," I said. "Go, and have fun at the dance."

I went towards Vincent's room, and as I got closer, I heard "Can't You Hear Me Knocking" by the Rolling Stones. I went in and started singing along like I was Mick Jagger, and he looked up, smiling and said, "Yo, Donna!" and got up to give me a hug. Then, he sat back down and went back to working on some picture he was drawing.

I sat down and started yapping about how great college was and suddenly, this strange guilt came down on me like a falling tree. I knew I shouldn't feel guilty for liking college. I knew he had a good time in college, even though it took him a long time to graduate because he kept taking time off for stuff like protests and hitchhiking across the country. But seeing him living back at home and not doing much of anything with his degree made me feel bad.

He lived near the college he attended for a couple of years after he graduated, doing odd jobs, painting houses, making pizza, until he ran out of money and moved home. He was still sticking with the overalls and work boots, and his hair was bigger than ever. His room didn't feel as empty as it did when he used to only stay here during college breaks. The walls were still bare, but books, albums, and instruments filled every available space.

"I mean, it's all right," I said, suddenly telling a different story about my college life. "Some of the people get on my nerves, and I don't love all my classes or anything."

"That's lousy." He arched his eyebrows with mild surprise. "This should be the best time of your life. There's nothing more fun than learning." As he said this, an amazing idea came to me. He could be a college professor like I planned on becoming.

"Hey, Vincent," I said. "You ever think of teaching in college one day?"

"Nah, I wouldn't be any good at that." I was sure that Dad had gotten to him with all his put-downs. I wished he never moved back home. If he talked to me before doing it, I would have steered him in a different direction.

"Hey, check this out," he said, showing me a drawing he made of a character from *The Lord of the Rings*. It was a young man with a crown and a blue-and-orange robe, waving a sword in the air, his mouth wide open as if a dragon or something else horrific was heading his way. His name was Fingolfin, and he was so animated like all the people Vincent drew. Even though the picture was drawn with markers on sketch paper, it looked like something that could have hung in a museum.

"I love it," I said. "You're so talented and smart. That's why I think you'd make a great professor. And you love learning. You just said how fun you think it is. So, you'd be a natural teacher."

No response. He just put his hand over his mouth as he laughed his galloping laugh.

"What's so funny?" I asked. "You have to do something for a job."

"Oh, can it with the job thing, Donna. You're bumming me out. Dad got me a job at the bakery in town."

"A bakery?! You're a college graduate!"

"Yeah, but I studied philosophy. Besides, what's wrong with being a baker? Grandpa was a baker."

"Yeah," I said. "But he was right off the boat. I don't think he could have had a lot of choices."

"Being a baker is gonna be cool. I'll get to make bread and pies and doughnuts. What else can be better?"

"Sure, it's all right, but you're like really smart and talented. Don't you want anything more? I mean, don't you think you deserve more or that you can do better?"

"C'mon now. Can it. You're bumming me out." He got up to put a different album on while asking me if I heard the new one by the Kinks.

"No," I said blandly.

He put it on, and I listened to Ray Davies sing about the fucked-up state of Hollywood. He then asked me if he ever told me about the time he went to Colorado, and I wondered if the song and Colorado were somehow connected but couldn't figure out a relation between the two things. I told him I never heard the story, and he told me how he was hitchhiking out west and ended up in some one-horse town near Denver.

"So, the sheriff said to me, 'We don't have any long-haired freaks around these here parts, so I'm going to turn around and count to sixty, and when I turn back around, if you're not gone, I'm going to have to take the law into my own hands.'" All the time he was talking with his eyes open wide like he was amazed by his own story.

"Weren't you scared to death? I mean, it sounds like he was going to kill you!"

"Nah," he said, smiling. "I did get out of there pretty fast, though." He laughed with some snorting thrown in.

"Did you make it out to California?"

"I turned back after that incident."

"Did you like it out there?"

"Yeah, I slept under the stars at night. Some nights on a mountaintop but others, on the back of a pickup truck."

"That sounds nice—the mountaintop thing."

"So, what's your favorite class?" he said.

"That's easy. My Modern American Novel class. My professor's the best too. He has so much passion about what he's teaching. A real inspiration."

"Good deal," he said. Then, he got up, turned the album over, and lit up a cigarette.

"I thought you quit!" I snapped.

"I tried," he said, taking a puff. He didn't seem to care that his attempt at quitting was unsuccessful. I'd be hating myself.

"Well, you should try again."

He looked down at the floor like he was thinking of something else to say, and in the brief silence, a sadness came over me and pulled me in like quicksand. It wasn't just because he was living at home. It was the fact that he was excited about the prospect of a bakery job and that he was smoking again. I thought that if he could just get out of the house, he'd be so much better off.

"How long are you going to stay at home?" I asked.

He put his hands up in the air, his palms facing the ceiling, a question mark on his face. I really hated the idea of him living with Dad.

"Do you want to stay at home?" I said.

"I don't have a choice right now. I'm broke."

"Maybe Mom could..." I was thinking she could sneak some money from Dad to help him out, but I wasn't sure how to say it.

"Could what?"

"Could get some money out of Dad's account and... you know."

"I'm all right here for now."

But I was sure that he wasn't all right, and the fact that he didn't know he wasn't all right made him even less all right. Even worse, whatever I said in an effort to get through to him about his situation just bounced right off him. I could hear Dad off in the near future saying how he never made anything out of himself and how his predictions were right all along. I wished Dad's insults could have made him angry. Then, maybe he would have been motivated to make a change, to get a better job, to call Dad's prophecy bogus!

The next morning, I woke to the smell of curry and knew right away that Mom was making Carmen's favorite breakfast—scrambled eggs with curry. He was out when I got in last night, so I didn't see him. In fact, I hadn't seen him all year because we'd kept coming home at different times. He finished college and started working at a life insurance company right away. He looked about the same as he did a year ago except for this cheesy mustache he grew that was long and skinny, nearly reaching from one side of his face to the other.

"Hey, Carmen," I said to him as I walked in the kitchen. I gave him a hug, and he asked me how college was.

"It's great. It's a lot of work, though."

"I wish I was back in college," he said, eating his eggs. "It's like being in a country club."

"I never thought of it that way," I said as I poured some corn flakes and milk into a bowl.

"Want to go to the mall later?"

"What, are you crazy or something? It's the day before Christmas."

"I didn't have time to get any presents."

"All right I guess, after I go for my run though," I said, getting a cup of coffee. "Maybe Vincent can come."

"He's at a bakery or something. That's what I heard Dad say."

I didn't know he'd be starting so soon and hoped it was going well but not too well, so he wouldn't stay there long and would get something better. I was tempted to sit and wallow in thoughts of him working at the bakery, but I had to get ready for my run. I kissed Mom goodbye, put on my sweatsuit, my down vest, and went out the back door to get hit in the face with a blast of cold air.

The cold made me run extra fast through the neighborhood that wasn't where I lived anymore but still felt like home. I ran past the parking lot of the tennis courts where I learned to drive, past the public school, that I always wanted to go to but couldn't because we all went to Catholic school, and past my friend Rinna's house. We'd graduated high school together, and she went to college in North Jersey, where she joined the crew team, which she loved and talked about all the time. I wished I belonged to a team at college, but I stunk at all sports. The only time I was part of a team was in ninth grade when I tried out for softball just to get out of math class. I played third-string right field. The few times the ball would come out in my direction, I'd run away in a panic.

I was laughing to myself thinking of me trying to play softball when I heard a clamoring sound and looked over to see a guy who looked about my age, dressed in a leather jacket, working on his motorcycle. I moved closer to see that he was somebody I went to school with. He was a year ahead of me, and I didn't even know his name or care to know it. But seeing him hunched over his bike, doing something that must have involved some mechanical ingenuity, his black-and-brown hair creeping into his deep-set eyes that were transfixed on the bike, made me want to know everything about him. Without thinking, I ducked behind a tree, took my hat off and freed my long hair to sway gracefully over my shoulders. I unzipped my vest and tried to make myself feel as sexy as possible while wearing sweatpants and running sneakers.

"Hi there," I said, walking by him. He barely looked up, so engulfed in working on his bike. I wasn't used to being ignored by guys, but I liked it in a weird way, and it made me feel really determined to get his attention, so I walked right up to him and said, "I'm Donna." He looked up at me, and our eyes met, and we stared into each other, but it wasn't like the kind of stare that tries to figure something out about someone. This was pure and innocent, with no agenda, like we were trying to come together through our eyes.

"I'm Frank," he said, mouth open as if he couldn't think to say anything else. I stared at his thick lips, and the thought of kissing them kept creeping to the front of my mind, even when I tried to force it away with unsexy thoughts of gross stuff, like Dad picking his teeth.

"I think you used to go to Saint Paul's," I said, managing somehow to speak despite my intrusive fantasy thoughts. I wondered if he was home from college like me or if he just lived at home and commuted to a local college or if he didn't go to college at all and just lived at home and worked at McDonald's or some other place like that.

"Yeah," he said, still speechless. The silence made me nervous, so I started talking up a storm, about how I was in my third year of college, majoring in English literature, and how I went to a liberal arts college, which was tough for me because I had to take math and science, neither of which was I good in. He just stood there, nodding and saying "yeah," so I asked him about himself in hopes of getting him to talk more.

"Do you go to college?"

"Yeah," he said. "La Salle."

"Oh, in Philly?"

"Yeah," he said, still deadpan.

"That's kind of near to where I go," I said. A smile peeked through on his face for a half of a second, and then he went back to staring, and while I was flattered, it made me uneasy, and I thought I'd run out of stuff to talk about with me being the only one talking.

"Do you like it?" I said.

"It's all right."

I waited for him to say more or to ask me where I went to college, and when he didn't, I said, "I go to Saint Joe's, also in Philly."

"Oh, cool." I started to think that this was the best I'd get in terms of conversation.

"What's your major?" I asked.

"Sociology. I want to go to law school." Excitement spilled over inside of me, and when I told him how great that it was that he was headed to law school, he smiled shyly, and I thought that the ice had finally broken, but then it went right back to dead silence with me worrying about getting back home to go to the mall with Carmen. I didn't want to leave until a date was made but wasn't feeling too hopeful that that was going to happen, even though I knew he wanted to ask me out. So, I tried this trick Randi taught me—I said I had to go and started walking away, all the while hoping and praying that he'd stop me. I was about twenty steps away from him and nothing, but then when I got to the next block, I heard him calling my name.

"Donna!" he said. Goosebumps, that had nothing to do with being cold, covered the skin on my arms. I turned to see him coming towards me. "Are you busy tonight?"

"Well, it's Christmas Eve."

"Oh yeah," he said, like he forgot. "And tomorrow night's Christmas. How about after Christmas? Saturday night?"

"Sure," I said, trying to conceal my excitement.

"Great," he said. "I'll pick you up at seven then on my bike. And don't worry because I have an extra helmet."

"I won't worry, but my mom will. She doesn't like motorcycles." She hated them, in fact. "There's no way she'll let me get on one."

"No problem," he said. "I can borrow my dad's car."

"Great."

"See you soon."

"Merry Christmas," I said, smiling as I walked away.

"Oh yeah, Merry Christmas."

Carmen and I got home from the mall later than we'd expected. We practically had to park on the side of the highway because there were like a million cars in the parking lot. We walked in the kitchen to find Mom already cooking the Seven Fishes dinner she cooked every Christmas Eve. I asked her what I could do, and she had me bread and fry oysters and smelts. Batter caked on my hands, thick like mud, as I dipped the little fishes in egg, flour, and breadcrumbs. Gloria was making Caesar salad, and Nancy was setting the table.

The kitchen was so alive with all of us doing our own thing while working together at the same time as Mom orchestrated with a spirit of festiveness. The air smelled of white wine and butter sautéing and of course, fish but not the bad fish smell of Chinatown in a heat wave. This was the scrumptious fish smell that could only come from a very fine restaurant or from Mom's kitchen.

Soon, the feast was served. Dad said grace, and then we began with shrimp cocktail, succulent and tangy and onto the Caesar salad—deep green romaine leaves brushed with creamy dressing and anchovies. We were all home for the first time in a while, and we had to use the extra leaf for our table because with Anthony and his fiancée, Sharon, there were nine of us. He was some big shot attorney in Manhattan, working really long hours, oftentimes sleeping over at his office. He looked tired, hunched over his plate, pale complexion and glassy eyes. Still, a light shone in his face as he talked about all the great places he'd go for lunch during his work week.

"In New York, they have these rice balls that you buy in the pizza parlors, and I get one almost every day for lunch. They're deep fried."

"Oh, the rice balls," Sharon said. She spoke fast and nervously, her words racing into each other. "They're delicious." She was a pretty, petite woman with jade green eyes and a warm smile.

"They sound great," Mom said, putting a big bowl of clams and spaghetti in the center of the table. They were always my favorite, and I went for them before anyone else had a chance.

"Hey you're really cleaning up there," Dad said to me as I scooped chopped clams out of the serving bowl. He was half joking and half serious. As always, he couldn't care less about the food. His focus was on whatever he drank, which appeared to be something with gin or vodka.

"What was the mall like?" Nancy said to me and Carmen.

We both answered at the same time. I said "A madhouse" and he said "Crazy."

"Why would you go to the mall today of all days?" Gloria said as she twirled spaghetti.

"Carmen didn't have time to buy any gifts before he came home," I said.

"Oh, that damned mall," Dad said. "I could have got that piece of property right near there for a song and a dance." He looked down, rubbing his forehead against the palm of his hand. He was always regretting some piece of property he could have bought for cheap.

After devouring a substantial portion of the clams and spaghetti, I was onto the fried oysters and smelts (that I did a really good job on), followed by the sautéed bluefish. While we were all chowing down, Anthony started choking on what I could have only imagined was a fish bone. When he lay on the floor clenching his hand around his neck melodramatically, I knew it was a joke, but poor Mom was ready to have a heart attack, and when he saw this, he got up and started laughing.

"Oh, that was real funny," Mom said sarcastically, and then she started laughing with the rest of us.

"I thought so," he said through his laughter.

The scallops were served last, which was smart because our appetites were mostly satiated, so we wouldn't pig out on the greatest delicacy of the meal. They were soft and buttery and delectable. I counted how many were on everyone's plate to be sure no one was being greedy.

After dinner, Gloria, Nancy and I helped Mom with the dishes, and then Vincent said we had to add some tinsel to the tree. He always loved tinsel and would say that the tree wasn't complete without it.

"Put some more over on this side," he said to me as he threw bunches of it on our tree. It was a nice full tree, but according to Nancy, it started out being scrawny and bare, so Dad drilled holes in it and stuck branches in the holes. Only Dad would have done such a thing.

"Remember the time we went out and sang Christmas carols?" I said to Vincent as I hung the silver strips.

"Christmas carols," he said, throwing all the tinsel he had on one of the few uncrowded spots on the tree. "That's what we need. I'll be right back." He went off into his room with a sense of urgency and returned in a minute with his guitar. He grabbed the Christmas music book off the piano, opened it, and started playing "Silent Night."

Dad popped his head in around midway through the song, and by the end of the song, he was sitting down on a chair across from where Vincent sat on the couch. He stared and smiled at his son as he played, sitting still for once and even leaning back. When the song ended, he said, "Play the 'We Three Kings' song," like a little boy who was hearing music for the first time. Vincent found the song in the book and started playing it, and I stood beside him and started singing. Dad listened as he sipped his drink that was on the table beside him, all the while smiling at Vincent.

The day after Christmas, I ran errands with Mom, which was basically going to a bunch of shops and returning unwanted gifts. I told her that people should return their own gifts and that she did too much for everyone. I decided adamantly that I'd never be doing that when I became a mom. After we finished returning stuff, she took me out to lunch at this fancy, old-time restaurant with big, bay windows, hardwood floors, and a bar that stood in the middle of the room like an island. We sat in a small room off to the side, lit with Christmas lights and filled with poinsettias.

"I'm glad Christmas is over," I said to her as I buttered a piece of bread.

"Yeah," she said reluctantly, looking up from the menu. Her olive skin glimmered in the warm lighting. "I love Christmas, though. I love the way it's so cold and dark outside and so warm and light inside." I looked around at the twinkling lights in the restaurant, thinking how I rarely saw anything good about Christmas because the whole holiday thing annoyed me—the cornball songs I'd hear everywhere, the crowds of crazed shoppers, the frenetic fights in our house.

But Mom's eyes could pierce whatever ugliness lay in their way, clear through to the core of beauty. It was probably why she could cope so well with being married to Dad.

"Yeah, that's sweet, Mom," I said as the waiter approached.

"May I take your order?" I looked up to see a tall, thin waiter dressed in a black suit with tails. I ordered roasted duck, and Mom ordered filet of sole, and when the waiter left, I asked Mom what she thought of Vincent working at a bakery. Her gentle smile vanished and was replaced with a strained expression that made her worry lines pop.

"I think it's a start," she said. "It's something...it may not be forever...he might really enjoy it, and it'll be great to have a baker in the family." By the end of her sentence, she was smiling strong again.

"I just thought he could do so much more, you know."

"I know, but maybe he can't. Maybe this is all he can do, and that's all right." I wished I could be more accepting like her.

Even though I felt differently, I told her that she was right and then added, "Dad helped him get the job, he said. That's great that he's helping him out."

"Yes, it is. And yesterday, he told me one of his apartments might be coming available, and he said Vincent should move in."

"Really?" I said with mixed feelings. I knew that living in one of Dad's apartments wouldn't be optimal but thought it would be better than living at home. "What's brought about the change in Dad?"

She took a big sigh and looked at me in the eyes and said, "I told him that when he gets to the pearly gates, Saint Peter is going to say to him, 'Cosimo, you did everything right, except that you could have been a better father to Vincent.'"

"And he went for that?" I said, laughing.

"Yeah, well it's the truth, right?" She was half-smiling, but I knew she really believed all that stuff *was* the truth, even the virgin-birth story. I would have never told her, but since I went away to college, I hadn't been to church once.

"Do you think it's such a good idea, though, for him to be living in one of Dad's apartments?"

"Oh, it'll be fine," she said, as if she were trying to convince herself.

As soon as Mom and I got home, I started getting ready for my date with Frank. I didn't know exactly what we were doing, but I was pretty sure it would be something mellow. I dressed so I looked good without trying too hard in my green-and-black-striped turtleneck with jeans tucked in my high-rise boots.

I was putting my gold hoop earrings in when I heard a car that I knew was his coming up the driveway. I liked that he was picking me up at seven like he said he would—no weird games or fake late excuses. He drove a bright red Monte Carlo, and I had to remind myself that the car belonged to his dad and that his own taste surely wasn't so gaudy. When I got in the car, he seemed much less nervous than he did when we'd first met, leaned back in a gray, corduroy jacket and blue jeans. His deep brown eyes matched his thick shoulder-length hair that was combed back and tucked behind his ears.

He asked me if I was up for seeing *Carrie*. I'd been dying to see it since it came out but was too busy with school. When I told him this, he lit up like a carnival ride, and I thought he was pleasantly surprised because most girls weren't much for horror movies. I always loved them, though—not the slasher kind but the supernatural ones, like *Carrie*. We headed to the mall to see the movie because there were no movie theaters in town. In fact, everything was at the mall. If you want to do just about anything, you had to go to the mall.

"How has your break been so far?" I asked, trying to sound calm and casual.

"Good," he said.

I waited a few seconds for a follow-up question, but when there was none, I said, "Did you do anything fun?"

"Not really, just relaxed, worked on my bike, helped my mom out around the yard."

"Same here," I said. "I mean, I didn't work on my bike or help my mom in the yard, though." He laughed, and I relaxed a bit. I didn't feel much like talking about school, so I asked him about what kind of music he liked.

"A lot of different stuff," he said. "Lately I'm listening to a lot of Coltrane."

"Oh," I said with confusion. It didn't seem right to me that somebody who rode a motorcycle would be listening to jazz.

"What do you like?"

"The Beatles, Dylan, Neil Young. I could go on forever."

"Cool," he said. "I love all of them." I was overjoyed at hearing this, and we talked about music for the whole rest of the drive, which flew by with the speed of a falling star. Before I knew it, we were sitting in the theater, munching popcorn, with the movie about to begin.

When Carrie started bleeding and crying in the shower and the mean girls started throwing tampons at her, I wondered what Frank was thinking. Right after the shower scene, he took out a bottle of beer that was hiding in the inner pocket of his jacket. He offered me some, but I didn't want any. When all the students were shopping for prom attire, he put his arm around me. He felt so warm and strong, and inside, I danced with delight. He kept his arm around me for the whole rest of the movie, and after the mean kids poured pig's blood on poor Carrie, he pulled me closer to him, so I put my head on his shoulder. When Carrie turned over the car that John Travolta was driving with the power of her mind, he held my hand tight. But he never tried anything else, unlike other guys, who were always trying to get to first base on the first date.

The way back was even better than the way up because a lot of the first-date nervousness was gone, and we both knew that the night would end in a kiss. Exhilaration filled every corner of the car like tiny, twinkling lights that only we could see. We talked about the movie and joked that we wished we had telekinetic powers.

When he got to my house, he parked the car on the street because he didn't want to wake up Mom and Dad. He walked me to the front door and said good night. We stood looking into each other's eyes for a flash before it happened. Initially, it wasn't the most romantic kiss with our noses colliding, but once we got into it, it was incredible, and I was thrilled to find that he really knew what he was doing. He used just the right amount of tongue without slobbering on me like a dog. In fact, he was damned good—probably the best kisser, by far, I'd ever been with.

After we kissed, he asked me if he could see me again. He didn't presume that I'd automatically agree like some arrogant jerk. Of course, I said yes, and we made plans for a few days away. I knew we both wanted the next date to be sooner, but we were being smart and sensible about pacing ourselves.

I went to bed, racing with thoughts of the night, of Frank, and of that kiss. I barely slept, but when I woke the next morning, I jumped out of bed with all this energy as if I'd slept for days. I got ready for church, making myself look extra good just in case I saw him there. He wasn't there as I hoped, but still, the mass seemed to last only minutes, and the glazed doughnut I ate after we got home tasted better than any doughnut I ever had. All day, a light and unfamiliar, warm sensation lived in my stomach, and a plastic smile was glued on my face. Carmen even made a wisecrack at my expense during Sunday dinner.

"That must have been some date," he said, looking smug. I blushed like a tomato in the hot sun, and everybody laughed.

That night around six, Mom and I were in the kitchen finishing up the dishes when Vincent came through the back door smiling, holding a white paper bag like there was some great treasure in it.

"I got some fresh-baked bread I made," he said, his eyes gleaming with pride.

"Fresh-baked bread!" Mom said as she opened the refrigerator and got out some butter. "You made it?" Delight floated in her voice like a cherub bouncing from cloud to cloud.

"Yeah," he said, sitting down at the table, still smiling.

"Oh yum," I said, sitting down. "Let's crack into it."

Mom put a cutting board and two knives on the table—one to cut the bread and one to spread the butter. Then, she placed the bread on top of the cutting board like it was a priceless sculpture and called it a work of art. I cut into the center, feeling the slightest bit of warm steam on my hand. The heat of the bread softened the butter making it spreadable. The crust was soft, and the inside even softer and warm and with butter, it was truly divine—not just my taste buds playing tricks on me because I was on love-sick cloud nine. Mom and I couldn't stop telling him how delicious it was and talking about it as if it was some new state-of-the-art invention.

"How did you make it?" I said, buttering my second slice.

"Oh boy," he said, taking a big sigh. "First, I make the biga yeast the night before."

"Biga?" I said. "Never heard of that."

"Oh yeah. You make it with yeast, flour, and water. You gotta let that rise overnight. The next morning, you make the dough, and let it rise like four or five hours."

"What if you get it too soon or too late?" I asked.

"Then, you make a lousy loaf," he said, laughing. "Anyway, it's really cool, just waiting for it to be ready." That would drive me crazy. I couldn't stand waiting for things to happen.

"What do you make the dough from?" Mom said.

"The biga yeast, water, salt, and more yeast," he said, having one of his massive-sized bites of bread.

"How long does it take to bake?" I said.

"Just like twenty minutes."

He really seemed to like talking about making bread, so I asked some more questions. I asked him about the other kinds of bread he made, which ones were most popular, and about the history of breadmaking. He said he also made rye, raisin, and baguettes, and said baguettes were by far the most popular. He said bread started being made in 300 BC. All the while, I listened, my mind spun, trying to get how four simple ingredients could become something so rich, complex, and wonderful.

He talked on about the bakery and all the other stuff he'd be making eventually—pies, doughnuts, cakes, pastries. We listened contentedly while polishing off the entire loaf. There was a quiet that rarely, if not ever, lived within our house. Outside our window, it was dark and cold, but inside, it was all light and warmth, and in that moment, I understood, fully and deeply, what Mom loved about Christmas.

CHAPTER FOUR: 1980

Vincent and I were sitting in the kitchen of his apartment. It was a sunny July afternoon, but you'd never know it because all the shades were tightly drawn. He said he was afraid the bright sun might damage his instruments. I told him it wasn't even that bright and that some sunshine would do him and the place some good, but he didn't agree. The place was one of Dad's apartments—a two-story old house painted white that had turned to gray over the years. He lived on the second or top level and had moved in about a year after he started at the bakery.

He stayed at the bakery for about two years— until they went out of business. The owners said they were driven out of business by a supermarket that opened down the street that had its own bakery. They said they couldn't compete with their prices and that people cared more about prices than quality. Vincent was on unemployment for a few months, giving him plenty of time to study the stars and play his instruments. Then, he got a job at a cookie factory in town. He said it was just factory work and you'd think that making cookies would be fun but, in fact, it was a real drag. I imagined him placing perfectly shaped globs of cookie batter on an assembly line with hair-netted ladies on either side of him. I thought that if he got his hair cut and got some decent clothes, the job market would have opened up to him, but every time I gave him any sort of advice, he'd just tell me to can it.

"Hey, what happened to your hair?" he said, looking at me with squinted eyes.

"I got a perm," I said. It was actually a little bit tighter than I thought it would be, but I thought it looked nice, until then. "What's wrong with it?"

"Nothing, I guess." He looked at my hair like he was making a study of it, then in an instant, he stopped and said, "Want some tea?"

"Yeah, sure."

"Did you see *The Lord of the Rings* movie?" he asked me as he put a kettle of water on.

"No, I'm not much into cartoons, but I read *The Silmarillion*." I couldn't wait to get this into one of our conversations, but it seemed like he couldn't care less.

"Did you see the movie though?" He fished a cigarette butt out of an old Maxwell House can he was using as an ashtray and lit it.

"No, but I'm sure you did."

"Yeah." He grinned, and his eyes glimmered with a self-possessed zaniness. "Sixteen times!"

"Sixteen times. Wow." That may have been the most pathetic wow I ever spoke in my life. All I could think of is how he should have been spending his time making a better life for himself—not seeing the same cartoon movie over and over.

"Sometimes, I'd just sit in the movie theater after the first showing and watch it again."

"You never got sick of it?"

"No. I got it on VHS. Want to watch it?"

"Sure," I said, grateful for being able to delay what I came there to tell him—that I would be marrying Frank in a few months. I didn't want to tell him because I felt guilty for getting on with my wonderful life while he was stuck in one of Dad's apartments, alone, working at a cookie factory, and smoking cigarette butts. I tried telling myself that I shouldn't feel guilty, that I was living the life I set out to live, that this was the life he chose, and if he just cleaned himself up, he'd look like a goddamned Italian movie star and would have been able to get everything—a good job, a house, a nice lady, and eventually, children. But all that self-help talk didn't help, and my guilt bubbled over like a chemistry experiment gone wrong.

I didn't think I'd be marrying Frank so soon, although I knew he was the one after he had a motorcycle accident, and I went to visit him in the hospital. It'd happened a few months after we'd started dating. In his drugged-out state, with eyes half-closed, he'd mumbled to me, "When I woke up in the hospital, I didn't know what was happening or even where I was. All I cared about was seeing your beautiful face again." His eyes shone through his bruised face. His broken leg, wrapped and elevated, hung like a part of himself he'd forgotten about. He'd gone on to say that when the doctor had told him he might walk with a limp for the rest of his life, he didn't care about that either. He'd just cared about seeing me again. He'd sounded like a desperate love song, but I was touched and moved beyond words.

Vincent turned off the screaming kettle, made two cups of Darjeeling tea, and brought them to the table. We left the kitchen and went in the TV room to start the movie. This was the main room in the place, and it was crammed full of all things Vincent: various stringed instruments, some displayed like trophies; a rainbow of crystals, with one big crystal ball prominently positioned in the center; two bookshelves crammed with Bibles, Bible concordances, Castaneda, star guides, sheet music, everything Tolkien ever wrote with some things in duplicate, books on saints and the tarot. The same leather-bound album cases he had in his room in our old house were on his floors, along with cassette tapes alphabetized and stacked inside wooden cases. On his walls, a small crucifix hung beside an even smaller round picture of Mary, which was next to drawings he made with markers. The one of Fingolfin was beside another with two Medieval monks standing under an archway, calligraphic words on either side of it that read: "And now all the days of a life to fulfill, setting my feet to the steep of the hill, beyond death's cruel severance I think on you still, as ever I will, Sweet Molly."

He started the movie, and I was surprised to find that I immediately got into it, and it even got my mind off everything. Vincent said it was really true to the books, and nobody would know better than him. After the movie, we were both hungry, and I offered to take him out for some pizza, but he said he had plenty of food and got out a can of tuna fish, a baguette, and some olives.

I was about to tell him my news right after we started eating, but I stalled, making small talk about light tuna versus albacore and how I preferred the

light—which was what we were eating—to the
albacore, even though most people were the other way
around. I then went on about how I was giving up meat
and only eating fish.

"What for?" He asked. "Lent's over."

"You know I'm not religious," I said, thinking of
how I'd probably have to get religious as soon as I
started having kids.

"Maybe you can be," he said, getting ready to
say something funny with a smile that reached across
his face, a slanted head, and hands on his hips. "You can
be a member of the tuna fish religion." He laughed
heartily at his own joke, and I joined him, but my
laughter was weak and joyless.

"Yeah, that sounds like a good religion for me."
I could feel the fake smile on my face fading fast.

"But say you'd have to pick a religion to
practice," he said, turning semi-serious. "What would it
be?"

I looked up at the ceiling and said, "I really can't
think of any. Maybe if the Romantic Poets formed a
religion, I'd be into that. They were really into being
anti-establishment and pro-individualism and—"

"Yeah." He waved his hand in the air dismissively. "They sound like a bunch of hippies." He laughed and asked me how I liked the movie.

"I loved it. It flew by. Now I want to read the books. I only ever read *The Hobbit* and *The Silmarillion*."

"Oh yeah," he said, paying less attention to my mention of this book than he did the first time I mentioned it. I really hoped for a more enthusiastic response from him for reading this book, especially considering I read it mostly, so I could talk to him about it. "So, what was your favorite part of the movie?"

"Mm, hard to say." I knew this answer wouldn't do.

"Just name one."

"Ah, I really liked the scene with the elf lady in white."

"Oh yeah, that's a good scene," he said. "Did I ever tell you about the time I met an elf?"

"Yeah right." I laughed.

"No really," he said, turning serious. "I met her on the bus on my way home from college one day."

"Did she have curly ears that point up?" I said, smirking.

"Kind of. And she was really tiny too."

"So, why's an elf taking the bus, anyway? Shouldn't she be running through some forest with a bow and arrow?"

"No, really, Donna. She was telling the truth." He wore a mystery smile that turned into a laugh, and I wasn't sure what to think.

"You're spending too much time in Middle Earth," I said. At this, he laughed like a madman, and I told myself that this would be as good of a time as any to tell him about me and Frank getting married.

"So, I kind of have some big news. I'm getting married to Frank." I spoke quickly, announcing my major life-changing event like I was talking about the price of tomatoes.

"Yikes!" he said. "When's that happening?"

"In a few months. I would have told you sooner, but it's going to be a really small thing. Just our two families and a couple close friends. We're not having any of that cornball wedding party stuff or else you know you'd be in it." Frank and I both thought big weddings were so impractical and preferred to save our money for a down payment on a house, rather than spend it on one day of festivities.

"Bring him over, and I'll crack out a bottle of Bailey's."

"Really?! That'd be great, Vincent. Thank you so—"

"Oh no!" he said suddenly. "We should go outside and see if there are any bats flying around. I saw a couple last night. This is the time they come out."

We went outside where it was hot and dewy, and my clothes stuck to my skin. The sky glowed pink with hints of soft blue coming through in places. Crickets sang, and an occasional car drove by slowly, songs playing from their radios, warping in the wet heat. We stood in the most open space we could find, so our view would be unobstructed and arched our backs to look up at the sky like something magnificent was going to occur. We watched for bats until it turned completely dark, and we were ready to hang it up when we spotted one, and then another. Their wings were white flickers against the blackness. The moon shimmered on Vincent's face while his eyes were joyfully transfixed on the bats flying through the sky like little frenzied kites.

I started my drive back home, which was in the part of Jersey just outside Philadelphia, where Frank and I had a little apartment with little being the operative word. The whole place was two small rooms with ceilings so low that Frank could reach them by stretching his arm up. When we first moved in, I was scared that we'd drive each other crazy in the tiny space, but after a couple weeks, I realized that the size of our place didn't matter because we always wanted to be in the same room with each other.

I moved in with him soon after graduating college. Randi and I planned on getting an apartment together, but things kind of fell through, and she ended up moving back home. He had me moved out of college and into his apartment in a flash. Together, we had emptied out my dorm room and shoved my belongings in the back of his muted-yellow hatchback. It was a warm day with the sun struggling to show itself through the dark clouds that threatened rain. After we unloaded the last bit of stuff into his apartment, the rain had started. I considered being able to get my stuff safely inside right before the rain started as a sign that I was doing the right thing moving in with him. That it wasn't too soon as I'd worried it might have been.

"You want to just keep all these books boxed up?" Frank had asked me as we both began unpacking my stuff, hoping that was the case. "I mean, my book shelves are crammed with law books, and I use them all the time, and these just look like a bunch of novels. Maybe you can just take one out if you want to read it or something."

"Okay, I guess." I wasn't too sure of myself and would have rather had my books out on shelves because seeing them inspired me, but I could see where he was coming from. Besides, I knew I wasn't going to have too much time for reading while preparing for the test to get into graduate school. I needed to get a master's degree in literature so that I could teach it in college. I'd planned to take the test in the fall and start school in the spring, but when test time came, I got a terrible flu that started in my head and quickly flooded every inch of my body.

"I told you, you should have gotten the flu shot," Frank had said, perched over me lying in bed with a tall glass of ginger ale.

"Well, I didn't," I'd snapped back. I never could stand the *I told you so* thing at any time, but especially when I'd felt like crap. I couldn't get mad at him though because of the way he cared for me when I was sick, almost like he enjoyed bringing me tea and dry toast, holding my hair back while I vomited in a trash can, and cleaning up all around me. Men in my family would never do that kind of stuff. The next test date wasn't until February and by that time, Frank had already hinted that he'd be asking me to marry him. I didn't want to start anything new while I was planning to get married, so I'd decided to wait until after we were wed.

I got home to find Frank asleep, lying on our futon mattress in front of the television blasting the MASH theme song that competed fiercely with his snoring. His hair covered half his face, and his "I Shot JR" T-shirt was pulled up so that his belly button showed. I went into the kitchen to find six empty cans of Budweiser sitting on top of the garbage, and I reminded myself that he was only drinking so much because he just finished law school only a couple of months ago and was still in celebration mode. Besides that, he worked two jobs—one as a legal assistant in some downtown firm that specialized in criminal law and another waiting tables in a restaurant up the street. Drinking helped him relax and unwind like it did for most people.

Personally, I never did get the whole drinking thing. I guess I was always turned off to it because of Dad. At college, I remained sensibly sober while all the other students would cheerfully sneak bottles of cheap wine into their dorm rooms, go haywire at the keg parties, and fabricate fake ID cards so that they could go out to bars.

"Hi, Sweetheart," he called out from the other room in a grumbly voice.

"Hi, Frank," I said, staring down at the empty cans crowded together.

"You just get home?"

"Yeah," I said, not taking my eyes off the cans. "Vincent wants us to go to his place tomorrow night. You don't have to work, I hope?"

"No," he said, getting up and walking into the kitchen to give me a kiss. He *did* end up sustaining a limp from his accident, but it was barely perceptible, not just to me but to everyone. It wasn't only because he was so fun to be around; it was something more. As soon as he opened his mouth and started talking, all eyes and ears were on him as if whatever he was talking about was either highly fascinating or some sort of crucial information. Any handicap could hide well beneath his charisma.

He smelled like a brewery but didn't seem even slightly tipsy, and in fact, after he kissed me, he opened the refrigerator and grabbed another can of beer. Before I could say anything, I was hearing that can-opening snap and watching him gulp beer like he was trying to put out a raging fire in his stomach.

"Frank," I whined. "Don't you think you had enough already?"

"Oh sorry, honey," he said. "This will be my last. I'm just feeling frazzled from work."

I said all right with reluctance, and we headed out of the kitchen and into the everything- else room, and I asked him about his day.

"So today, one of the lawyers there is on the phone talking to who must have been a client, and every other thing out of his mouth is 'very interesting.' This guy thinks everything's so goddamned interesting. A paper clip could fall on the floor, and he would say that it's very interesting. Poor joker's just bored out of his fucking mind, and he doesn't even know it!" I laughed so hard that my stomach hurt, and he kept on about this guy who he nicknamed "Very Interesting." No one ever made me laugh as hard as Frank. That may have been what I loved most about him.

Another thing I loved about him is how he liked to do fun things all the time. I was never much into spectator sports, but he started bringing me to Phillies games last year, and I was surprised at how much I enjoyed watching a ball fly around in the giant stadium sky while a bunch of guys tried to either catch it or avoid it. We did all kinds of things in the City. A weekend ago, we'd gone to South Street, where all the punks hung out and got matching Ramone's T-shirts at a store called Zipperhead. Then, we'd had water ice at some stand, and Frank had started talking to the guy working there like they were old-time friends, asking him how long he'd been working there, where he was from, and the name of his favorite bar in the neighborhood.

I smoked some grass and turned on a Bob Dylan album. While listening to "Like a Rolling Stone," I said, "Do you ever wonder how many times you will have listened to this song by the end of your life?" I loved to get into deep conversations when I was high, but Frank wasn't so big on them, and he just started kissing my neck and said, "No, but I do wonder how many times I will have kissed you by the end of my life." It was tough to tell him to be serious and to try to get into a deep conversation when he was being such a sweet romantic.

When Frank and I got to Vincent's, my stomach knotted, and my brain swelled with a strange kind of worry about what Frank would think of Vincent once he saw all the stuff in his apartment that most people would consider weird. I was grateful that he didn't have any pet rats with names like Jezebel or that the black robe he wore while gazing into his crystal ball, that looked like something that belonged to a warlock, hadn't been out on display recently. I rang the doorbell and heard him yelling out the window, "Yo, Donna. Be there in a minute."

We stood outside on the grey wooden porch in the hot, still air for only a minute before Vincent's big footsteps came clomping down the hardwood steps. He opened the door smiling and saying "Yo" to Frank, and then we all headed upstairs, my mind buzzing with anxiety. When we got to the top, I gave Vincent the bottle of Bailey's we brought.

"Ah, thanks for that," he said, taking the bottle. "I already had a bottle of Bailey's but guess you can't have too much."

"That's for sure," Frank said in strong agreement. "And we also brought some Guinness, in keeping with the Irish theme." I didn't want him buying any beer. I told him Bailey's would be enough and that there was no theme. He insisted, though.

"Hey guess what?" Vincent said, getting out some glasses from one of his cabinets. "I've been practicing." He poured the creamy whiskey drink into three small glasses and took one into his little living room. I took one of the glasses and followed him.

"Hey, Vince, mind if I put the beer in the fridge?" Frank asked.

"Yeah, sure thing," Vincent said from the other room.

Frank came into the main room with us and started looking at his surroundings with the hungry curiosity of a child in a museum for the first time in his life. I wondered if he was going to try to figure out what kind of person my brother was based on his extremely eclectic collection of stuff. I hoped that he'd quickly figure out that Vincent stood on his own and wasn't someone who could be categorized, given the absence of a single category that included Catholics, pagans, bibliophiles, hippies, musicians, Renaissance types, artists, and amateur astronomers. I was quite sure I left something out.

Vincent started playing a song on the guitar and singing with a slight Irish brogue. I took a big sip of booze and looked over at Frank, who to my relief, didn't look freaked out at all. He was standing over me looking at Vincent play like he really admired his talent. I took another sip and delighted in the warm sensation in my stomach and was able to relax and even enjoy the music. I recognized the song from one of Vincent's albums. After he finished playing, he told us that it was an old English folk song called "Sheep-Crook and Black Dog."

"That was great, Vince," Frank said, raising his glass as a form of applause.

"Yeah, it sure was!" I said with too much enthusiasm. I tried to think of a follow-up question about the song, but my mind was as blank as a shiny-clean chalkboard, and I got uncomfortable in the brief silence. I turned to see Frank looking in the direction of the crystal ball and feared he was going to ask a question about it, and sure enough, he did. He asked Vincent if it was real crystal, and he said "Yeah," and I prayed he wouldn't start talking about any funny stuff like seeing the future when he looked into it. I slammed the rest of my drink down and went in the kitchen to get a beer, and when Frank heard me open the refrigerator door, he asked me if I could get him one.

"Sure," I said. "Vincent, you want a beer or more Baileys."

"Both," he said. Frank started laughing like it was the funniest thing he ever heard, and I could only imagine how much he must have loved Vincent's response. I knew the two of them would be boozing it up. Usually, I'd get down on Frank for drinking too much but not that night. I just passed drinks out like a cocktail waitress and got settled back in my chair as Frank was asking Vincent if he played anything else besides the guitar.

"Fiddle, mandolin, bass guitar, Celtic banjo, dulcimer, penny whistle. That's it for now."

"For now?!" Frank said, laughing. "That's incredible! So, what's next?"

"I gotta learn the harp." He spoke in his most matter-of-fact tone.

"Oh, I love the harp," I said.

"What's a Celtic banjo?" Frank said.

"A banjo with four strings," Vincent said. "For playing Celtic tunes."

"You like to play Irish music then?" Frank said.

"Oh yeah," Vincent said. He was the most Italian-looking person I knew, and his name was Vincent Tucci, but he loved Irish music. Crazy, huh?

"What do you play, Frank?" Vincent said, like he assumed that he must play some instrument.

"I just play guitar," Frank said as though he was saying that he played the kazoo. "But I haven't played in a while." Vincent didn't respond. He just got up and handed the guitar he was playing to Frank and grabbed a bass guitar from his closet.

"Thanks, Vince," Frank said. "Nice one. A Martin."

"What about something for me?" I said, half-jokingly.

"Wait a minute," Vincent said, getting up from his seat. He was back in a minute with a penny whistle, which I hadn't played in years.

Together, we all fumbled around for about an hour or so, playing mostly early Beatle songs. I ended up being the singer in our little band and only playing the penny whistle once in a while. Initially, Frank was messing up left and right, but as the night went on (and so did the drinking), he got better, and when he didn't know a chord, he'd look at Vincent, who would mouth the name of the chord back to him. In fact, we all got better, and I thought we sounded really good, or at least we did inside my own drunken head.

We had so much fun making music that three hours just danced by, and when Vincent went to use the bathroom, Frank told me we should head home soon because it was getting late. The thought of ending this wonderful night and leaving Vincent alone made me go from jubilant to sad in an instant. I never didn't want anything to end as much as I didn't want that night to end. But I knew Frank was right, and when Vincent came back from the bathroom, I told him we had to go soon.

"Let's just play one more," Vincent said, sitting down.

"You name it," I said to him.

"'Animal Farm' by the Kinks," Vincent said. I wanted to jump up and down at the suggestion because I always loved that song, and I knew all the words. Frank said he wasn't sure if he knew it, so I told Vincent to play the record for him in hopes that he'd recognize it.

"Oh, I know this song," Frank said, after it played for about a minute.

Vincent started the song again, and we played with the record, and then we played it on our own and one more time with the record. The last time we played the song, it was perfect, and it swallowed us up in one magical gulp and blurred any lines that lived between us. It didn't matter that Frank would soon be a lawyer and that Vincent made cookies in a factory or that Frank and I would be married and living in a nice house while Vincent stayed alone in his same run-down apartment. It didn't matter who we were or where we were going because the music leveled everything out, made us indivisible, and let us float gloriously above this world.

When the song ended, Vincent walked us out to our car where we hugged goodbye and drove away while I waved a limp, sad wave. I felt tears growing inside of me, which I held back, but as soon as Vincent was out of sight, they came pouring out, fast and furious as if angry at me for trying to hold them back. Frank looked over and asked what was wrong.

"I just get sad sometimes when I see Vincent all alone," I said through my sniffling. "I wish he had somebody. I try to think of girlfriends to introduce him to, but he's just so different than anyone I know, and I just get sad is all. I…" I began fully crying with sobs and all. I wanted to blame my tears on the alcohol but knew that they were a long time coming.

Frank pulled over, stopped the car, and reached over to hug me, which consoled me but made me cry more. He continued to hold me and eventually my crying reduced to a whimper. He didn't try to make it better or tell me to stop crying or tell me that I shouldn't be sad because maybe Vincent was happy that way. He just held me and my sadness and my pain. He just let it be, and in that sorrowful moment, my love for him grew huge, like a mountain that lived high among the clouds.

CHAPTER FIVE: 1984

"Where's the beef?" I said to Vincent, mocking the old lady on the commercial for Wendy's that played every five minutes on TV. We were eating square-shaped burgers from that very same fast-food chain, sitting on the back of his red pickup truck by the Atsion Lake. Bee buzzes muffled in the warm air, and every so often some ducks swam by us, some in little families grouped together as if connected by an invisible string. An occasional gentle breeze rolled off the lake that rippled to the shore in perfect half-circles.

"Oh yeah, that commercial," Vincent said, smirking. His hair was the shortest it had been since high school, and I could see him again, and with his hair cut away, his face returned to the boyish innocence of his youth, his cheeks full and his eyes squinting into the sunlight that shined in them. He also returned to the clothes of his youth—no more overalls and work boots. He was back to jeans and T-shirts, and he even had Reebok sneakers like everybody else wore, not Converse high-tops that people wore back in the sixties. He took a bite that was about a quarter of his burger and looked out on to the lake.

I never ate junk food, but being pregnant made me crave the stuff with a ferocity that bordered on addiction. Still, I wasn't eating nearly as much as I did during my first pregnancy, when I could eat half of a pepperoni pizza without suffocating in fullness. I worried that I'd turn out a big, fat, colicky baby because of all the crap I ate, but instead, I had Angie, with her pink smiling lips and big, bright eyes looking out at the world, ready for all it had to give her. I wanted to name her after Mom but knew she'd be in for a lifetime of people mispronouncing her name by saying it with a hard *G*. So, we named her after Frank's Dad, Angelo. For my second time around, I was expecting a boy, and Mom begged me to name him after Dad because none of their own were named after him. I was fine with Dad's name, but I planned on Americanizing it from Cosimo to Cosmo.

Although I wasn't eating like I did during my first pregnancy, polishing off a burger and fries was still no problem, and I was overjoyed by the fact that leggings and oversized sweaters were the style so that I could be comfortable as I grew out. Being comfortable was crucial because I spent so much of my time reading and writing papers since I started grad school. Three days a week, I'd drop Angie off at Mom's and drive into

Philly for my classes. In between classes, I was at the
library working on papers while I ate peanut butter
sandwiches I brought from home and jammed small
paper cups full of vending-machine coffee that tasted
like liquid cardboard—just like in my college days.

I loved my classes even more than I did in my
college days too. Some of them had only six students
and everybody was so passionate about literature. A
week ago, we'd had the best discussion of Huck Finn in
my 19th Century American Literature class. My
professor, Mr. Jones, had asked what Huck was really
after in the novel.

"Freedom," my classmate, Lisa had said. "The
same thing Jim's after."

"Good," Mr. Jones had said, his dark eyes
glowing with mystery like he was hiding something.
"What else?"

"Happiness," I'd said.

"Very good, and how does he find that
happiness?"

He'd looked at me for an answer, but nothing
came and so, he'd looked around at the rest of the
class, and my classmate, Duane had said, "He found
happiness in his friendship with Jim." He'd said it more

like a question than a statement as if he'd known it wasn't the answer our teacher was looking for.

"He could only be happy living the pioneer life that he wanted to live," Mr. Jones had said. "He wasn't like everybody else, and he didn't want to live up to society's expectations of him." A wave of light had swept over me, brilliant and shining, like a cloud on fire.

Frank was working at a well-established law firm in Cherry Hill, and we'd recently moved into a red-brick ranch-style house in our hometown with a big front yard and an even bigger backyard that reminded me of the one in my childhood fantasy.

Vincent was still in the same old apartment that belonged to Dad, and every time Dad got mad at him, which was like all the time, he'd threatened to kick him out, and he couldn't afford to move out and go anywhere else, so he just stayed and put up with it. Some months he couldn't even make rent, and I was certain that the only reason Dad let him stay was that Saint Peter crap that Mom had told him years earlier. I thought Vincent could have afforded to move out if he got a decent job, but he was still working his same old jobs. He left the cookie factory, saying that a robot could do his job, and started painting houses with some round, sweet man named Johnny Molatzo, but it was only here and there—nothing full-time.

"Do you ever think of going for a job in the casinos?" I asked as I ate the last of my fries. I knew those glitzy shit-hole palaces were the complete opposite of him but thought there had to be something he could do there that wouldn't be so awful. "I'm not saying getting a job as a Black Jack dealer but maybe something in one of the restaurants or something like security."

"That cornball place?" He waved his hand in the air.

"It might not be so bad. You'd have more money and health benefits. Carmen worked there. Nancy worked there during her summers in college." I was expecting him to tell me to can it, but instead, he asked me if I wanted to come with him to the music store in Pleasantville, where he wanted to buy a new mandolin.

"A new mandolin?!" I snapped back. "You haven't worked in months." He barely had money to eat. I forked over for Wendy's. He wanted to pay, but I wouldn't let him. Mom kept him stocked up with boxes of macaroni and cans of tuna fish or else he'd go hungry.

"I work. I paint houses. I have money to get a new mandolin." The tone and volume of his voice remained the same even though he was defending himself. In fact, he even chuckled.

"You know if you worked at the casinos, you'd be able to buy more instruments."

"I told you, those casinos are a lousy deal. I'd feel like a real horse's ass working there." He took a drag from his cigarette and blew smoke out towards the lake.

"I thought you were going to quit."

"I am...one day." He hunched over and laughed, half of his face hiding behind his hand.

I really started to get tired of trying to convince both him and Mom to quit. Surprisingly, Dad quit a few months ago. Cold turkey. I thought if Dad could quit, Mom and Vincent should have been able to do it too. I was wrong.

"C'mon," he said, ignoring my nagging. "Let's go to the music store."

At that, we both got in the truck and drove off. Soon after leaving the cookie factory, he'd learned to drive and got the big old clunker that we were sitting in. Right after he got the truck, he wanted to drive to upstate New York to see Robin Williamson, the guy who started The Incredible String Band. He talked me into going, and we drove and drove as the surrounding mountains grew larger, and the winds outside grew colder.

"I thought you said it was just a few hours away," I'd said, sitting in the passenger seat, freezing because the heater didn't work so great. "I just saw a sign for Canada!" He'd laughed and told me we were almost there. We'd got to some little dark tavern with a bunch of old mountain hippies sitting around, and when Robin came out, Vincent was in his glory listening to him sing old Scottish ballads, tell stories, and play the harp. In between sets, the two of them talked like old pals, and I'd found out that they'd known each other because Vincent's old landlady in Pennsylvania was good friends with the guy.

We were quickly approaching the music store that was in a crummy neighborhood on a busy street. There was nothing charming about this place, but according to Vincent, they carried top quality instruments. The salesman was an adorable old man dressed in a maroon suit and a bow tie, and he gave Vincent a break on the mandolin because he was a regular and could pay in cash.

We went straight back to his place and were barely through the door when he took the mandolin out of its case and started tuning it. The air in his place was stale and stuffy as always, which figured because he was a smoker who rarely opened the windows. Bad smells bothered me more than usual during my pregnancies, so I opened a bunch of windows and expected him to say something back, but he was too engulfed with his new instrument.

I went into the kitchen, put on some water for tea, and sat down at his kitchen table, which was always completely covered with papers, pens, markers, books, guitar picks, cups, and boxes of tea. Beneath all this stuff was a really cool, vintage, white Formica table from the 1950s. I got out two English Breakfast tea bags and put them in a couple of clean cups that weren't easy to find. I opened the refrigerator for milk to find it was bare, except for a container of milk, a head of partially brown lettuce, a couple tomatoes, and a jar of mayonnaise.

"Can you put sugar in mine?" Vincent yelled out from the other room. "It's on the table." The sorry-looking, little sugar bowl sat on the over-crowded table without a lid and sugar that looked like some coffee spilled into it. I carefully spooned out some clean sugar for his tea and brought the two cups in the other room, where he was still tuning his mandolin. I sat down which, since I'd been pregnant, was my favorite thing to do. I looked around at Vincent's place, and for some reason, the place didn't look so bad to me. It could have been the sun's rays coming through the room, reflecting on a piece of rose quartz that sat on one of his tables or that it was a little neater than usual or that I was feeling happy in my pregnancy, and the happy feeling made me see the place differently.

"Hey, listen to this," Vincent said as he started playing a melody.

I sat and listened and sipped my tea as sunbeams danced across the room. After he finished the first song, he started playing another, and whenever I'd tell him how great he sounded, he'd say "I've been practicing." I could have sat and listened to him play all day, but I had to get back home. It was Saturday, so Frank was able to watch Angie while I got out for a while, but soon, she'd be up from her nap and too much for him to handle on his own.

I hugged Vincent goodbye and said I'd see him tomorrow which would be Easter Sunday.

I entered the back door of my house holding a large framed print of Monet's *Water Lilies* that I bought for our living room. The back door entered into the kitchen that was in the center of the house. When I'd first stepped foot in this room, I knew we'd found our home. The beady-eyed Realtor had opened the door saying, "I got a good feeling about this place." Outside, it was icy, but the kitchen, with its homey wooden cabinets and burnt red tiled floors, made me feel warm inside.

It was quiet, so I knew that Angie was still napping, and I walked lightly through the kitchen and the dining room, where a picture window framed a view of our backyard worthy of a painting. Pressed up against the window was a honeysuckle bush in full bloom, and beyond that, a dogwood tree was flowering in the palest shade of pink. A crystal chandelier hung in the center of the room, chains of cut glass gracefully hanging from it, letting the light dance rainbows on them on sunny days. I walked through the den where built-in dark brown bookshelves housed some of my favorite classics, copies of *National Geographic,* and a set of encyclopedias—a gift Mom gave us when Angie was born. Finally, I got to Frank's study where he was leaned over a case law book and a yellow legal pad.

"Look what I got!" I announced, holding up the painting for him to see, but he only looked at it for an instant and said, "Oh nice" and then put his head back in his book. I couldn't get upset at him because he was busy preparing for some big murder trial, plus he was always indifferent to things like décor. I sometimes felt like I could bring home a velvet picture of Elvis or the Last Supper sold by one of those side-of-the-road vendors, and he'd just say it was fine.

I went into the living room to hold the print up on the spot on the wall where I planned to put it and seeing how well it complemented the olive-green carpeting and yellow velvet chairs made me tipsy with feelings of self-praise. When I started to think I missed my calling as an interior decorator, I had to rein myself in. I looked out our giant front window that I loved to sit by on weeknights while waiting for Frank to come up the driveway. Beside our long driveway was our front yard where a sturdy, old oak tree sat in the center with branches that sprawled out in all directions and leaves that turned a brilliant shade of orange in the fall. A rose bush grew on the side of our house with roses a color somewhere between beet red and deep violet. They smelled way better than any roses that came from a flower shop. They smelled sweet, spicy, and timeless. They smelled like love.

I entered Mom's house carrying a bag of Easter candy in one arm and Angie in the other. The smell of baking ham and gravy filled the air. Mom pranced around the kitchen like a fairy working hard to get miracles to happen until she saw her granddaughter, who wore a white dress with embroidered flowers. Her eyes glistened joyfully as she walked towards me. Angie bounced in my arm and held her hands out to her grandma. I offered to finish up the artichokes, so Mom could dote on her for a little while.

After I finished the artichokes, I went into the living room and looked out the window to see a big, dull green shape coming down the street. As the shape got closer, it turned into Vincent dressed in some kind of Medieval-looking costume. He came up the driveway to the front door, and I dashed to answer it.

"What are you?" I said, answering the door for what felt like an overaged, oversized, trick-or-treater.

"Oh, I'm an elf," he said too casually for the occasion. It made sense when I looked more closely at the outfit—a short army green robe fastened with a leather sash and a matching cape draped over him. Being tall should have made him an awkward elf. I could have easily imagined him dressed as a grand and towering wizard, but he managed to pull off the elf thing beautifully.

"Definitely not one of Santa's," I said as he came inside.

"No, from *Lord of the Rings*." He made a hearty laugh and hunched over, making his costume wrinkle in the dim light of the foyer.

He carried an egg carton full of what could have only been Easter eggs. He walked into the kitchen, and I followed him, marveling at the costume that he must have made himself and wondering how he could have made it without a sewing machine. He didn't own a sewing machine that I knew of anyway.

"Well, hello," Mom said as he entered the kitchen. Her eyes were big and full of surprise but not too much surprise. This was, after-all, Vincent.

"Yo, Mom," he said, setting the carton of eggs down on the table. Nancy appeared under the archway on the side of the kitchen wearing a floral blouse with football-player shoulder pads. She just broke up with her boyfriend, which I think is what prompted her to dye her hair platinum blond. It was either the breakup or her infatuation with Madonna. I wasn't sure, but I was sure that she was still pissed at me for something that happened over two months ago.

She'd called me up to complain about her then-boyfriend, and she was going on and on, without even stopping for air, and I could hear Angie waking up from her nap. So, I'd said, "Nance, I have to go now. I'll call you back," and she'd got really weird as though she was mad at me for having a life of my own. She'd said, "Oh okay, sorry to bother you. Have a nice day," in this very formal voice. I'd called her back to apologize—like I'd really had something to be sorry for—and got her answering machine and had left a message, but she'd never called me back. I'd gone from hearing from her eighteen times a day to not hearing from her at all. She was still being snide to me while being nice to everyone else. She asked Vincent if he made his costume.

"Yo, Nance, Oh, yeah, I made it." He said it as if saying he sewed a patch on a pair of jeans.

"That's great," Nancy said, wide-eyed and smiling. "Did you walk down the street like that?"

"What?" he said, looking around, and then quickly without giving Nancy a chance to ask the question again, he said. "Oh yeah," as if he'd heard her but just asked "what" for the hell of it.

"Well, I think it's wonderful," Mom said to Vincent. "You must have your grandfather's talent." Mom's dad was a tailor, who worked for two dollars a week during the Depression. Nancy and I agreed with Mom, but he barely acknowledged our fussing over his talent.

Mom still held Angie, who looked at Vincent, her eyes bursting with fascination. She started clapping and bouncing up and down like a yoyo in Mom's arms, so Mom brought her over to Vincent, who took her and held her up, so their faces were right across from each other. They smiled at one another, like they were the same age or on the same wavelength, both communicating in a secret language that only they were privy to.

Dad came in through the back door and looked at his son like he was a giant talking bird and said, "What's going on here?" in a comical voice that eventually broke into laughter. Vincent laughed and we all joined in, and I wished Carmen, Anthony, and Gloria could have been there. They would have gotten such a kick out of his costume.

Vincent gave Angie to me and opened up the carton of eggs he brought, which were filled mostly with pastel-dyed eggs and three eggs with intricately painted designs and flowers on them.

"Those three are too beautiful to open and eat, Vince," Nancy said. "Too bad you can't save them."

"I took the egg out so you can," he said to her. "You can have one." He handed her one, warning that they were super fragile. She thanked and hugged him, and he gave the other two eggs to me and Mom.

"Thank you so much, Vincent. I want to get a little stand for it and put it in my curio cabinet when I get home. It's so precious." I asked him to hold Angie, so I could put mine in Mom's china cabinet until we were ready to go. I handled it like it was a butterfly that had come apart and been glued back together as I placed it between a golden King Tut head and a statue of a bluebird. Next to the china cabinet, Mom had a row of African violets that sat on the window ledge, flourishing and sparkling in the afternoon sun.

When I returned to the kitchen, everyone but Mom was gone. I asked her if she needed any help, and she said no and that I should just go into the living room with everybody else. I knew how she felt about having her space in her kitchen because I'd become the same way in my own. So, I went into the living room to see Angie sitting on Vincent's lap and reaching her hands out towards the piano.

"I think she wants to play it," Vincent said, carrying her over to the piano bench. When he got close enough to the piano for her to reach the keys, she started banging away on them with her tiny fingers.

"Watch out there!" Dad said swiftly. "That's a Steinway. It cost a lot of money."

"Sorry, Dad," I said as I grabbed Angie, who started to cry as soon as I took her away from the piano. "C'mon, sweetie," I said, trying to comfort her.

"She should play the piano," Vincent said. "That should be her instrument."

Dad shook his head, smirking and had a sip of his drink.

"That would be great," I said to Vincent. "One day you two could play together."

I heard a car coming up the driveway and through the living room window, I saw it was Frank. He wanted to come later, so he could have some time to work on his upcoming trial. I went to the kitchen to see him get out of the car. He came towards me, limping like a loser in a barroom brawl. Stress exasperated his limp.

I was so glad he didn't care about skipping holidays with his family, which was dominated by his miserable mother—wobbling around her house, picking up fallen crumbs with licked fingers, and still wearing black for her husband who died years ago. I only met him a couple of times and thought he was a real sweetheart, but according to Frank, his mother always complained about him when he was alive. Whenever I'd try to talk to her, she came back at me with one-word responses like she was talking to some pushy used car salesman and never—I mean never—said my name. Sometimes I wondered if she even knew it.

The last time we went to see her, we brought Angie. When I'd asked her if she wanted to hold her, she'd said, "Oh no thank you, I've held enough babies in my time," in her dried-out voice. I couldn't imagine her having any; she was about as maternal as a shoelace. She'd shown up late to her own granddaughter's baptism and sat in the back of the church with her continual frown that, while a part of her, was its own miserable entity. I was surprised she'd come at all considering she'd missed the ceremony for Frank's graduation from law school.

"Hi, honey," I said, as he came in through the back door. He was holding a bunch of flowers in his hand and gave them to Mom who hugged him saying, "Thank you so much, Frank." She looked at them with a combination of gratitude and contempt as they were mostly chrysanthemums, which she hated—one of her superstitions. She'd call them flowers for the dead. I was sure she'd toss them as soon as we left. Still, I offered to put them in a vase in the living room.

I got back to the kitchen to see Frank talking to Vincent about his costume while feeding little pieces of Easter bread loaf to Angie, who sat on his knee. Dad poured him a shot of amaretto, which he thanked him for, and drank down in a blaze, without interrupting his flow of talking to Vincent and feeding Angie. Dad gleefully poured him a second shot, and he drank this one down too, so quick and seamless, invisible to everyone in the kitchen but me.

"Maybe you can make costumes for people who go to Renaissance fairs," I said to Vincent. "You would love that, and you'd be able to show off your talents— not just making costumes, but you can do acts, like juggling and playing the dulcimer and doing some Shakespearean acting. Didn't you act in Hamlet or something once?" I got more excited as I talked, my words blurring together like a school of fish in cloudy water.

"Oh, don't talk to him about all that crazy stuff," Dad said. "He needs to get a regular job."

"But he can make money doing these fairs," I said.

"I never even heard of these things. They sound like nonsense to me," Dad said, slamming a shot of amaretto.

"They're really cool Dad. Everyone dresses up like the Renaissance times, and they play music and eat big drumsticks of meat. On the news the other night, they showed this one in Lancaster County." I couldn't believe I was trying to convince Dad that something was cool.

"He needs a job with health insurance," Dad said, walking out of the kitchen. Then, as he trailed off into the other room, he yelled, "If something happens to him, who do you think is going to have to pay? Me, that's who. And how much longer can I live?" He'd been saying that thing about not living much longer since I was about ten.

"Dinner's ready!" Mom called out.

We all headed into the dining room, where the table was covered in a white linen table cloth with matching napkins and Lenox place settings trimmed in little turquoise designs. A big fine-china dish full of ravioli sat in the center and off to the sides, deep-fried artichokes and a ham topped with pineapples. Right after we sat, Dad said grace.

"Name of the Father and Son and the Holy Spirit." He spoke in his most subdued voice, but after a couple glasses of wine, he loosened up and started in with his stories of the old times.

"Remember the time you made that good report card in high school," he said to Vincent. "That was a first for you." Vincent wore a smile big as a clown's painted lips in spite of Dad's insensitive remark.

"I asked you what you wanted as some kind of reward, and you said you wanted this album." Dad looked up at the ceiling as he tried to remember the name of the album. "Some crazy title. It had the word wedding in it. Umm..."

"Oh yeah, the *Wedding Album.*" Vincent said, leaning forward with a laugh.

"Yeah, yeah," Dad said. "I'll never forget. I drove through this blizzard—the year's worst—to some record store in Vineland. There's no other cars on the road. We get back, and I'm lying down, taking a nap, and all of a sudden, I hear, 'John...Yoko...John...Yoko.'" He spoke in a deep, mocking voice. "I said to myself, you got to be kidding me. I drove all the way to Vineland and back in a snow storm for this?!" There was a symphony of laughter with Mom's rich, deep laugh, Angie's baby-girl laugh, and Vincent's galloping laugh, rising and falling away like ocean waves.

We feasted into the early evening, until the remains of the day's light poured into the room. I think that the homemade raviolis were my favorite part of the meal. I must have had about twenty, each serving topped off with what was probably too much Parmesan.

"You're really going to town on the ravs," Dad said to me as he drank what I estimated to be his seventh glass of wine.

"Yeah, yeah," I said nonchalantly.

"She's eating for two," Frank said jokingly.

"Yeah, more like five," Dad said. "She always had a good appetite." His voice was dying down with what sounded like fatigue.

For dessert, Mom cut slices of a dark chocolate egg filled with coconut cream that was topped with a yellow confection flower. Outside, the sky was a wall of pink and fiery orange light—a stunning closing stage curtain to our Easter celebration.

CHAPTER SIX: 1989

Vincent took the bus from Atlantic City to visit me on a sunny February day that felt more like a day in late May—what I used to call a Greenhouse day—and the mild weather called me to be outside, but he wanted to stay inside because he said the sun was bothering his eyes. He sat at my kitchen table as I put on water for tea and broke open a fresh-baked loaf of banana-walnut bread. I put the loaf in front of him, and he said thanks and looked down at it with a great heaviness, like it was a list of daunting chores he had to complete.

"It took the bus an hour and a half to get here," he said as he cut a piece of bread. He looked tired, with purple circles that hung like drooping flowers under his dull, half-open eyes. He moved to Atlantic City a couple years ago and got a job as a security guard in a casino, soon after he had two root canals within six months. Mom paid but had to sneak the money from Dad, and Vincent finally realized that he needed health insurance.

"It kept stopping every two seconds," he said. I wish I could have picked him up, but it was nearly impossible to get out of the house with Angie, Cosmo and Silvia, whom I gave birth to only a few months earlier. I would have had Frank pick him up, but he was in court all day. I couldn't remember the last time I took a bus anywhere, but I did remember how shitty long bus rides could be. He had to give up his truck when he moved to Atlantic City because finding parking for it was too tough.

"At least you can read a book on the bus," I said, trying to be optimistic as I got a couple cups of tea together.

"Yeah, but it's hard to look down without getting motion sickness, and I'm so tired that every time I started to read, I just fell asleep." He was working swing shift for the past couple of months, so every couple of weeks, his schedule changed. For two weeks, he'd work graveyard, and for the next two weeks, he'd work days, and for the next two weeks, he'd work nights. This zombie-inducing work schedule kept him from ever getting good sleep, and fatigue not only showed in his face but in his slouched posture and his mood—apathetic with a tinge of grumpiness.

"How's your new place working out?" I asked, attempting a cheerful tone but failing miserably.

He lived in a room not far from the casino where he worked. It was an SRO (single resident occupancy), kind of like a boarding house where no meals are served and nobody talks to each other. He had to use a shared bathroom, and his room was super small, like a dorm room, so he left a bunch of his stuff with me and Mom because it couldn't all fit. He had a mini fridge and a hot plate and ate most of his meals out—greasy cheesesteaks and hoagies stuffed with fatty meats. Typical Atlantic City fare.

"All right," he said, with the emotion of a sleepy cow.

"How about work?"

"All right." He was still on the same piece of banana bread, taking small bites like someone with a stomach flu. "It's a job, and I got health insurance."

"That's right," I leaned forward and tried to look into his eyes in hopes of reviving them, but his head stayed tilted down as if he was trying to read a book on the floor. "Health insurance is so important. Nobody should be without it." He nodded his head in a sort of agreement that looked as if it'd been forced upon him. He seemed like some depressed imposter, and I just wanted to shake him.

"Is it possible to get a security job without having to work swing shift?"

"Not at the Claridge, right now anyway. Maybe at a different casino."

"Why don't you look then?"

"Well, because I'm thinking about joining the priesthood." It took me about a good minute to process what I just heard, partly because he said it as if he was thinking about buying a new jacket and partly because, although he was a good Catholic, he also had some beliefs and practices that the Catholic Church wouldn't be too big on—like gazing into crystal balls to tell the future, astral projecting, reading tarot cards, and casting spells.

"Huh?" I needed to make sure I wasn't hearing things.

"I said I'm thinking about becoming a priest."

"Is it anything to do with your new interest in woodworking?" This was the best I could do. I knew it seemed nonsensical, but I reasoned that Jesus was a carpenter and that maybe doing carpentry made him feel closer to Jesus and maybe that made him want to become a priest. He made beautiful things, by the way—a chair for Mom made of rich, deep walnut, an oak table for Dad's office, and a mahogany jewelry box for me, perfectly square and big enough to fit all the jewelry I acquired throughout my entire life.

"Huh?" he said, squinting his eyes. It was too much for me to explain the woodworking question, so I just asked him why he wanted to do this new thing.

"You remember that time I told you about when I was astral projecting, and I saw Joan of Arc?"

"Yes," I said with great caution, scared to find out what was coming next.

"Well, yeah that was one thing, and then just a few days ago, I did a tarot reading and asked about joining the priesthood, and the cards said it would be a great path for me."

"Do you know how crazy that sounds, Vincent?" I blurted out. "Seeing Joan of Arc through the way of something, which may or may have not been an acid trip, and a tarot reading. The Church isn't okay with all that occult crap, you know."

"I was completely straight when I saw Joan of Arc. I was astral projecting," he said through laughter. I was glad to see him laugh after being so despondent since he arrived, and with this, I felt that the depressed imposter was gone. "And you know I destroyed my crystal ball a while ago."

"You what?! Why couldn't you have sold it? That had to have been worth a lot of money."

"I had to crush it to renounce my pagan ways."

"You could have used the money."

"No, I had to, Donna." Laughter kept poking through his seriousness like raindrops coming through a crack in a wall.

"What about the tarot? You have a bunch of tarot decks. You're just going to throw all of them out? And all your occult books—you're going to toss them too?"

"Well, no." He paused for a minute. "I was hoping I could keep them here with you when I move into the seminary." When he said this thing about moving into the seminary, I knew he was really serious about it.

"Of course, you can." I looked at him straight in the eyes and said, "I just hope you're thinking this thing through really carefully. It's a really big decision, you know."

"I am," he said, drinking the last of his tea.

I feared he was searching for something he'd never find and thought that if he were happier, he wouldn't be going on this pointless quest. My efforts and energy to steer him in the happiness direction had dwindled over the years. I attributed this decline to having three small children and to the fact that all my well-thought-out advice usually resulted in him either laughing at it or telling me to can it. I did manage to convince him to get a job in the casinos, which I felt was a great accomplishment, until only a few minutes ago when I heard about his priesthood idea.

I could hear Cosmo getting up from his nap, and I told Vincent I'd be right back. I walked through the long hallway that connected all the bedrooms and into Cosmo's room, where a twin bed sat across from a tan dresser and a window that looked out onto a cherrywood fence. He yawned and rubbed his little head, which was covered with thick, black curls like his grandma and his Uncle Vincent. A tall toddler, he also inherited Vincent's height. When I told him his uncle was visiting, he smiled, showing his baby teeth like prizes he won and ran into the kitchen. I followed him in to find Vincent lifting him up in the air, both of them smiling at each other. Vincent seemed like himself again, his eyes all the way open, with some light returning to his face.

As soon as I sat down, I heard Silvia's sweet baby voice in our bedroom, and I went in to find her standing up in her crib, holding on to the railing. Our room was open and bright with a window that looked out on a rhododendron tree. We had a king-size bed that made Frank's snoring more tolerable and made it easy for Angie to sleep with us when she was having bad dreams. Silvia was sitting in her crib, looking around the room, her eyes sparkling like golden flecks in the sharpest sunlight. I picked her up and carried her into the kitchen, where Cosmo was sitting on Vincent's lap as Vincent fed him small bites of banana bread.

"Oops," Vincent said, looking up at me as I walked in. "I should have asked you if he could eat this first, huh?"

"He's okay to have a little bit of that. He's a good eater like you." I brought Silvia to Vincent, so he could see his niece, whom he only saw one other time since she'd been born.

"Who's this?" He spoke in a cutesy baby voice, slanting his head and making his eyes big.

"Silvia, meet your Uncle Vincent. Vincent, meet your niece, Silvia," I said. She put her little hand on his right cheek like she wanted to see if it was real and made a high-pitched laugh. Vincent made a silly face with his eyes open wide and his lips tightly closed, like a clown without makeup. Both Cosmo and Silvia laughed at him, which spurred him on to do more entertaining. I hated to interrupt the fun but glancing over at the clock above the kitchen sink, I saw it was time to pick Angie up from kindergarten. So, I put shoes and jackets on

Silvia and Cosmo, and we all got in the car with Vincent helping me to put them both in their car seats.

Frank bought me a Mercedes a couple years ago. He was so funny when it came to spending money—he'd buy dented cans of beans to save a dime but insisted on buying no less than a Mercedes. As soon as we got the car, he wanted to drive down to Florida and stay with his friend, Joe, from law school. He was a great guy—much too mellow and easy-going to be one of Frank's friends—but not so great on planning things to do.

One day, he'd taken us all to a cigar museum. Really thrilling stuff for toddlers. We went on a tour with some old man who'd talked especially slow—like one-syllable-at-a-time slow—making the already dull tour aspire to torture. Joe was asking him a bunch of questions, and out of nowhere, Frank started cracking up. In his bright red, Hawaiian shirt, he almost glowed against the backdrop of the place that was the same dull color as a cigar. So, the old tour guy had asked him if anything was wrong with a hint of a smile, and Frank had said, "My friend Dean. He smokes cigars!" and then he'd laughed some more. He'd told me afterwards that that was all he could think of to say and that he just found the whole situation—us having a tour in a cigar museum with the kids—to be too fucking funny!

As we drove, Silvia fell asleep in a sunbeam, Cosmo and Vincent stared out the windows, and REM sang about Orange Crush on the radio. My light feeling was replaced with heaviness that dropped in my stomach like a bowling ball as we passed the house of my old high school friend, Johnny, who died a few months ago of AIDS. He was my junior prom date, and because he hadn't told me he was gay until our senior year, I couldn't understand why he didn't want to make out after the prom.

I lightened when we arrived at Angie's school, which was the same kindergarten I went to over two decades before. It was a little white schoolhouse near the center of town and the public library. My kindergarten experience had been so much different than hers: I chewed my hair and my pencils all day, barely talked to the other kids, and couldn't wait for Mom to pick me up. Angie was so much more well-adjusted and seemed like she couldn't care less about me picking her up, and sometimes, I even felt like I was interrupting her play time.

When I arrived that day, she was playing tag with some other kids and had her coat off and thrown on the grass. As soon as we pulled into the parking lot, I got out of the car, grabbed her coat off the ground, and put it on her. The sun beat down on her beautiful, little face while I put her arms, that fell limp like hanging sausages, in the sleeves of her coat.

"I know it's not cold, honey, but you can still catch a cold." I kissed the top of her head and told her that Uncle Vincent was with us. She sparked up like a firecracker and ran to the car. I buckled her in between her pop-eyed siblings who sat in their car seats like human dolls in a land of toys, awaiting their next adventure.

"What did you learn about today, Ang?" I said as we drove out of the lot.

"A lot of stuff," she said in a sloppy little-girl voice.

"A lot of stuff?!" Vincent said playfully. "Like what?"

"Numbers and letters." She opened up her book bag, took out a wrinkled piece of paper, and gave it to Vincent. I glanced over to see that it was filled with capital and small letters of the alphabet.

"Yikes!" Vincent looked back at her after looking at the paper. "This is really great work you got here." Through the rear-view mirror, I saw her smiling proudly, her eyes glittering like polished pebbles in the sun.

"Pisa!" Cosmo blurted out from the backseat, as we passed Bruno's Pizza.

"Should we stop?" I said, like I knew what the answer would be.

"Yeah!" Cosmo shouted bubbling over with excitement. I didn't hear anything from Angie, and I looked back to see her frowning like a sad puppet.

"What's wrong, Ang?" I said.

"Cosmo," is all she said. It turned out that she was hurt because he interrupted her.

"C'mon, we'll get some pizza, Angie, and then you can tell us what else you learned today," I said while pulling over to park.

"Yeah, and it looks like you did a terrific job on those letters," Vincent said. In a matter of seconds, she went from pouting to singing to Vincent, in her cheerfully tone-deaf voice, some new song she learned in school. She sang as we parked the car, walked down the street, and entered the pizza place, growing in volume until I had to tell her to quiet down.

Inside, the place was bleached white, sparkling clean, and all business—no garlic bread, calzones, side salads, or any of that extra fluff—just the best pizza in the world. It was their own unique invention that was the perfect combination of tangy sauce, crust that was thin but had substance, and mozzarella with a dash of cheddar.

We were the only ones in there, being the odd hour of three in the afternoon. We got a table in the center, and I handed Silvia to Vincent while I put Cosmo in a booster seat. I went up to order with Vincent offering money as I walked towards the counter. I didn't respond; I just sneered back at him like he lost his mind. He laughed as he held little Silvia, who sat in his arms, silently looking around the restaurant with calm but curious eyes.

When I got back, Angie was still going on about what she did at school with Vincent listening as if it were highly fascinating and Cosmo nearly jumping up and down in his seat with pizza joy.

"I ordered a small because dinner's soon," I said to Vincent as soon as Angie took a break from talking.

"Sounds good," Vincent said. "What'd you get on it?"

"Half mushroom, half pepperoni," I said. "Wasn't that what we'd always end up getting when we were kids?"

"Sometimes, we'd get sausage," he said, gazing out at the empty space in front of him with nostalgia in his eyes.

Mrs. Bruno, an Italian lady with a heart-shaped smiling face and an apron that matched the bright white place, brought the pizza to the table, saying hi to Vincent in her thick accent.

"Yo, Mrs. Bruno," Vincent said as I took Silvia from him, so he could grab a slice.

"Where have you been?" she said.

"Oh, I moved to Atlantic City." He got a pepperoni slice and took a bite that was even huge for him, and I imagined how much he must have missed the pizza he grew up on.

"Oh, you must be working in the casinos then," she said.

"Yeah," he said, looking down at the table like he wished otherwise. Thoughts of him joining the priesthood invaded my mind like the police breaking into the house of a convicted felon. I pushed them out and cut little slices of pizza for Cosmo and Angie, who insisted that she was big enough to get her own slice. I started eating, (or at least trying to eat), while Silvia's little hands flapped merrily through the air, sometimes touching my food, sometimes hitting me in the face.

We finished the whole pizza, thanks mostly to Vincent's appetite, which I was glad to see was back to usual. We drove home with my mind taking a very rare break from the constant to-do thoughts that swirled in it like clothes in a washing machine. As soon as we walked in the door, Silvia's meek cries started, signifying her hunger that she so kindly waited to have until we got home. I thought I birthed an angel sometimes.

Vincent stayed with Cosmo and Angie while I breastfed Silvia in my room. When I was finished, I walked into the living room to find Vincent watching Cosmo play with his Legos on the floor, while telling Angie that she had the perfect fingers for playing the piano. She smiled, and her eyes sparkled like stars against the darkest sky as she held her hands up and looked at them as if she were seeing them for the first time. I put Silvia in the playpen and sat down on the couch, and as soon as I did, Angie flopped beside me and said, "Can we get a piano, Mommy?"

"One day, but not right now," I said, looking over at Vincent as if to say "Thanks a lot" facetiously, and he, in turn, laughed, hiding his face in his hands.

"I have to play the piano," Angie said, hopping off the couch and twirling around in circles. "I have the perfect fingers for it."

"All right, sweetie," I said to her. "One day soon. I promise. Why don't you play with your brother now?"

"I'm too old for Legos," she said, very sure of herself.

"Oh no," Vincent said, sitting beside Cosmo, who was trying to smash two unfitting Legos together. "You're never too old for Legos." As soon as he started to play, Angie joined in, and in a flash, forgot that she was too old for the plastic toys. I wished she could play nicely alone with Cosmo, so Vincent and I could continue our discussion about the priesthood, but she seemed to have a tough time doing anything with her little brother. I was grateful for Vincent playing with them and for Silvia being able to entertain herself in her playpen, holding her stuffed animals, looking around the room, her eyes shining bright with wonder.

"Uncle Vincent, are you staying over tonight?" Angie said, daintily sticking a red Lego onto a blue one.

"Not this time," he said.

"Oh c'mon," I said. "Why don't you stay? You're off tomorrow, I thought. We'll go see Mom."

"She's sick with a bad cold and told me to stay away. That's why I didn't go there today. Besides, I gotta get back and feed the mice."

"I thought you had rats," I said.

"I used to. Now, I have mice," he said, staring down at the miniature red and blue plastic village he was making.

I sat back, attempting some kind of mild relaxation when the kitchen phone rang. Getting up to answer it seemed to take all the energy I had left, especially because I feared it was Frank with some bullshit excuse of why he couldn't make it home for dinner.

A hello was halfway out of my mouth when I heard, "Hi, honey, it's me." He was speaking in his bad news voice—saccharine and affectionate. "I'm so sorry, but I can't make it home for dinner. I'm working on that same case—the drug possession one I told you about."

"Frank, you knew Vincent was visiting us tonight."

"I know, but what can I do? I don't want my client to go to jail. And tomorrow I got an arraignment for that assault case, and after that, I got to go to the prison to meet up with a new client who's facing thirty years to life!" I was constantly hearing about his never-ending work itinerary.

"Can you at least get home soon, so you can bring him back to Atlantic City?"

"I thought he was staying over."

"No. He has to get back, and I don't want him taking the bus."

"All right," he said. "I'll be back by eight."

"Okay, I appreciate that." I was silent, fishing for an "I love you," which he'd been saying to me less frequently.

"Okay, bye, hon—"

"Don't you want to tell me something?"

"Oh, I'm sorry. I love you."

Ever since he got his own practice, staying late at the office became a pretty common occurrence. I thought he'd be working less, or at least that's what he told me when he signed the lease for his office space. He stayed at work late about three times a week and went out for drinks after work on at least one of the other two nights.

I thought fondly back on the days, that weren't too long ago, but that seemed like another lifetime, when he couldn't wait to get home and tell me about his day—his clients, his experiences in court, what he talked about with some judge. The day he'd got his very first own client, he'd burst through the door of our house wearing one of his only suits—some pinstriped thing that was semi-gangster looking—with a bottle of cheap Champagne in one hand and his briefcase in the other.

"I got my first case!" he'd announced, smiling so big that it almost looked like it'd hurt. "The first of my very own." Without even giving me time to respond, he'd gone on to tell me how it was a shoplifting case in which his client had switched the price tags on two different items in the accessory section of a department store.

I went back into the living room for a little while before going into the kitchen to warm up the pot of lentil soup I made the night before. I got out a loaf of rye bread and butter and put a salad together.

"Dinner's ready," I said, picking Silvia up from the playpen and putting her at the table in a high chair made of off-white plastic.

"Where's Daddy?" Angie said, walking into the kitchen. When I told her that he couldn't make it home because he had a lot of work to do, she said, "Again?" I ignored her and started doling out soup for everyone.

"Oh, homemade lentil soup," Vincent said cheerfully like he hadn't polished off a pizza only a couple hours ago. "Looks great."

"Yeah, Mom's recipe," I said with the enthusiasm of a dying bug. I buttered Cosmo's bread and watched him as he took great efforts to eat soup with his plastic spoon. I looked towards Vincent and asked if he'd spoken to Mom about his decision.

"Talked to Grandma about what?" Angie said as she broke her bread into little pieces, small enough to feed to a baby chick.

"About none of your business, honey," I said back to her. "And if you keep playing with your food, you're not going to get any dessert." She lived for dessert, so she got that threat a lot.

"Oh yeah," Vincent said. "She thinks it's great."

"What does Grandma think is great?" Angie said.

"Angie, please!"

"It's okay to tell her," Vincent said. He then turned to her and told her that he was thinking about becoming a priest. She slanted her little head, and her eyes puzzled in confusion.

"Those men who wear black and say mass, honey," I explained to her.

"Why?" she said, turning to her uncle, face still flummoxed.

"That's what I want to know," I said.

Vincent laughed and turned to Angie and said, "Because," in a cartoon voice with playful eyes. Then, she said, "Because why?" This could have gone on forever.

"Honey, please let your uncle and I talk," I said to her with real pleading in my voice. At this, she turned away from her uncle, looked down at her plate resentfully, and began to eat some of her soup, which I was sure had turned cold.

"Do you think the priesthood will make you happy?" I said to Vincent.

"Yeah, sure. I think it'll be a lot of fun," he said, as if he was thinking of joining a circus.

"I hope you give it some more thought before you make your decision. That's all I'm saying." I started clearing plates from the table. I wished I could talk to him longer, but I had to start getting the kids ready for bed.

"Angie, go brush your teeth," I said, as I loaded dishes into the dishwasher.

"What about dessert?" I got out a carton of strawberry ice cream and robotically put a small scoop in a plastic bowl for her.

"Frank's going to take you back to AC," I said to Vincent, who replied that he didn't mind taking the bus. I ignored his comment and told him I'd be right back as I picked up Silvia.

I brought her into our bedroom, changed her, kissed the top of her head while whispering an "I love you" in her little ear, and put her down. I brought Cosmo in the bathroom and brushed his teeth and went back into the kitchen where Vincent sat with Angie who was talking to him about her favorite kinds of ice cream—a list which included all five kinds she had in the course of her very short life.

Vincent suggested that we all go outside and look at the stars because it was such a clear night. So, we put coats on, went out in the backyard, and sat on the picnic bench while Vincent pointed out all the stars to us. We followed his big hand moving across the starlit sky in perfect synchronicity. Cosmo's eyes were open wide, brimming with a curiosity and exuberance I never saw in him before. We weren't outside too long when I heard the sound of Frank's car coming up the driveway, blasting through our placid star-gazing time.

As soon as he got out of the car, Angie ran up to him, shouting "Daddy!" He picked up Angie and continued on towards us as if he were in a walking race. His worry lines hid in the darkness, but as he got closer to me, they showed, thick, dark, and deep as if drawn on his face with a black marker. Frank and Vincent said hi to each other, and as we all turned to go inside, Cosmo began to cry, which was a true rarity for him.

"It's okay, honey, we'll come out tomorrow night, and you can look at the stars again." I tried to console him, but he just kept crying and continued even after we were inside. Even Vincent couldn't get him out of his crankiness with his clownish antics.

"How's it going, Vince?" Frank said loudly above Cosmo's crying.

"Not bad," Vincent said. "How about you?"

"Can't complain," Frank said. "Just tired of having to stay late so many nights."

"I don't know why you can't bring your work home," I said.

"I wouldn't get anything done." It was tough to buy this excuse because up until a couple years ago, he brought his work home all the time, and it seemed like he was getting it all done just fine.

"Did you eat something?" I asked Frank.

"No, I'll just grab something on the way back," he said and then turned to Vincent to ask him if he was ready to go.

"Sure thing," Vincent said, turning to me and the kids to say goodbye. He picked up Cosmo, who was still sobbing lightly, and Angie grabbed on to his waist. I joined the group hug that, like the star-gazing, felt cut short by Frank's silent hurrying. We all watched as the two of them walked to the car, and the car drove off, Vincent waving, his smile shining in the faint light of the moon.

After they left, I read *Goodnight Moon* to Angie and Cosmo, who calmed down as I read in my most soothing bedtime-story voice. Although calmer, he was still thinking about the stars in the nighttime sky and made me promise him three times that we'd go out to look at them more often. After tucking the two in their beds, I finished the dishes and went to take a bath.

As bath water ran, I looked in the mirror to find a tired, worn-down woman staring back. I took my hair out of the ponytail I constantly wore and let it hang down on my shoulders. Fine lines had started to form around my eyes—fanning out like perfectly curved creases—and that morning I plucked the first gray hair out of my head.

I immersed in the bubble-filled tub, the one and only luxury I had left, and felt a mild sadness come over me. It wasn't about my saying goodbye to Vincent. I didn't get sad at saying bye to him when he was the one leaving. It was because I saw Frank for a total of twenty minutes all day, during which we'd interacted with each other with the dry mechanization of a person ordering from a fast-food drive-thru window. Pictures of our past flooded my brain—good pictures of how it used to be: making love by candlelight, bringing me breakfast in bed on Mother's Day, sitting with me and Angie, our little family cuddled together like animals trying to stay warm on frosty nights.

At some point, we'd started breaking apart and doing our own thing. I knew that alcohol was the cause of our divide. I'd go to bed alone, and he'd fall asleep in front of the television with a six-pack beside him. I told myself we were independent. I rehearsed, in my mind, what I would say to him to get him to stop drinking or at least cut back, but it was never the right time. There was always some great excuse—a big upcoming trial or some other lame reason—that surrounded and guarded him like knights protecting a fortress.

And then there was Vincent joining the priesthood. I envisioned him in one of those black priest outfits. It didn't fit him right, and he looked uncomfortable and sad in it. But then I saw him living in the SRO, eating food out of a can, and working crazy hours. Suddenly, the priesthood looked all right. Inspiring even. I imagined him playing holy songs on his guitar, giving really meaningful sermons, getting into good conversations and debates about philosophy, maybe even teaching in a Catholic college one day. Best of all, he'd have something to be proud of, kind of like that loaf of fresh-baked bread he made for me and Mom.

CHAPTER SEVEN: 1993

Vincent's apartment in Ventnor was in one of those typical South Jersey shore beach houses—a big, old, white place lovingly weathered by the salt air. I loved it! It reminded me of the summer rentals we'd get when I was a kid, usually something right on the boardwalk. Lying in the sun in my yellow bikini, eating ice cream sundaes, walking the boards at night, we three girls driving around the little shore towns with Carmen in his rust-colored Toyota. I could still see the beach-worn copy of *Watership Down* on his dashboard. He never read it, but it remained on his dashboard like a fixture, and when he lost it, he went out and got a replacement copy that he also never read.

I laughed thinking of it as I rang the doorbell and waited on the front porch. Someone named Barbara, who lived in one of the downstairs apartments, answered the door. I met her before—a soft-spoken lady who claimed to be an alien abductee. I made my way up to his apartment on the second floor and knocked on the door, which he answered immediately wearing a smile that took over his entire face and a Bart Simpson T-shirt. Behind him was the brightest and biggest apartment that he ever had and like ten times bigger than his room at the seminary.

His strange interlude at the priesthood may have even been worth it after all—not because he enjoyed his time there but because he didn't. I could still see the look on his face when I said goodbye to him. His eyes had the fear and confusion of a child who was just separated from his mother for the first time in his life. Not the slightest hint of excitement like the time he left for college. Anthony and Nancy drove him up. I would have gone, but both Silvia and Cosmo were sick, so I couldn't get away.

Mom and I had gone to visit him once and would have gone more, but visiting wasn't encouraged by the staff at the seminary. It was up in North Jersey, near Newark, which wasn't too far away but seemed like it was on another continent. Maybe it was because it had been further away from me than any other place he ever lived, or maybe because it was its own special kind of world, insulated in a way from the real world that buzzed around its perimeters. It was so tough to believe that this peaceful, little place was only a stone's throw from New York City.

When we arrived there, he showed us around the grounds and inside the stunning cathedral—stained glass windows, ornate chandeliers, marble floors. The kind of church that made me wish I were a good practicing Catholic. Mom wanted to bring him out for lunch, but he'd said that kind of thing was frowned upon, so we all ate in the cafeteria of the school. The food, just about all of which came out of a can, was bland and overcooked, but Mom and I had pretended to like it.

"This is really good," I'd said as I ate a spoonful of creamed corn.

"Yes," Mom had agreed.

Vincent had nodded in sad agreement. Mom and I had tried to seem enthusiastic, but I was sure he'd seen right through us. He sat there eating like a sleepwalker, his eyes dull and empty like those of a cow. The whole time, he'd never laughed and barely talked, and when he did, he'd mumbled his words, his head fixed downward as if a great weight were pressing down on the back of it. He smiled once, but it was a half-broken smile, weak and pointless.

I was jubilant a month later when he'd told me he'd wanted to leave. Of course, I was encouraging and told him not to feel bad for leaving. "You tried something, and it didn't work out," I'd said to him on the phone.

"Yeah," he'd said, deadpan. "I'm just doing the best I can."

I knew he felt bad, but I also knew that once he was out of that place, it wouldn't take long for him to get back to himself. I was right. He came back to Atlantic City with a renewed sense of appreciation for the place and decided, on his own, that he would get a real apartment, not an SRO.

The first words out of his mouth after "Yo, Donna," were, "I've been practicing." I said, "Let's hear some tunes," and he played "And Your Bird Can Sing." He sat near a small oak table he made that had various crystals displayed on it, an amethyst in the center of them all glimmering strong in the early afternoon sun. When I asked him if he was getting into any of the crystal healing stuff that had become so popular, he said, "Nah, I just like the way they look."

I sat down on one of the three chairs in the room and listened to him play. Iridescent strips of light danced across the room, on the stereo, the TV that sat in the center, the bookshelves, and of course, Vincent, who was playing like a real pro. This place had become a type of sanctuary for me—an escape from the rollercoaster that my marriage had become with Frank,

Mr. Mood Swing, and his constant temper tantrums over nothing.

A week ago, he'd slammed through the door like a tornado, got a tall glass out, filled it with scotch and about a sip of orange juice. He drank down half of it in one giant gulp. Then, he'd started complaining about this new judge, whom he'd claimed was out to get him. Whenever I'd tried to say something in an attempt to console him, he snapped back, "You don't know what you're talking about!" or "You can never understand!" or "I work my ass off going around to all these little shit courthouses all over the fucking place! You don't know what that's like! How could you know?!"

He'd left without saying goodbye and didn't come home until midnight, smelling like the floor of a fraternity house after a keg party. It killed me because every time I'd suggest going out for a nice dinner, he'd complain about money—how taxes were due, or we needed a new roof for our house—but when it came to pissing money away in a bar, he had no problem.

As a highly functioning alcoholic, he wasn't drunk a lot—usually, he was just in maintenance mode, which required numerous drinks evenly spaced throughout each day like a diabetic on insulin shots. When he was drunk, how his behavior would manifest was anybody's guess. That night, after he'd slipped into bed, he'd started groping me. I'd felt violated, not just because he'd been a bastard to me that morning but because being drunk turned him into a hateful imposter. I'd told him I didn't feel well, but he continued, so finally I got up and went to sleep on the couch. When I'd seen him the next morning, he'd acted like the day before hadn't happened, and I wondered if, in his drunken state, he'd forgotten, or more likely, was just pretending to have forgotten. He'd just stood at the sink, drinking his coffee, staring out the window, distant as some far-away exotic island that only exists, for most people, in pictures.

And then there was Cosmo and Angie with their constant fighting, her screaming, "Mom, Cosmo cut the hair off my Barbie!" followed by his response, "She started it! She drew all over my comic book!" or Cosmo's lack of response because he knew it annoyed her more to be ignored than to fight with her. Silvia was still easy, though. She could sit for hours drawing and coloring.

"I think Silvia inherited your artistic talents," I said to Vincent, searching my bag for a pack of cigarettes. I started the habit I was always so viciously against, it effortlessly slipping into my life like a magician making something appear from nothing. I thought I was too old to get hooked, but one day I found myself lighting up and puffing away without thinking or even knowing what I was doing.

"Yo, what are you doing that for?" Vincent stopped playing, suddenly. He never did that. The world could be coming to an end, and he wouldn't let it interrupt his playing.

"What?" I played dumb. "Oh this. I'll stop next week."

"When did you start?"

"Last month. It's only been a month, so I can quit anytime I want." I lied. It had been over a year. I started when he was at the seminary. I had been able to refrain during our past visits, but now, I was really hooked. Of course, fucking Frank was the reason I started.

One night, when he didn't come home, I'd sat in our living room, staring out at the driveway waiting to see his car pull up, biting my nails down so far that one of them bled. I'd imagined him dead by the side of the road after he'd drove his car into a tree or a pole because he was drunk. I couldn't leave the house with the kids there, even though they were all in bed, or else

I would have driven to his office and the local bars he frequented in search of him.

I'd found a pack of cigarettes in his drawer that he'd smoked once in a great while when he'd drink more than the usual excessive amount. Before that, I'd only smoked a couple times in college and never cared for it and thought cigarettes stupid and gross, but I couldn't think of anything else to do, so I'd smoked one and then another and then one more because I always did things in threes.

I'd felt like such crap the next day and told myself never again, but when we'd had our next fight a week later over me spending too much money on clothes for the kids, I'd gone out to Wawa's (our local convenience store) and got a pack of my own. I'd stood at the counter staring up at all the options for cigarettes like I was studying a train schedule, when the pimpled salesclerk asked me what I wanted in a squeaky voice. I went with a pack of Salem's because that's what Mom smoked.

"It's not like that," Vincent said seriously. It was so rare to see him serious, so his words carried extra weight. "I've been trying to quit for years now. I did hypnosis, the patch, everything. It's tough to quit. I heard cigarettes are more addictive than heroin."

"That's crazy," I said, taking a reluctant puff. "Mom said it's easy to quit."

"Then why does she still smoke?"

"She quit before, but she chose to smoke again."

He waved his hand like he thought that was bullshit and said, "Does she know you started smoking?"

"No." I'd like to tell him the reason I started and how stressful my home life became and how the love was slowly (and sometimes quickly) draining out of my marriage, but I couldn't. So, I just promised him that I'd quit next week. He looked really skeptical and seemed like he wanted to go on about it, so I changed the topic to something I felt sure he'd be interested in.

"Hey, you know that the character name, Homer Simpson, comes from this really cool novel by Nathanael West called *The Day of the Locust?*" He wasn't interested, but at least he stopped talking about the dangers of smoking.

"Wanna go to White House?" he asked, standing up and putting his guitar in its case.

"Sure," I said, putting my cigarette out. "I haven't had a cheesesteak in years."

As we were almost out the door, I saw a sketchbook on one of his tables, and I rejoiced inside to know that he was drawing again. We went out the door and down the steps to find the sun shining bright and the air heavy with damp, warm ocean breezes. I offered to drive, but he said we should walk, so we started up Atlantic Avenue, passing by three-story houses with windows that wrapped around them, brown-stone apartment buildings, and the occasional shop, one of which was a shoe store.

"Let's go in," I said, looking in the window.

I needed a new pair of sandals to replace the ones I wore that were falling apart. Shopping for myself, as opposed to shopping for Frank and the kids, was something that happened with the infrequency of a solar eclipse. I was looking for something plain, drab, and practical like my falling-apart ones when a pair of royal blue suede clogs popped out at me. They were completely impractical and way too warm for the season, but I had to have them.

"Do you have these in a nine?" I said with urgency to the closest salesperson I saw.

"I'll go check," she said turning to me, her straight blond hair falling into her very tanned face.

"Thank you so much," I said. I looked over at Vincent, who sat by the door looking out the window. It was so nice to be shopping with someone who wasn't yanking on my arm, telling me to "C'mon, Mom, we have to get to the toy store before it closes!" or something like that.

When the saleslady came back with a box, I was ecstatic and had to contain myself from grabbing the box out of her arms like I was going to steal the shoes and make a run for it. I put the clogs on to find they fit perfectly and looked great on my feet that had grown a full size since having three kids. I walked around the store, looking in every short shoe mirror and every tall mirror, loving what I saw. I went over to where Vincent sat to show him the clogs, and he looked at them and then up at me like he wasn't crazy about them.

"You're just jealous because I can sing the Elvis song," I said as I stared in the mirror to see myself looking transformed by the shoes, my skin glowing luminously like flower petals in the morning light. He laughed. I bought them and put them on and tossed my shitty old sandals in the first trashcan I saw. I felt like I was walking on water as we went down the street, singing *Blue Suede Clogs,* me staring in every reflective surface we passed.

When we got to White House, I was a little bummed because I had to stop walking. I glanced at the giant, cartoonish hoagie on top of the little stone building and stepped inside to a place filled with orange vinyl booths and walls covered with photos of celebrities—the Beatles, Tony Bennett, Jerry Lewis, Jimmie "J.J." Walker to name a few—all of whom supposedly ate there at one time or another. The smell of cheesesteaks and fried onions permeated the air, and being there felt like a special occasion even though it was just a hoagie joint. I barely ever went out to eat, and when I did, I went to one of those annoying kid-friendly restaurants with placemats that could be colored in and with Frank, Mr. Big Spender, scrutinizing the prices on the menu. A few weeks earlier, he'd come bursting through the door, holding a stack of coupons for McDonald's as if they were some sort of grand prize.

"I'm not feeding our kids that crap," I'd said to him. "Just go without us." He had come back with a large soda without ice and a Big Mac. He'd eaten about half of it and had complained of heartburn for the rest of the night, with loud, long, painstaking burps like an alien monster was trapped inside his stomach and struggling to make its way out.

We sat near the back of the place and a waitress with lipstick the same color as the orange booths came over to take our order. We both ordered cheesesteaks with fried onions and Cokes, and then Vincent told me he had to go get something across the street. A minute later, I was sipping my Coke, when he came to the table with a whole carton of cigarettes.

"And you're lecturing me?" I said. "At least I don't buy a whole carton."

"Yeah, but it's too late for me. I'm hooked," he laughed.

"All right," I said. "Let's both quit then."

"Okay, let's quit tomorrow."

"No! Today. Or tonight. I just don't know what you're going to do with that whole box. Why couldn't you just get a pack?"

"I'll just leave it somewhere. I always do that."

"Why do you like to throw your money away?"

No answer, just a laugh. The food came, and we dug in. The bread stole the show, so fresh and soft that it may have even held a second place to Vincent's magical loaf of fresh-baked bread. After we finished, we fought over the bill, and I let him win because I didn't want to make a scene but made him promise that drinks would be on me.

"Where'd you wanna go?" he asked.

"The Irish Pub," I said, without having to think of the answer and knowing that he would be in great favor of this choice.

We went outside to see a group of teenagers who all looked identical to one another, all wearing overalls with one strap hanging down. That was some weird fashion statement of the day, and after they passed us, we just looked at each other with silent laughter. We walked on past the oversized beach houses, storefronts, restaurants, and picturesque alleyways where white sunlight bounced off the walls of the concrete buildings. Soon we were sitting in the warmly lit pub filled with rich brown, wooden furniture and tiffany lampshades that shone like lanterns on a moonless night.

"What'll be mate?" the freckled bartender said in a thick Irish accent.

"Two Bailey's," I said, handing the bartender a twenty.

"Hey, guess what I saw the other day?" Vincent said soon after the bartender left to get our drinks.

"What?" I lit a cigarette without the smoking shame I felt earlier that day.

"I saw a lady hit the jackpot in one of the slots, and she must have had a heart attack or something, because she put her hand on her heart, and she passed out."

"Shit, that's awful."

"And then the lady behind her started taking all her quarters."

"Wow, that's sick." I took a sip of my drink and tried to imagine the scene. "What would possess somebody to take a dying lady's money?"

"I think the casinos can make people crazy. They're kind of designed that way." He lit a cigarette and took a puff.

"They sure are." All the times I went out to the casinos, I'd be so excited to get there, but once there, I couldn't wait to get out. I could never find the way out either because every glitzy room looked like every other glitzy room, a labyrinth of sleaze. I was just glad Vincent was kind of removed from the casino floor because he worked in security and spent most of his time looking in security cameras. Besides, working there was way different than going there for fun.

"It's sad, really," he said.

"Oh yeah," I said in strong agreement.

"I mean some of the people come in there thinking they're gonna win a million dollars playing craps, and all their problems are gonna go away."

"What about the winners?" I used air quotes around the word *winners*. "Do they seem happy?"

"It's hard to tell with the high rollers."

"They're probably so into the whole thing that they don't even know if they're happy or not. Like they can't ever get enough money. That's the way it always goes, right? Like I have five million dollars, but it's not enough, because I know somebody up the street that has ten million, and that's not fair because I should have what that guy has. You know what I mean?" I felt like I was back in college using the phrase, "You know what I mean." I used it all the time when having a meaningful conversation with somebody, and I wanted to make sure we were on the same wavelength. Having meaningful conversations was another activity that discreetly faded out of my life like a music box unwinding.

"Maybe they think if they get enough money, they'll live forever."

"Wow! So, it's an attempt to immortalize themselves? Brilliant." I wanted to keep talking about this, but he stood up and said we should head back to his place and watch one of the shows he had on tape.

"Sure thing," I said. "Let's walk back on the boards."

The boardwalk was crowded, but it didn't matter because having the endless ocean beside us made me feel like I had all the space in the world. Roasting peanuts, salty air, and cotton candy combined to create a potpourri of smells that brought me straight back to my childhood. I looked beyond the dunes of tall grass that gracefully blew in the air and the field of sand that stretched out to the sea, its waves forming, breaking, and traveling to the shore, playing its unending melody that cleansed my head of all the worry that lived in there and that was sure to return as soon as I got home.

The last time I was on this boardwalk was when Frank and I first started dating, and he took me to the Atlantic City Pier. We rode some really scary ride that went straight up in the air, fast and swift like a rocket, and he'd played the shooting game until he eventually won a fuchsia-colored teddy bear for me. Then, we'd walked on the beach, and he'd started carrying me on his back when I'd told him my feet were tired.

"Hey," Vincent said as he took his big, galloping steps. "Did I tell you I'm studying Greek?"

"Wow!" I said. "That's amazing."

"Yeah, it's a lot of fun."

We stopped by an arcade, where boundless noise blasted in the air, so Vincent could play some game called Mortal Kombat. Afterwards, we went in a fudge shop, where some teenage boy was stirring a big, brass vat of fudge in the window. I got a couple boxes of saltwater taffy, one for the kids and one for me and Vincent that we ate as we continued on. We passed a bunch of stores selling everything you could want on the boardwalk—T-shirts that said Atlantic City, ice cream, macaroons, taffy, fudge, pizza, roasted nuts, and even the future with a palm reader every few blocks. We passed tall, boxy casinos that clashed terribly with the shack-like storefronts, like misfit skyscrapers, and a guy dressed up as a giant peanut standing outside of one of the nut-roasting places.

As we got closer to Vincent's place in Ventnor, the casino crowds started to lessen and were replaced by more locals, mostly joggers and bike riders in hoodies. We'd just about gotten through the door to his place when he started showing me some new toy truck he got.

"Look at this," he said, guiding the miniature plastic truck around his apartment with a remote control he held in his hand.

"Here, let me try it," I said. He gave me the remote, and I drove the poor little thing right into the wall. It was harder than it looked, but once I got the hang of it, it was fun, and I decided to get one for Cosmo and play with it myself when no one was home.

"I'm going to get one of these for Cosmo," I said.

"Oh yikes, you reminded me," he said, walking out of the room with a strong sense of purpose. He came back in carrying a large paper bag with a handle. He took out a box with a portable keyboard piano and said it was for Angie. Then, he took out a blue plastic telescope and said it was for Cosmo. I tried, unsuccessfully, to fight my guilty feelings at receiving such wonderfully thoughtful gifts. I never was very good at accepting gifts but also thought he should be saving his money instead of spending it on presents for my kids.

"Vincent, these are wonderful. I don't know what to say. I—" Before I could finish, he pulled out a sketchbook, along with a bunch of coloring books and a jumbo-sized box of crayons and said, "These are for Silvia."

"Oh my God! Did you know how much she loves to color and draw? I think she inherited your artistic talents." He paid less attention to me saying this the second time than he did the first time.

"Yeah, hope they like everything," he said, collapsing in the only armed chair in the room.

"Are you kidding? They are going to love everything. I don't know what to say."

"I got it all in the same toy store where I got my truck. It's just up the street."

"Thank you so much. You'll be getting thank you cards from each of the kids too." I wanted to sneakily slip some money under one of his crystals, but I reminded myself that he was one of those rare people that loved giving to others and that I shouldn't take that away from him. Besides, his birthday was around the corner, so I'd just be sure to get him something extra nice and special then.

"So, I got a bunch of stuff on tape," he said. "Did you see *Raising Arizona?*"

"We watched that last time I was here. Don't you remember?"

"I got a bunch of shows—*Seinfeld, X-files, Mystery Science Theater 3000, Doctor Who*—the Tom Baker years, you know the doctor with the long scarf. He was the best doctor." He spoke with authority.

"What's that thing with the weird title? Mystery science?"

"Oh, you gotta see this." He didn't bother explaining it to me. He just put a tape in, and we started watching these robots sitting in front of a big movie theater screen, making a mockery of some really bad B movie called *Manos: Hands of Fate*. Once I got into it, it was really funny, and I laughed so hard at one point that my eyes started to tear.

After the show, he turned on a Donovan album he said he got last year. It was a new collection of old songs called *Troubadour* and listening to it brought back memories of being a little girl and listening to Donovan in his old room. He went in the kitchen and brought a couple of Snapple's back, handed me one, and took a sip from the other.

"Ouch," he said, putting his hand on his right cheek. "I got a shooting pain in one of my back teeth. Probably another root canal."

"Another?" I said. "How many have you had?" I didn't have any myself.

"I had three so far." He said this like he was planning for more.

"Shit. That's not good."

"Good thing I have insurance."

"That's for sure," I said, looking at him and noticing how handsome he looked, even with his juvenile Bart Simpson T-shirt. His eyes shone bright with his spirit that had been graciously freed after his time in the seminary. He lit up a cigarette and said that it would be his last night for smoking. So, I joined him in having a last smoke and making a promise that I wasn't too hopeful about keeping.

Afterwards, he walked me to my car, and we hugged goodbye. I got in my car and looked back at him smiling, his big hand waving in the darkness, and I was surprised to find that I didn't feel sad for him like I always felt when saying goodbye. But feelings of sadness still stoked within me, a lame fire that refused to neither burn out nor become magnificent. It burnt for me having to leave behind not only Vincent but that part of myself that would have to go dormant again as soon as I walked through the doors of my house. Sure, I missed my kids and wanted to get back to them, but I wasn't dying to get back to Frank and to being a maid and a slave and to having no time to laugh, or play, or get into good conversations, or go out for cheesesteaks and drinks, or to buy a pair of blue suede clogs.

CHAPTER EIGHT: 1996

Frank was in the kitchen losing his mind as I sat in our bedroom, holding little Vincie close to my chest, one hand over his head, trying to shield him from the sounds of slamming cabinet doors and screaming rage: "Fuck this goddamned place! Shit's always disappearing on me here! I can't find anything in this fucking place!"

I shook from the inside, like a dying lightbulb crazily flickering, as I held Vincie, and feared he might have been sensing my anxiety, soaking it in through his thin, delicate baby skin. My mind stirred with indecision about staying put or going in the kitchen to try to calm Frank down, but I remained as frozen as a mannequin until I heard the sound of shattering glass. I put Vincie down, which started him crying, loud and automatic, and ran in the kitchen to see every cabinet door open with Frank searching inside of them like a starving raccoon.

"Can I help you find something?" I tried to sound like a calm, composed salesclerk, but my voice crumbled in fear, and my stomach flipped like an acrobat.

"What the hell happened to that bottle of vodka I had in the liquor cabinet?!" His eyes were bottomless black, dark and hollow like tunnels that go nowhere.

"I'm sure you just misplaced it somewhere, Frank."

"What are you kidding or something?! I never misplace anything! I bet you that Cosmo is doing something with it. One of his goddamned science experiments or something!" His arms flailed in all directions like an orangutan. He continued on his search, sidestepping the broken glass, with his heavy feet pounding the floor from one side of the kitchen to the other.

"Maybe you drank it all and forgot about it." I regretted saying this the minute my words hit the air, but I couldn't think straight being one big tremble with my head feeling disconnected from my body.

"What do you think? I'm a fucking idiot or something. Jesus Christ, Donna!"

"Why don't you just calm down, Frank." Another stupid thing to say. I knew better than to tell a maniac to calm down.

"Why don't you just go screw yourself!" He banged his very heavy ring on our table, making a fresh, new dent, and stormed out of the house, slamming whatever doors he could on the way out. Then, he blazed down the driveway, and I made a big sigh of relief and collapsed while standing.

From the other room, Vincie's cries grew, and I ran in to pick him up and brought him in the kitchen to feed him. I bounced him up and down and spoke to him in baby talk to mask my crumbling voice and did the best I could to seem functional and together. I put him in his high chair and opened a jar of plum pudding—his favorite of all the baby foods. As I fed him, I told myself I'd confront Frank, once again, about his drinking that night. I told myself that this time would be different, but my hope was forced and contrived. How could I expect hope to come easily after all my previous failed attempts?

I approached him a few weeks earlier after he'd just won a big trial and was in an annoyingly cheerful mood, all smiles and hugs. I'd put the kids to sleep, brought him a big bowl of chocolate frozen yogurt in the den where he sat in front of the TV with a bottle of beer, watching snakes mate on some nature show.

"I talked to Nick today," I'd said. Nick was his brother and also a former alcoholic.

"Oh yeah?" He'd looked at me like he was sizing me up.

"Yeah, and he was telling me about how great the AA meetings have been for him and how he's going to be a speaker at one next week, and I thought we might go together."

"I knew that was coming as soon as you said his name." He'd stopped eating and looked up at the ceiling, bubbling over with frustration.

"What's wrong with AA? It changes lives."

"I'm not going to sit in some room with people moaning and groaning about their fucking problems."

"Well, then what about therapy or medication? Lots of people use medication to control their addictions."

"That's great for people with addictions, not for me."

"But, Frank, you have to do something. You have a problem. Can't you admit that?"

"I keep telling you that it's your problem, not mine. I drink because I enjoy it."

"Oh really? What about when you go crazy because you didn't get a drink on time?"

"I guess you and Nick talked all about it then? You must really have it all figured out."

"Can't you just consider go—"

"This discussion is over!"

"But, Frank—" I'd said, pleading.

"This is over." He'd picked up his bowl of frozen yogurt and his bottle of beer and left the room.

I finished feeding Vincie, and he started smiling and tapping his little hands on the table of his high chair. I had him last year even though Frank didn't want another child. I wanted one so badly, and as much as I didn't like to admit it even to myself, I needed one. Frank had his work. Angie had her friends. Cosmo and Silvia had each other. And now, I had little Vincie.

After I fed him, I dressed and put him in the stroller for our afternoon walk. The sun illuminated the clouds, making them glow like brand new snow. It was that confusing time of year between winter and spring, and the air was kind of mild while the trees' branches were still naked, some splayed out like an octopus's arms, others reaching straight up for the sky like a sunbeam in reverse. We usually went only once around the block, but he was being so good and seemed so content that we went around two more times.

When we got back, I had a message on my answering machine from Randi. She said she heard of an opening for a part-time adjunct English instructor at the community college in Philadelphia. She saw a lot of academic job announcements because she worked in the dean's office of our old college. A feeling of exuberance swept over me, and my mind raced. I just about gave up on the idea of teaching in college. I also never entertained the idea of working at a college in the City. It seemed far, but really it only took about forty-five minutes to get there.

I sat with the idea and imagined myself teaching at a college and remembered how I used to have that dream and how much it meant to me. I decided to apply, even though it felt like a longshot, and I decided that I wouldn't say a word about it to Frank. I thought he would have just tried to discourage me because he wouldn't like the idea of me getting a little independence.

I put Vincie in the playpen, called Randi back to ask her the deadline for applications and was relieved to find that it was two months away. I called the college to have them send me a copy of the announcement and an application. I got a bit nervous thinking of Frank seeing the letter in the mail, but he rarely, if ever, saw the mail before me. Based on what I knew, I started writing the cover letter. I called my old college and grad school for transcripts and dug out recommendation letters from my old professors.

Frank got home after ten that night when, thankfully, all the kids were asleep. I was sitting in bed reading, (or pretending to read), all geared up for a discussion about his drinking. He came into our bedroom with his hair a mess, a big white stain on his navy jacket, and his button-down shirt untucked. He looked like a businessman who fell asleep in an alleyway. He wasn't drunk but in maintenance mode. He said hi in his most aloof tone, and I told him I wanted to talk about that morning.

"What's there to talk about?" he said.

"Well, for starters, you were screaming at me for nothing at all, and when you left, you told me to go fuck myself."

"I never said any such thing," he said indignantly.

"Sorry, you said 'screw you' instead. Let's not get hung up on semantics, though. It's the same thing, Frank."

"The hell it is."

"So, you're not going to apologize then?"

"Oh, like you're so innocent in this whole thing. Talking to me like you're humoring a mental patient."

"What did I say or do to offend you?" I couldn't wait to hear what he would grasp for.

"It wasn't what you said as much as how you said it." It sounded like he couldn't even remember what I said.

"How was that?"

"It was as if I were imagining things or like I was crazy."

"You're projecting, Frank."

"So, you're saying I am crazy?!" He threw his hands up in the air.

"I'm sorry I told you to calm down."

He looked as if he didn't expect an apology, so when he got one, he was at a loss for words. Finally, he said thank you as if he had been terribly wronged and was finally getting some justice.

"Maybe it's a good thing that something happened to the vodka. I mean, don't you have enough to drink in the house already?"

"That's a weird thing to say." He shook his head and looked at the floor with disappointment as if his searching the kitchen like a lunatic for a bottle of vodka, when there was plenty of other alcohol in the house, was completely normal.

"Can you just consider cutting back on your drinking?"

"There you go, calling me an alcoholic again." He raised one suspicious eyebrow.

"I never said that or implied it." Even though I knew he was a text-book alcoholic, I couldn't say it to him. "I just think you have a drinking problem is all."

"Now who's getting hung up on semantics, Donna? I'm not a stupid man. You can't fool me, you know."

"A drinking problem is different than being an alcoholic," I said, disregarding his moot but valid point about semantics. "Anyway, the point is, have you ever thought of cutting back?"

"Why? What for?"

"For you and us and the kids. Your problem is getting worse and worse."

"I don't have a problem. I have a stressful job getting clients out of jail or seeing them go away to jail. Alcohol helps me with my stress. I could do a lot worse you know. It's not heroin for Christ sake. I didn't kill anybody. It's not a problem for me either, like I always tell you. It is for you, though." He got up from the chair and paced the floor with his hand on his forehead. I knew that my sitting still and remaining seemingly calm was making him more anxious.

"Maybe it is a problem for me, Frank, but isn't that enough?" I spoke in my most pleading voice and tried to look into his eyes and win him over with whatever love remained between us, but his eyes were fixed on the floor. There was a good full moment of silence, and he looked hard and thought about what to say next.

"I am who I am, Donna, and I drink because I like to drink. I'm sorry if it's not good enough for you." He walked out of the room.

Sadly, that may have been the closest thing to an apology that I ever got from him, so I felt some sense of accomplishment. Also, he was relatively calm throughout the discussion, and this gave me a glimmer of hope that I could eventually get through to him. Something like this would take time, and I'd just have to keep working on it like I was so strongly determined to do. Mom always said that when I put my mind to something, I could accomplish anything. I held on to these words as my mind drifted off into sleep.

When the phone by my bedside woke me at five in the morning like a scream in a nightmare, I knew something was wrong. I answered it to hear Nancy's crying voice.

"What happened?" I said, quickly sitting up.

"Mom!" she said, and then she broke into hysterical crying. I felt strangled with fear at what would come next. I jumped out of bed and stood up, trying to make myself feel more comfortable, but I felt worse standing. I was afraid to ask what had happened and afraid not to ask.

"Nancy, tell me! What happened!"

"Mom's gone!" She started crying again, but I could barely hear her sobbing. Her voice was drowned out by the blast of shock in my head. I sat frozen, my mouth wide open, like I wanted to say something, but I forgot how to talk. I gasped for air, took a bunch of shallow breaths, and then joined Nancy in hysterical crying. Frank woke up and asked what happened.

"Mom!" I said to him, just like Nancy said to me.

"What happened?!" He sat up with his mouth hanging open.

"Is that Frank?" Nancy asked through her crying.

"Yeah," I answered her, and then turned to Frank and said, "Mom's gone!" and continued crying into the phone. Like Nancy, I couldn't use the word *dead*, or *deceased*, or even *passed*.

"What?! How?!" His face was all twisted up as if his own mother died. No, worse. He didn't even like his own mother. He loved Mom.

"I don't know." I didn't want to know because I thought that that knowledge would make it more real, but I had to ask. "How did it happen, Nance?" I said into the phone.

"A heart attack," Nancy said loud enough for Frank to hear. "Listen, I have to go. I'll see you at the house."

"Yeah," I said to her in my broken voice. "I'll be there soon. I love you."

I turned to Frank to see him crying for the first time in our lives together. Tears streamed from his swollen eyes and down his razor-stubbed cheeks. He grabbed me and held me tight, and I held him back, and we cried together. All our past years of fighting faded like fog clearing in the sunshine, and I felt his love for me and for Mom, and in our grief, we were one, the way we used to be.

We stayed that way for a while, and then I told him that I had to get the kids up, so we could go over to my old home. I couldn't call it Mom's anymore, and I realized that my life would be divided into two parts from this day on—the time before Mom died and the time after. I pushed this thought aside and forced my mind to be blank, so I could do what I needed to do. I moved like a slow robot, just going through the motions. I felt better moving than sitting still because moving somehow allowed me to flee that strange new pain that was way beyond words—a big hollow space, down deep inside me, waiting to be filled while knowing that it never would be.

I dreaded telling Silvia because she was so close to Mom. I could see them sitting on the beach together, Mom in her canvas chair, smiling down at Silvia as she made little sand sculptures, the two of them eating strawberry shortcake pops, little Silvie not wanting to ever leave her grandma's side, and Mom secretly favoring her over the other grandchildren. She would never show it, but I knew. They had such a strong bond. I heard myself thinking about her in the past tense, and the thought of having to speak about her in the past brought on a round of fresh, new tears, which I wiped from my face like I was angry at them.

I went into Silvia and Angie's room to find both girls awake and sitting up in their matching twin beds as if they were waiting for me to come in and give them bad news. They must have heard the phone ring or the sound of me and Frank talking and crying, or maybe they just knew because as children... were intuitive.

"Girls, I have some very bad news." I tried to make my voice strong, but it was beaten down like a defeated boxer. I sat down on Silvia's bed, held her hand, and said to them, "Grandma is no longer with us."

Silvia looked up at me with eyes, helpless, shocked, and confused all at once. She burst into tears, crying "No! No! No!" I held her as close as I could without suffocating her, and through our nightgowns and our skin, I could feel her pain. I could feel her little heart, that had never even been chipped, breaking. Angie got out of her bed and hugged her from behind, and all three of us cried together.

Then, I got up and said to Angie, "I have to go tell the boys, honey. Please help Silvia get ready. We're going to my old house."

"Yes, Mom," she said, in a shaky, crying voice, while tears slid down her porcelain cheeks.

I went into the boy's room and told Cosmo, and he just sat quietly with tearing eyes. When I hugged him, he felt numb, and in his face, he looked like he was trying to make some kind of sense out of death. I told him I loved him and to get himself dressed. I picked up Vincie, who was standing in his crib and thought him so lucky because he wouldn't remember any of this.

Outside, the smell of coming rain hung in the air. The sky was gray with black end-of-the-world clouds, and there was a cold, damp stillness like everything had stopped. Driving to my old house was like driving to some terrible, unfamiliar place. I tried telling myself that I was just having a bad dream and fantasized that when we got there, I'd see Mom, and she'd tell me that there was a big misunderstanding at the hospital. She'd make a pot of coffee and a pancake breakfast to celebrate, and we'd all be together in a kind of love we never knew because we'd appreciate her in a whole new way.

"Why don't we see someone's true greatness until they're gone?" I said to Frank quietly so that the kids wouldn't hear me.

"Got me," Frank said in a voice devoid of emotion. "Maybe just another shitty trick God plays on us."

Vincie started crying and snapped me out of my thoughts and back into the drive of doom. I turned to where he sat in the back between Angie and Cosmo to stroke his head and saw a kind of sorrow in his face as if, in his own way, he knew what happened. I started crying, joining him and Silvia in their tears.

The drive was only a few miles, but it seemed to take a really long time. When we arrived to a driveway packed with strange cars, the whole thing became more real. Soon, I'd be walking back into my childhood home, knowing that Mom wasn't there and that she'd never be there again. I didn't want to get out of the car, and I sat longer than anyone. Finally, Frank said, "C'mon, Donna. We got to do this."

He helped me out of the car, which he never did before, but then again, I'd never needed help getting out of a car before that time. He held my hand as we walked towards the back door. Angie carried Vincie, and Cosmo held Silvia's hand. Her face, bright red from crying, shone in the gray light of the sky.

We opened the door to hear Dad screaming from the living room, "Take me too, Lord!" A couple of his friends sat in the kitchen, drinking coffee with Sambuca. Nancy was standing off to the edge of the room with her husband, Jason. I walked right over to her as if she were the only other person there. We hugged and walked in the dining room together.

"How did it happen?" I said. "Were you here?"

"It happened quick. At four this morning, I heard Dad screaming, and we ran in to see Mom lying in her bed having a heart attack." She clutched her chest and spoke in a trembling voice, the whole time in tears and taking shallow, sobbing breaths. "Jason tried to give her mouth-to-mouth. I called an ambulance. Me and Dad went with her to the hospital. I knew it was over though. I knew it before we got to the hospital." I put my hand on her shoulder and asked her when she got here.

"We came last night. Something was telling me I had to come down. So, I got to be with her on her last night." I couldn't help but feel cheated that I wasn't there for Mom's last night. I lived in the same town as her too. Nancy lived up in North Jersey. While happy for her getting to be there, I also envied her.

"You should have seen her last night. She was dancing around the living room and eating pepperoni pizza and dark chocolates. You know how she loved dark chocolate. I think she knew, Donna." Her eyes sparkled as if she witnessed some kind of miracle.

I told her that Mom probably did know it was her time and put my envy aside to tell her how lucky she was to have been with her on her last night. I then asked her where Carmen was, and she said he was in his old room. I knew he needed alone time, but I needed to talk to him before Vincent arrived, so I went to the doorway of his old bedroom to see him crying on his old bed like a little boy, face down, occasionally banging the mattress. I didn't want to interrupt his crying, so I waited outside until I heard him getting quiet, and then I said hi to him. He got up slowly, his body incapacitated with pain, and hugged me, breathing new life into my grief that poured out of me like a deluge with no end in sight.

"Did you come alone or with Karen and Jessica?" I asked, pulling away.

"I came alone. Jessica is really sick. They're going to come later."

"Does Vincent know?"

"Nancy called his place and the casino and found out he's working until four today. She didn't want to tell him while he was at work." He rubbed his hand across his face to dry his eyes.

"Do you want to go together to AC and pick him up? I don't want him to be alone when he finds out."

"Sure," he said, looking down at the floor.

From the kitchen, I heard Grandma and Grandpa coming inside, and I went in to see them, with Carmen following. Mom's mom was a big, Sicilian lady with an even bigger voice, and her dad was a calm, little man who never said much or showed much emotion. But that day, an endless stream of tears rolled down his shriveled, old face. Grandma was forcefully grabbing everyone by the shoulders, kissing them on both cheeks and saying, "She was beautiful on the inside and outside," in her broken English. She grabbed me and pulled me towards her soft, plump face, looking as if someone had poured a bucket of water over her.

Dad came in and our eyes met, and in one tragic movement, he came towards me and collapsed in my arms crying, "My Gilda!" Dad, once mighty and powerful as a mountain, became a weak and feeble child, and I couldn't imagine that I had, at one time, been afraid of him. I couldn't imagine feeling anything for him except unending sympathy.

More people came from the outside and piled in the kitchen. I knew some of them from my childhood, and some of them were strangers. Some sat and some stood. They shared one common expression of grief and awkwardness. Frank sat at the table drinking coffee and

Sambuca. I couldn't believe that his alcoholism was my biggest problem only the night before. In an instant, my world changed, and the world as I knew it, would never be again.

It rained during the drive to Ventnor—hard rain, loud like nails falling from the sky. It wouldn't have been any better though if it was bright, blue, and warm outside. Carmen and I were mostly silent, and when we did talk, we'd talk about how we were going to break the news to Vincent and how Dad was going to survive without Mom. In a weird way, I felt grateful for having problems to talk about because they were a distraction from my pain.

"I can cook for Dad and help him around the house," I said, staring out at the road.

"He's not going to want to stay in that house without Mom," Carmen said, his voice still shaky from crying.

"I can't imagine him living anywhere else." I couldn't imagine him staying with us because he and Frank couldn't stand each other. They really liked each other when they first met, and then for no apparent reason, they started disliking each other. I wasn't sure who decided he didn't like the other first, or maybe it was just more of an organic happening. But it was clear. Frank would talk about what a bad husband Dad had been to Mom, and Dad stopped treating Frank like his long-lost son and started treating him like an intruder.

"Maybe he can get an apartment in town or something," he said, like he was trying to convince himself of this possibility.

"Can you imagine that?"

"Not really."

I was still trying to imagine him living without Mom. They met when she was sixteen, and he was eighteen. They eloped two years later and would have had a proper wedding, but the two families couldn't stand each other. I thought of them like Romeo and Juliet. I knew that he wasn't any sort of ideal husband but also knew that he loved her fiercely. I saw pictures of them together, when they were young with that unmistakable in-love look shining in their eyes, filled with the warmth and excitement of new romance. They had all of us kids together, and when Dad's secretary quit, Mom went to work in his office. They were inseparable, and the few times Mom would stay home from the office, Dad would be calling the house every two seconds. I'd pick up the phone and hear, "Put Mama on?" Not even a hello. He was lost without her.

"He'll probably just stay at home and get someone to come in once in a while and help with the housework," Carmen said. "Who knows? Maybe he'll learn to cook for himself. Sometimes he used to try to cook. Remember?"

"Yeah, and Mom would always kick him out. She'd say 'Get out of my kitchen!'" We both started to laugh, and then my laughter turned to crying, and Carmen reached over from the driver seat to pat me on the back. We got off on the exit for Ventnor and got to Vincent's place just as he was walking up his street, undoubtedly on his way home from work. As he approached, I realized how lucky our timing was and how careless of us not to call before we came up. We could have missed him. He could have gone out to eat or something. But it was tough to think straight.

"Hey, Vince," Carmen said, getting out of the car. He spoke in a somber tone, which was a huge departure from his usual lighthearted one, and that, coupled with our tear-stained faces, was enough for Vincent to know that this wasn't just some surprise visit. His face filled with confusion as he tried to make sense of what was happening.

"Vincent, something happened last night," I said.

"Mom had a heart attack," Carmen said. He didn't need to say anymore. Vincent understood completely, his face heavy with pain and his eyes empty as if he were blinded by the shock. I went to hug him, but he felt stiff and lifeless like he, himself, was dead. He was lost and alone, and I wanted to stay holding him as if by doing so, I could absorb his pain and take it onto myself. But Carmen said we had to get moving. So, I backed away and said, "Vincent, it's going to be all right. We're here for you. We'll always be here for you." His eyes were still empty, and he remained motionless as if in a conscious coma.

"Vince, let's go in and get your stuff," Carmen said. "You can call work, and tell them you'll be out this week, and we'll all go back home." That sounded so good to me—us all going home to be together, all except for the person who made the house a home. Without her, our home was just a house, a nameless structure, an abandoned warehouse. She was what made it home. She was what made us a family. I knew that without her, our family, that for the most part was only being held together by strings, would fall apart.

We went up to his apartment where he called work and packed, and then we drove back together in the rain, which seemed to have worsened—falling steady and forceful, almost like the sky was angry. The ride back was quieter than the ride to Ventnor with none of us talking and with Vincent staring out the window, silently crying.

When we got back to the house, the driveway was so full that we had to park on the street. In the driveway were two cars with New York license plates that must have belonged to Anthony and Gloria. When we went inside, I saw the two of them sitting next to each other, their sorrow-soaked faces crinkled like the pages of a book that fell into a pool of water. They both came up to us and we hugged, and then we all talked about how we had to start making arrangements. I looked over and saw Frank sitting in the dining room, looking like he was sleeping while sitting up, his eyes only half-open. Vincent walked into the living room, and I wanted to follow but waited until we finished talking.

When I did go into the living room, I found Vincent sitting on the floor with Silvia, who was drawing a picture. As I got closer, I heard him telling her how she should make the eyes on the picture, and when I got even closer, I saw that it was a drawing of Mom. Silvia's little face was still red but no longer filled with anguish. Angie sat close by watching Vincie as he played with blocks, and Cosmo sat across from Angie, going between staring out the window and watching his little sister draw. Vincent looked up at me as I stood watching him with Silvia. His eyes were still sad and dull, but I saw a tiny gleam of light peeking through them.

By the end of the night, my old home started to feel less like an abandoned warehouse and more like my old home again. We all filled up the place with the energy of what our family used to be and paved a path for Mom to grace our home with one final visit. I felt her spirit, falling around us like invisible rain. I could almost smell her cooking, and little Vincie kept looking up at the ceiling as if he were seeing something amazing, which I thought must have been his grandma—a brightly shining angel. Silvia was no longer crying, and she was drawing more pictures of Mom with Vincent coaching her along.

When I finally got into bed, my mind raced, and I toyed with the idea of taking a sleeping pill, but in the end, I decided not to. I wanted to feel my grief because it connected me to Mom. I let the tears and the sobbing come on as a glorious slideshow of Mom's life played in my head.

I saw her getting ready to go out with Dad on a Saturday night in front of her dresser with the portrait of her from her sister's wedding. I always thought her the most beautiful woman in the world, and I still did. I saw her dusting the house while she danced, doing yoga, reading tarot cards on her bed, going up the steps at Sainte-Anne-de-Beaupre on her knees, and singing in church. I saw her sitting in Dad's office, filing papers, typing away, and doing crossword puzzles in her down time. I saw her shopping in the local grocery store and talking to all the people in the store as she shopped. I saw her cooking in the kitchen, flitting around, performing for us all. I saw her reaching her arms out as far as she could, and I saw her hands, so big that they could hold the sky.

I looked at my own hands and noticed, for the first time, how much they looked like Mom's with their long, thin fingers and protruding veins and, in that moment, I felt her with me, closer than ever, comforting me the way she used to when I was a little girl and couldn't sleep. I drifted off with a feeling of unearthly peace that I knew was sent to me from Mom.

A couple months later, all of us Tucci's gathered at my old house and went to church and then to the cemetery. I had gone to the cemetery a few times during the past two months, but this was the only time since the funeral that we'd gone together as a family.

It was a sunny day, not at all like the one she died on. But despite the sun and the flowers beginning to blossom, we all stood limp and lifeless, like dried-out, dying plants without the hope of ever being revived by the rain and the sun. We stood and stared at the stone while a sea of sadness washed over us. The Virgin Mary's face was carved into it, and half of it was saved for Dad because he wanted to be buried right near her.

As I looked at the stone, I saw a bug crawling over Mom's name, and when I got closer, I saw it was a ladybug, and apparently so did Nancy, who screamed, "A ladybug!" Everyone else got closer to the stone to look at it and see that it really was a ladybug. We all came to life and smiled in sync. We didn't have to talk about it either. We knew it was a sign from Mom. Vincent kneeled beside the stone where the ladybug crawled and let it crawl onto his finger and then his hand. He smiled down at the bug, and we all watched it crawling on his hand, and then it flew away and faded into the horizon.

Carmen and I drove Vincent back to Ventnor after we left the cemetery. We went up to his apartment where he made us some coffee in a percolator on his gas stove. I always made coffee in a regular drip coffee maker, set to go off automatically every morning, so I could get my tired ass out of bed. It didn't taste like anything to me anymore, but Vincent's coffee tasted really rich and smooth, and without thinking, I had a cup too many and got jittery and craved a cigarette, but I couldn't smoke around Vincent because I told him that I quit. Again!

"I got this thing in my ears called tinnitus," Vincent said, his hands touching his ears. "I hear this ringing sound. I'm sure it's from all the noise on the casino floor."

"Oh no," I said, trying to sit still without fidgeting. "Did you see a doctor?"

"Yeah, there's not much they can do, and it's happening like all the time now. I need to get out of there." He drowned his face in his hands, and when he sat back up, he lit a cigarette, and then I just had to ask him for one. I thought that if I asked him for one, he wouldn't know about the ones I had in my bag, and then I could tell him that I quit but that all the coffee I drank made me want one.

"I thought you quit?" Vincent said.

"I did. I'm just jittery from drinking so much coffee." I was pulling off my cleverly orchestrated lie really well until Carmen chimed in.

"No, you didn't," Carmen said through a cynical smile.

"Why'd you tell me you did?" Vincent said.

"Because I thought if you thought I quit, you would quit." It was tough to lie with him staring me down with those big honest eyes.

"That's crazy. Besides, smoking's worse for you than for me," he said, blowing smoke out of the side of his mouth. He put his cigarette down, sat forward in his chair, and told me the reasons it was worse for me than for him, while keeping count of the reasons on his fingers. "I'm older than you. I did just about everything I wanted to do, except for learning the harp and maybe the bagpipes, and I don't have kids!"

"Just because I have kids doesn't make my life any more important than yours!" I snapped back.

"Yeah, it kind of does, because then they'd have to grow up without a mom." He spoke as if being childless didn't bother him in the slightest. I was so focused on feeling bad for him that his words bounced off me.

"He's right," Carmen said. "Imagine if Mom died when we were kids." This sunk in, and suddenly I didn't want a cigarette as bad. But then I considered that Mom was a chain smoker her whole life, and she still lived to be sixty-two, and that wasn't so bad. Still, I knew they were right, and I wished I could have told them why it was so hard for me to quit this stupid habit. I wished I could have told them that my marriage was crumbling and that I even thought of leaving once or twice but that the thought of leaving just made me want to smoke even more. I looked up at Vincent and felt guilty for feeling bad for myself when his life was no walk in the fucking park. And now, he had this tinnitus thing. What if he had to quit his job because of it? What would he do then?

"All right," I said. "I'll quit. I promise." Of course, like all the previous times, I seriously doubted I could keep this promise, but at least I could try.

"Mom would still be here if she hadn't smoked," Carmen said to both of us in an instructive tone with stern eyes.

"All right. All right. I'll quit if you try to quit also," I said, turning towards Vincent. I wondered how many more times I'd have to make this same bargain with him. He agreed, and I said, "Now, can we stop talking about dying and start talking about living please?!"

"Yeah, what's the thing you said about the tinnitus?" Carmen asked Vincent, sitting back. He looked uncomfortable, and since we arrived, he'd been resituating himself in his chair.

"Yeah, I got this ringing in my ears, and when I'm stationed on the casino floor, it sounds like...like I don't know, like just awful and blasting and shrill, really shrill."

"You have to get out of there. You deserve so much more, and you can't be happy there." I didn't mean to say this. It just slipped out with my coffee nerves.

"I'm happy. I mean I know I don't have the perfect job or the perfect life, but I'm happy, Donna." It sounded like he was trying to convince us and himself of his happiness, and I heard a crack in his voice when he got to the last three words.

"I know you are," I said, raising my voice to show strong agreement despite wanting to cry at hearing his voice break on these words.

"You ever think about doing a workman's comp case?" Carmen said.

"No. That's a good idea, though. Maybe I should," Vincent said.

"Then maybe you can look for a job that you'd like better," I said.

"Yeah, that sounds good too." Vincent spoke in a tired, flat voice as if, even though he liked our ideas, he didn't have the energy to pursue them.

"I could help you with the workman's comp case. Frank can, I mean." I spoke loud and quick, trying to get him to liven up.

"Oh yeah, thanks a lot," he said, and then looked down at the floor and said, "Hey, do you ever wonder if Mom can hear us talking now."

"I think she probably has better stuff to do now or at least more exciting stuff," Carmen said.

"I think she'd want to be with us though," I said, turning to Carmen. He shrugged and tilted his head in reluctant agreement.

"I talk to her like she's right here," Vincent said. "I talk out loud even."

"I hope not when people are around." Carmen said with a straight face.

"Nah," Vincent said. "Well, maybe sometimes." He took a puff and went on, "I mean really. Think about the way we're all talking here now. How do I know that you're both really here and listening?"

"Because that's what your eyes and ears tell you," I said.

"Yeah, but your physical perceptions may be wrong," Vincent responded quickly as if he had this answer prepared for some time.

"Oh, that's crazy," Carmen said.

"Is it really?" Vincent had a mysterious look in his eyes like he knew some great truth.

"Go on," I said to Vincent, who got excited when I showed interest in his theory.

"Well, our physical perceptions may or may not be accurate because they can change, and the whole world is just this man-made construct that was designed so we could all live in it. Think about the concept of time. It doesn't really exist, right? So, if everything we perceive may or may not be true, then I can't really rely on my perceptions, so I rely on my beliefs. I believe I can talk to you, and you can hear me. I believe I can talk to Mom, and she can hear me."

"Wow," I said. My mouth hung open. My mind was truly blown, and I felt like a little girl again being wowed-away by my cool, big brother.

CHAPTER NINE: 2000

"Look at that tree!" I said to the kids as we drove by a cherry tree in bloom on the way to school.

"Oh, that's so beautiful," Silvia said, turning her neck as we passed it, so she could see it as long as possible. I smiled down at her little head of brown, wavy hair that was still turned back towards the tree. I loved the way she readily saw beauty everywhere, so much like her grandma. Maybe she was thinking of how she'd draw or paint the tree. She was my little artist child, and since Vincent suggested I send her to art school, that was all she talked about.

"What kind of tree is it?" little Vince asked. He sat in the back between Angie and Cosmo. I couldn't call him Vincie anymore. A couple years ago, he said it made him feel like a baby. At four years old, he didn't want to feel childish! He was always asking me lots of questions and soaking up everything with an unending thirst.

"It's a cherry tree," I said to him. I imagined his eyes lit up with curiosity.

"Mom! Cosmo's turning his eyelid inside out again!" Angie screamed from the backseat. I looked in the rearview mirror to see Cosmo fixing himself, so he could tell us all that Angie was just imagining things.

"C'mon, Cos. You can do better," I said. "You're too smart for that kind of behavior." At fourteen, he was smarter than any of us—always winning science project awards and helping me out on our computer. But I had to remind myself that he was still just an adolescent boy out for whatever trouble he could find. I saw him smirking and ducking his head with mischievous eyes.

"No, he can't," Angie snapped. "He can't not be a gross jerk. He doesn't know how." She wore her cheerleading outfit because on that day, there was a pep rally at school. Her long dark hair was back in barrettes, and her makeup was on perfectly as it was every day she went to school. She was, after all, to be the prom queen that year.

"Ang, you know better too," I said. I saw her looking out the window at the school playground like she couldn't care less about what I had to say. She looked like she was going to jump out of the car before I had a chance to stop, so she must have seen her friends on the playground. The second the car stopped, she sprung out like a piece of bread popping out of a toaster. Cosmo got out and walked alone to the playground because he was too cool to be seen with anyone else. He walked just like Vincent, bouncing along as if life were something that just happened in his own time.

After I dropped Angie and Cosmo off, I drove down the street to drop off Silvia and Vince at their school. I gave them each a kiss, and then we all joined in a group hug. The two of them walked to the playground holding hands, while I absorbed the moment, staring at my two little angels, dressed in denim and brightly colored T-shirts, not even knowing how lucky they were because they didn't have to wear uniforms to school.

Then I got on the expressway and headed to work, which was the teaching job at the community college in the City that Randi told me about four years ago. After some really rigorous interviews and a long waiting period (things move really slow in academia), I got the job and had been working there for nearly three years. I loved everything about it, including my colleagues, one of whom told me about a part-time job in the audiovisual department of another community college, which was near to where Vincent lived.

He was back in the same apartment he lived in before—the one Dad owned. Fortunately, Dad mellowed out a lot, and the two got alone all right or at least better than ever before. Anyway, I told him about the job, he applied, and got it! It was perfect for him, and I was so glad he got out of the casinos because his tinnitus was just getting worse.

The one fly in the ointment of my life was Frank, whose drinking problem had grown like a hard-working weed. I was also pretty sure he'd been cheating on me. I didn't have any proof, just a strong feeling. It was just fine with me though because I really didn't want to be intimate with him and couldn't even recall the last time we'd had sex.

In fact, the closest thing I had to a sexual encounter was during the previous summer when we'd all gone to Disney World and the Three Little Pigs had surrounded me and felt me up with their grubby little paws. Crazy as it sounds, it really happened. It got better too. Frank had started chasing them down, and they ducked into some staff-only area. So, then he'd gone to the information center and had told the staff about it, and they'd said that the Pigs would be severely reprimanded and possibly terminated, but that wasn't good enough for him. He'd started thinking about suing Disney World! In the end, he'd decided not to. "I have enough on my plate," he'd said. "Besides, I don't want to be like one of those sleazy lawyers who goes around suing anyone and anything they can. Those bastards went and ruined the whole goddamned legal profession."

I wish he cared half as much about our marriage as he did about his stupid, fucking profession. But he didn't. He'd been on a real tear a couple of weeks earlier, and we'd all had to leave home and stay in a hotel overnight. We'd snuck out when he was in the bathroom throwing up, which was right after he'd turned the kitchen table over and tore the phone out of the wall.

"C'mon, Angie wake up," I said, cajoling her out of bed. "Wake your sister. Get your stuff. We're going to a hotel tonight." I'd then gone into the boys' room to get them up. They all got ready like high-functioning sleepwalkers because they knew the drill, it having been somewhat of a regular occurrence. I questioned whether I was a bad mother by subjecting them to Frank, but the alternative, I thought, would have been much worse for them—leaving him might mean him getting custody and them living without me there to protect them from the monster Frank had become. Besides, I reasoned all of us Tucci kids had grown up with Dad and turned out all right.

I drove over the bridge, and at the first stoplight, I put lipstick on in the rear-view mirror.

Driving in the City made me feel claustrophobic and frustrated at having to stop every two seconds, and I couldn't help but feel a mild resentment towards the pedestrians who seemed free as birds in a tropical paradise. I started listening to classical music and jazz and that kept me pretty calm and sane, while allowing me to learn a little something about the two genres of music I was mostly ignorant of.

Outside, the pale, blue sky and bright sun enlivened the mostly gray city streets, as I passed by parking lots and building after building, some plain and modern, others stately colonials, pre-revolutionary war structures standing strong and proud as the day they were built. Soon, I was pulling into the staff parking lot and walking to class.

"Better to pass boldly into that other world, in the full glory of some passion, than fade and wither dismally with age." I was standing in front of my Survey of British Literature class, quoting from James Joyce's *The Dead*. Sunlight came into the classroom, reflecting off the shiny white desks and onto the young faces that looked forward at me with eyes open wide and alert. The room was silent, which meant that my students were either really bored or really engaged, and that time, I was sensing it was the latter, so I took the opportune moment to ask them about the meaning of the story.

"Who is really dead in this story?" I said. They stared back at me with confusion, probably knowing it was a trick question. I looked at the clock to see that class would be ending in minutes, so I gave them a hint. "It's not Michael Furey." Still nothing for a few seconds, and then bright-eyed Olivia, who always sat in the front row and was always engaged, raised her hand and said, "The people at the party."

"That's right, Olivia! Excellent," I said. "So, the people at the party who are alive are figuratively dead, and Michael Furey, who died, is alive, living on in Greta's memory and in her heart." There was a stillness in the air, and I could almost hear their eager brains churning like the gears in a machine coming to life. I felt electric as I spoke, my mind and heart weaving together into one beautiful thing. I continued despite the ticking clock.

"What can you call this?" I said. "It starts with an i."

"Oh, oh, oh!" Xavier called out. Covered in dreadlocks, he was another one of my other favorite students, who reminded me of Horshack from *Welcome Back Kotter* every time he raised his hand.

"Yes, Xavier," I said quickly for fear of our time constraints.

"Irony."

"Great!" I said as they all began to pour out of the classroom. "See you all next week."

Frank steamrolled in around dinner time, and as usual, he was the last one to sit down at the table. He didn't have to get up to get anything because I always had everything anyone could ever need out, but he always found excuses to scramble around the kitchen after we were all seated, and that night, he busied himself by fucking around with one of the utensil drawers. He was forever testing the integrity of stuff—the kitchen drawer, the rear-view mirror, the window latch—as if hoping to break that thing, so he could then complain about how everything was made like crap *these days*. He finally slammed the drawer closed and went over to the refrigerator to search for something as if he didn't have a complete inventory of everything in there.

"What are you looking for?" I said, knowing that he wouldn't have an answer. I sat as still as a statue, eating the dried-out chicken that I overcooked once again.

"Nothing," he said, his head still busy in the refrigerator. Finally, he grabbed a bottle of Budweiser out, walked over to his seat taking slow careful steps, and sat down. We already began eating because I didn't want our food to get cold, and we were all used to him pulling his before-dinner shenanigans. Usually, he didn't mind us eating before he was seated, but that night, he had something to say about it: "Couldn't you wait to eat until I'm sitting down?" He sighed and stared at me with the evil expression of a comic book villain.

"I didn't want our food to get cold, Frank." I remained calm and distant, which made him more anxious than he was already because I wasn't giving into his need to fight. I knew when fighting was a necessity for him as opposed to a desire because I could read him like an open book in large print. He didn't respond to me. He just looked off in another direction and snickered, as if mocking me in his own head.

"Today at school," Cosmo said, "We—"

"Don't talk with your mouth full," Frank said, fast as a rubber band snapping. Cosmo rolled his eyes like it wasn't the first time he heard this from his dad. It wasn't. Frank saw his rolling eyes and complained that his son had no respect for him.

"You did the same thing when Mom said she didn't want our food to get cold," Cosmo said. Actually, Frank sighed whereas Cosmo rolled his eyes, so it wasn't the same exact thing, but it was meant to have the same effect. Still, I was ready for Frank to yell back at Cosmo, making clear this distinction when Angie spoke.

"Dad, how was your day?" she asked, taking a bite of her baked potato. I really appreciated that she was asking him about his day and might have been getting his mind off Cosmo's comment, but I couldn't help but think it was her way of getting one up on her brother. I couldn't figure out why she would have done such a thing because she didn't need to compete with her brother for Frank's approval. She was Frank's favorite, and Cosmo was his least favorite.

I always thought that the whole favorite thing was a form of child abuse, but Frank didn't, and he played favorites. A week earlier, Cosmo had come home with a ninety-seven in his physics test. He was taking physics in ninth grade and was so smart that he always ruined the curve. Anyway, I was fussing over him, and when Frank came in, I'd told him about his son's accomplishment, and he'd said, "Too bad you can't do that good in your other classes." I'd thought I was hearing things. I'd taken Cosmo out for pizza that night and explained to him that his dad just had a tough time expressing himself. He didn't seem to fall for it though. I should have known he'd be too smart for that bullshit.

"Thank you, Angie," Frank said, enunciating each syllable as if trying to make some point that went way beyond thanking her. "I appreciate that someone has the decency to ask about my day. It's no surprise that it's Angie." He looked back at me with eyes that were meant to penetrate me, but that only boomeranged off me. When he saw I wasn't bothered, he got more fired up. "Because you know I'm just the one supporting the whole household. That's all I'm good for is bringing money in."

"How was your day?" I asked Silvia who was sitting quietly beside Vince.

"It was good," she said through her purple braces. "Wednesday is my favorite day because we have art. Today we worked with watercolors. My picture's drying at school, but I'll bring it home tomorrow. I made a—" Frank walked out as she was talking, making such a clamor—moving his chair out, sighing, slamming his empty beer bottle down on the table—that everyone looked up at him, and Silvia stopped talking.

"You can continue, Silvie," I said to her in an effort to divert attention away from Frank.

"I just made a really nice painting." She spoke quickly, the enthusiasm drained out of her voice.

"Uncle Vincent said she should go to art school," Cosmo said. He was naturally good at ignoring Frank and had become a kind of inspiration for me.

"I heard that about art school!" Frank yelled out from the living room. "I'm not going for that waste of money! I work hard for my money!"

I looked down at Silvia, who appeared as if she were about to cry any second, and I quietly but firmly said, "You will go to art school. I promise."

I was getting out of my car and walking up to Vincent's apartment when I saw a white bird feather flying in the air. Pushed along by a gentle breeze, it continued floating through the air, landing on the ground, and then a bush, and then the ground again, and then Vincent's car—some old, pale, blue tank that played

"Rock Around the Clock" every time he turned on his right turn signal. I knocked on the door, heard his footsteps coming down the steps, and when he answered, I was still staring off at the feather.

"Yo, Donna," he said, opening the door. I turned to look at him, with his Einstein hair jumping out at me. He looked good, like he just got back from some very restful vacation. He finally grew out of his pale, thin self, and even the purple circles, which usually hung under his eyes, were mostly faded. He barely drank at all anymore, and he quit smoking for good a few months ago. I tried to quit also but failed. As usual, I told him I stopped though because I didn't want to ruin his own motivation to stay off those shitty cancer sticks.

Anyway, I didn't smoke that much, partly because I had to sneak-smoke around Silvia and Vince as they both hassled me every time I lit up. I wished I could have been done with them, but as long as Frank was a hell-raising drunk, I needed something for my stress, and I thought that I could have done a lot worse.

"Hey, Vincent," I said, hugging him. I followed him upstairs to his apartment, which looked almost exactly the same as when he lived there previously. There was, however, more of everything: books, crystals, and instruments, the most notable being a beautiful harp. I barely sat down when he said, "I've been practicing," and sat on the chair behind the harp and started playing.

His playing was nearly flawless, and I was floating in peace and harmony as I closed my eyes and melted into the music, and when I opened them, I looked out his window to see the rest of the world and remembered that beyond this room and the outside of this apartment, beyond the singing birds and the leaf-filled trees, Frank lived. My upper stomach soured like I drank a gallon of vinegar, and my head felt dizzy with angst. So, I closed my eyes again, and the feeling dissipated, and I was being lulled by angels in a timeless place without any knowledge or concern about the drama and chaos that lived outside of the window. After playing for what felt like too short of a time, Vincent stopped and said he was going to put a pot of water on for tea.

"Play another song," I said loudly, so he could hear me from the kitchen. He poked his head in, smiling with eyes glinting into the sun that poured in the room and said that he would as soon as he got a couple cups of tea together. I told him to just put milk in mine, and he said he already knew that. He brought in two cups of tea and sat down to play the harp some more. He said he only knew a couple songs, so I'd have to hear the same ones again. I said I didn't care if he only played the same song over and over.

I was listening with my eyes closed and feeling relaxed, but then I heard Frank's raging screams going on about something, too abrasive and stirring to be drowned out by the lovely music. He kept breaking through to my sanctuary. That bastard! So, I opened my eyes and focused on Vincent playing the harp as if I was a student trying to learn to play. I studied his fingers as they moved so delicately from string to string, and then I glanced up at his light-filled face, and the feeling of ease returned. I looked over at a CD cover that was lying on the floor—*Liege and Lief* by Fairport Convention— and went to pick it up to view it more closely. Vincent stopped playing and said he'd turn it on and that he was ready to quit the harp for the time being.

As soon as the first song started, I knew I loved it. As I listened, joy rose up inside of me like a geyser, and I couldn't believe I never heard this album before. I had something else by the same group called *Heyday,* and when I told this to Vincent, he said very seriously, "Stay away from *Heyday,*" like he was warning me against taking a drug with fatal consequences.

"They could only make music like this in the sixties," he said through a smile.

"Like what?" I said.

"Like this. Like if they had rock and roll back in the Renaissance times, it would sound like this."

"Yeah." I tried to think of a more recent band that achieved this same kind of sound, and nothing came to mind, but that could have also been because I wasn't up on anything new. Still, I felt sure he was right in saying that there was nothing recent like this out there. The first song finished and transitioned invisibly into the second one like a sunset changing the sky from bright orange to pale pink. I looked at Vincent listening and thought of all the great music I heard because of him. Hours of staring at album covers, while music, deep and light, fast and slow, sad and uplifting, moved me in a way beyond this world.

"All the songs are adapted from traditional British and Celtic songs," he said.

"They really breathed new life into them." I imagined a group of young British folkies sitting in a room—homey but bare of anything nonessential to create great music—recording the album when Vincent said, "Hey, check this out, Donna." He pulled out a large coffee table book from his book shelf and handed it to me. It was an annotated version of *Alice in Wonderland,* which he knew was one of my favorite books.

"Oh, this is great," I said, as I started flipping through the book. He asked me if I wanted it, and when I didn't respond right away because I did want it but didn't want to say so, he told me to have it.

"Thank you so much, Vincent," I said. "This is really great. I love it!" I sat down and started looking through the book, when he said that we should play chess. He was a chess master who couldn't be beat. Once, when I was in high school, we'd played for four hours, and I'd won one game, but I knew that that was only because he'd let me win. We got settled with a couple more cups of tea and started playing.

"Hey, did you hear? They're making a *Lord of the Rings* movie," he said as he set up the chess board. "It's going to be in three parts—one for each book. It's going to be a real movie with real people. No cartoon this time. There's big talk about it. They said it's going to come out next Christmas."

"Wow," I said, thinking of how excited he must have been about this movie.

"Yeah, it's gonna be made by some guy named Peter Jackson. He does a bunch of funny horror movies. I've been renting them. I got one now if you want to

watch it, I can put it on after we're done playing chess."
I told him next time. I looked down to see the whole
board was set up, and he told me I could go first. He
always let me go first and gave me any other advantage
he could, probably, so the game would last longer than
five minutes.

"Ever play the penny whistle anymore?" he said
after he moved one of his pawns.

"Not so much," I said, looking down at the
board. "I'd be so rusty if I picked it up now. Not as rusty
as I am at chess, though."

"Why don't you learn the flute?" he asked. The
idea of learning the flute sparked something in my mind
like a single white firecracker streak lighting up the sky.
On the chess board, he was just about ready to
checkmate my queen, but I didn't care because I was
busy imagining myself playing a beautiful silver flute,
and I could almost hear its delicate whistling sound. I
was so excited about the prospect of learning
something new—something just for me, not for
everybody else in my life. I could take flute lessons and
practice every night. I could play duets with Angie on
the piano. I could—

"Checkmate," Vincent said. "Play another?" I
looked at my watch to see that I had time for one more

game, but that would be it, and when I told him this, he said that we should skip the game, so he could show me these things he'd been building.

When he brought his new building projects out, I wasn't really sure what to make of them as they were, for the most part, indescribable. They were made up of these circuits that were put together with electrical cords, and somehow, this thing, whatever it was, made a light go on.

"That's amazing!" I said, trying to wrap my head around how he built it. I had no mechanical ingenuity and couldn't begin to imagine how I'd build any such thing. I never realized, until then, how mechanically-inclined Vincent was. I thought that I should have been encouraging him to go into some kind of engineering trade school all along or to take an electrician course or something like that. Then, he could get a really good job and a nice place to live and maybe even have enough money to buy a house. It wasn't too late, I reasoned. People changed careers all the time.

I was all ready to tell him when this voice inside pulled me back and told me to just let him enjoy his creation instead of telling him how he could capitalize on his talent. I looked at him looking at the thing he created with his eyes sparkling as they had when he carried in the fresh-baked loaf of bread he made for me and Mom.

I then got a vision of a little boy building a sand castle. He smiled at it and was filled with pride, and just as he was about to put the crowning touch on it, some other kid came along to tell him it wasn't good enough, that it wasn't what it should be, it was too big and impractical and that no one lived in castles anymore. The little castle builder walked away, defeated and crushed, the smile erased from his face and the shine gone from his eyes.

Now, I knew this was far from how Vincent would have reacted if I told him that he should become an engineer or an electrician. He ignored most, if not all of my suggestions or just laughed them away. It was just that I grew tired of telling him what to do and not to do, what to be and what not to be. My days of knocking down castles had come to an end.

CHAPTER TEN: 2001

I got home to find a red eleven blinking on and off on my answering machine like a light on top of a police car. Frank was at work, and the kids were at school, so I was all alone and afraid to check my messages because I knew something bad had happened. My fear, however strong, didn't impede me from darting to the machine and pushing the play button. The first one was Carmen. He said, "Donna, call me on my cell when you get in." His voice was flat, somber, and more serious than I ever heard him speak. He didn't say goodbye or anything. He just hung up. The second one was a repeat of the first one. I played three more that were all from him, with each one my stomach dropping further and further until it hit the ground like a heavy rock falling from a skyscraper. I knew it made no sense to keep playing messages when there was apparent urgency to call him, but something in me was too afraid to dial his number. When my shaking hand did dial his number, my body was stiff and frozen as someone who had been left in the tundra without a coat. He answered in only one ring like he'd been waiting for my call for hours.

"What happened?" I said as soon as he answered.

"It's Vince," he said. My heart raced, and I couldn't feel my body. I wanted to ask what happened, but I couldn't talk. I knew what he was going to say, and I just stood there with my mouth open, holding my head like it was going to burst, and then he said the words. He said that he was dead and that it must have been a heart attack. I held my breath as if I forgot how to breath, and he asked me if I was alone. I answered a shaky yes, and he said he'd be right over. I said okay in between heavy, shallow breaths.

I hung up, and a scream so loud and shrill that it felt alien, came out of me, a glass-shattering prelude to the wailing and streaming tears that followed. I lay, stomach-down on the floor, banging it a bunch of times with my fists while screaming "No!" into the air—the only witness to my pain. I was glad no one was home to see me or save me from myself. I always hated when people tried to cap grief as if it was a contagious disease.

I grabbed a roll of toilet paper and sat in a chair by the front window, eyes focused on the driveway, so I could see Carmen's car as soon as it arrived. I waited for his car for what felt like either hours or seconds, and as soon as I saw it, I got up and ran outside. He got out of the car, a broken man, in the world without his best friend for the first time. I hugged him so tight as if to squeeze the pain out of both of us and cried and sobbed so loud that I knew all the neighbors could probably hear, and I didn't care one bit. Eventually, he pulled back from our tear-soaked hug, and when he did, I saw his sad, worn face, aged with sorrow. I wondered why he was even in town. He didn't tell me anything about coming, and it was a weekday, so I asked him.

"I took off this week to do some stuff around the house, and I just decided to come down today on a whim and surprise you and him and Dad." He took a deep sigh as if talking was too much exertion for him.

I couldn't get over all the parallels between Mom's death and Vincent's: Carmen came to town right before instead of Nancy; I was robbed of spending their last nights on earth with them; and they both died of heart attacks—sudden with a fright that I hoped lasted only seconds. It seemed almost unreal, like my life was repeating itself, moving in one giant circle of tragedy. There was one big difference though—Vincent quit smoking for good; Mom never had and never really tried. I could still hear him telling me how he quit cigarettes and drinking and felt better than ever.

Carmen continued, "I went to his apartment and there was no answer, but he was home because his car was there, and his lights were on, and he never leaves his lights on. So, I kept knocking and knocking, and finally I went down to Dad's office to get a key to his place, and I went back and opened the door and..." He stopped talking and took another sigh and put his head down. Tears came from his eyes like they were forced out. "I went in and saw him sitting in a chair with his eyes open, and I knew he was dead, but I felt his pulse anyway. And then, I closed his eyes, and I kissed him on the cheek." He started crying, I hugged him, and we cried together again in one big beautiful mass of sorrow.

I closed my eyes and imagined Vincent sitting in a chair in his apartment, dead, and I opened them because I didn't want to see it, but even with my eyes open, I saw the same heartbreaking image. I stepped back and asked Carmen where he was. He said Vincent was still in his apartment and that he was waiting for me to call him back, so we could go to his place together. We got in his car and went to Vincent's.

The gray sky hung like a dirty curtain as we drove, the whole time me picturing Vincent getting a heart attack and how he must have been scared even though he never seemed scared of anything, and I wondered if he felt any pain or anything besides fear, and all those thoughts weren't the worst of it. The worst thing was that he died alone. I kept shaking my head like I was trying to get moths out of my hair in an attempt to get the thoughts and images out of it, but they continued to return, each time with greater ferocity.

"He died alone," I said.

"We all do," Carmen said, looking out at the road before him.

I knew that wasn't true but didn't have the strength or energy to argue. Mom had Dad and Nancy and Jason, and if it hadn't been the middle of the night, she would have had more. People that died in hospice centers had families and friends and nurses. Vincent died alone. Why couldn't I have gone to visit him last night? I thought of what I was doing when he was dying—probably watching TV with the kids. I wanted to bang my head against the window of the car at the thought. I could have been there, and when he started to get pains in his chest, I could have taken him to the hospital, and then he would have still been alive. It would have been so fucking easy! Then, I'd have him move in with us so that I could always keep an eye on him, and when he did die one day, he'd have me and the rest of his siblings and my family around him. He'd have us all right there.

Carmen pulled up to his driveway, and a dread that I never knew swept over me as if a swarm of killer bees were outside the car, and I had no choice but to walk outside and get stung to death. My body pulled me in opposing directions with one part of me anxious to go in and get it over with and the other half of me glued to the car seat.

"C'mon," Carmen said with reluctance in his voice. He got out, and I followed him through the front door and up the steps. An Amazon box that must have just come in the mail was pushed to the side of the steps, and all I could think of was how he was just ordering books online and living his life like we all do, never thinking that the next day wasn't going to be.

I thought of all the times I walked up these steps and came through this door, always excited to see him, to watch him play music, to talk about life, to laugh, to play chess, to drink tea, to watch movies, to get away from Frank. I never came up these steps feeling dread and anguish, and with each step, these feelings grew exponentially. An image of Mom going up the steps of Saint Anne's Cathedral came to me, and I thought that climbing these steps had to be way more painful than climbing all the stone steps in the world on my knees. I always knew this day would come but not so soon and not like this. He was only forty-nine. I planned on throwing him a big party when he turned fifty. I heard myself saying the word *was* and thought of how I'd be talking and thinking about him in the past tense from now on, just like Mom.

When we got to the top of the steps, Carmen turned to me and said, "I know this is going to be hard for you, but we're really the lucky ones—the only ones who get to see him so close to when it happened, and it's only right that it should be this way. We were the closest ones to him." This statement made me as strong as Popeye after he ate a can of spinach, and I loved Carmen intensely for making this into a good thing. He opened the door, and we walked through the little doorway, and when I saw Vincent sitting on the chair, his eyes closed, his face a grayish white, I repeated the words, "We're the lucky ones," in my head like a mantra. I walked over to him, still repeating the words, kissed him on his cold cheek, and stepped back to look at my brother one last time. All of the life had left his body, and it wasn't not coming back, and I was drowning again in tears, and through my tears, this other feeling rose up inside of me like an erupting volcano—anger.

I wished it was anger at Dad for not being a better father, but it was worse because it was anger at myself. I thought that if I tried harder, this wouldn't have happened. He could have had a different life, one in which he was happy, and he would have still been around because his will to stay alive would have been stronger. I tried telling myself that I already had a lot on my plate with my kids, crazy Frank, and my job, but the bigger part of me said that those things were no excuse. I tried to push my anger onto Frank for distracting me from my childhood ambition of ensuring that Vincent had what he needed for happiness, but my anger couldn't be pushed away, and it just continued to burn, like a giant torch, deep inside of me.

"Donna," Carmen said, like he was trying to get me out of a trance. "We have a lot to do. We have to call someone to take his body away. We have to talk to Dad about funeral arrangements and go to the funeral home up the street. We have to tell everybody." I wanted to respond, but I just stood there, eyes fixed on Vincent, with my mouth open, paralyzed and powerless. Carmen saw this but continued on anyway with an itinerary for us that, in my current state of dysfunction, sounded as impossible as building a bridge. "I'll go call the hospital now," he said in a tone devoid of emotion.

I didn't want to hear him making the call, but there was no place to get away in the small apartment, so I just stayed still and planned to stay that way until he came back to tell me what to do next. I stood motionless, staring at Vincent, part of me hoping that if I stared long enough the shock would wear off with the other part of me not wanting it to wear off. Once the shock was gone, there'd be nothing left but that unending grief pain.

Finally, I walked away telling myself that I wasn't really even staring at Vincent anymore, just the empty casing of the body he lived inside of for so many years. I went to sit in the main room in the same chair I always sat on when I'd visit him. I moved like a dying robot, slow and mechanical, just going through the motions of being a human alive in the world. When I sat, my mind became polluted once again with anger. Then, I got an image of Vincent laughing, and the grief tears came—pure and real, not like the contrived and ugly anger feelings. I knew that being angry at myself at a time like this was wrong, but I couldn't help where my mind went, and I continued to vacillate between feelings of grief and anger like they were two sides of a malfunctioning see-saw.

I'd have given anything to go back in time and save him the right way. I thought of how I could have called him more while he was in college and talked to him about his classes, all the while lending encouragement and guidance. I could have looked for jobs for him, not just told him to get one. I could have had him live with us instead of in cramped apartments or SROs. He could have lived in Frank's study, which hadn't been used in years. I could have gotten him out of the house and gone on walks and bike rides with him to make sure he was getting his exercise. I could have cooked him meals to be sure he was eating healthy. I could have—

"Let's go," Carmen said. He was on the phone all this time, and I hadn't heard a thing as I feared I would, being so immersed in war games with myself and with developing an alternative history of mine and Vincent's lives. I wasn't sure where we were going, but I knew he knew, so I just followed him out of the apartment and down the steps like a mindless idiot. He told me to leave the door unlocked in case the people from the hospital came while we were gone. I didn't want to obey because I didn't want any hospital people stealing Vincent's body away while I wasn't there, but I did what he said anyway.

"We'll go to Dad's office, and then we'll call everybody else, and then we'll go back to Vincent's house and to the funeral home," he said as he got in his car.

"Okay." My voice was so broken that it sounded like it didn't belong to me. As I walked to the car, my body felt like a thousand pounds. I was drained and anxious at the same time, running on nervous energy that felt like it came from some kind of contaminated fuel.

We got to Dad's office, which was right in town and down the street from Vincent's apartment, and I told Carmen I wanted to wait in the car. I didn't want to be alone with my pain, but I didn't want to see Dad either.

After he was done doing whatever he had to do in Dad's office, we went back to Vincent's just in time to see the paramedics carrying him out. I looked away, and Carmen held me until they were gone. He said some words to them, and they gave him their condolences. Once the ambulance was out of sight, he turned to me and said that he was going back to Dad's office to call everyone, and then to the funeral home. He assumed I would come, but I told him that I wanted to go up to his apartment. He said I shouldn't go up there and that it would just make me feel worse. But I really wanted to. I thought that some of his spirit had to still be there and that if I waited too long, all of it would be gone.

So, I made my trip up the steps alone, slow and long, my body heavy, my eyes focused on the door in front of me. I still heard Carmen in the driveway and for a quick second, I thought of turning back to go with him, but I couldn't. I knew I was choosing the tougher thing to do, but it was what I wanted. I opened the door, stepped in, and for the first time in my life, I was alone in Vincent's place, with all his things—his instruments and books and paintings and albums and crystals and the musty smell that lived in his apartment. I always opened the windows as soon as I got to his place and tell him that it needed to air out, but I wanted to keep them closed to hold onto all of him that I could.

I stood alone in the main room, waiting to feel his presence, but I felt nothing, just like I felt nothing when I came up a little while ago with Carmen. I looked at his harp and thought of how I'd never get to hear him play it or any of his instruments again. I thought about the group of local harpists he only just recently found to play with. I looked over at his book shelves and saw all the Tolkien books and thought of how he'd never get to see the *Lord of the Rings* movie. He was cheated. Why is life so fucking unfair? Then out of nowhere, I heard him saying, "Yo, Donna, can it, you're bumming me out." I heard him comparing me to Nietzsche or Sartre or one of those other miserable philosophers and couldn't help but crack a smile.

I put the kettle on for tea, even though it was really tough to do because I would only be making one cup, instead of two. I looked up at the shelf in his kitchen to see several different kinds of tea and decided on the Lady Grey. I went back and sat in *my* chair with my tea and closed my eyes and asked Vincent and Mom for strength, and then a fresh batch of tears came furiously out of my eyes—endless grief tears that left me dehydrated with a desert thirst.

I gulped a glass of water and went into his room where there was a big box off to the side and opened it to see lots of small unfinished, wooden boxes that he must have made by hand. I opened one and found a deck of tarot cards that was wrapped in a piece of golden silk material. I looked in a few of the other boxes to see the same thing in each of them.

I went to his desk, sat down, and started opening drawers. One had a bunch of letters in them, some dating back to the seventies, and most of them were from me. I sent letters to him when he went away to college and when I went away to college. He'd write back closing his letters with something like "I love hearing from you better than Breyers ice cream." I sent postcards from Europe when Randi and I spent a month there after our sophomore year. He saved every letter and postcard I ever sent him.

Underneath the pictures, there was an eight by eleven sketchbook, which looked like the same one I saw that day in his apartment in Ventnor. I pulled it out and flipped through it, seeing that it was full of drawings he made of himself at various stages of his life. They were made with markers and their bright colors stood out against stark white paper kind of like he stood out against the backdrop of the world. They were cartoonish but real, and I could almost hear and touch him through these drawings.

The first one was of him as a young teenager, dressed in blue jeans, a green-and-blue striped T-shirt, and Converse high tops. He was slouched out over an invisible floor, reading a *Thor* comic book with a look of contentment. Beside him were albums by the Beatles, Donovan, and The Incredible String Band, and a big hard-bound book by Tolkien. I could still see him as a boy reading that comic book in our den as I'd sat on the chair beside him reading *The Wind in the Willows,* looking down at his comic book occasionally to see all the cool pictures.

"What's it about?" I'd said to him, my eyes gazing down at the page.

"It's about this doctor who can change into a superhero," he'd said, turning towards me.

"What's a superhero?"

"It's somebody with super powers, like he's really strong and mighty."

"Why does he change into one?"

"To fight the bad guys." He'd never tired of my questions or made me feel stupid for asking them.

"Oh," I'd said. "Want to know what my book's about?"

"Nah," he'd said.

In the next picture, he was dressed in a big orange sweater, and he was playing the mandolin. His stance with one foot in front of the other somehow revealed his unassuming, humble nature. I could tell he was a young boy by his size in relation to the mandolin and by his facial expression—with two black dots for eyes and a couple of lines for a mouth, he was able to convey his childlike innocence and spirit. I thought of the time we'd driven to the music store in his big old Chevy truck, so he could get a new mandolin and how happy he was, once we'd got back to his apartment, just to sit and play it.

The next one was of him as a student sitting at a desk with a constellation globe, a large book, and a telescope. Behind him, a model molecule sat on top of another large book that was suspended in air. He was studying a star map and was deep in concentration, while pushing his long hair back, so it didn't obstruct his view of the page. I thought of the night he, Angie, Cosmo and I were stargazing in my backyard. I also remembered right after he'd started working at the bakery, he'd bought a telescope and invited me over to gaze through it on one clear night. He'd point it in a certain direction, tell me to peer through the lens, and tell me what I was looking at.

"This is Mars," he'd said. Then, he'd pointed it in another direction and said, "This is Venus." He'd moved it again and said, "This is Jupiter and the moons of Jupiter." It was dark outside, but the light in his face remained.

I turned the page to find an uncolored picture of him playing the bass. He looked like he was in his student days with a young face and shabby hair. He was wearing boots that looked like they belonged to an elf, long shorts, a vest, and a puffy button-down shirt. I wondered if he intended to color it in and just never got around to it. I thought of the night Frank, Vincent and I played music together—Frank on the guitar and Vincent on the bass. It was one of the best times of my life, and I could still feel that feeling I had of never wanting it to end.

Next, was one of him as a young man, scruffy hair, dressed in all blue, playing a penny whistle with his long skinny fingers. Carmen, who went to college with him, used to say that he'd play that thing all over the campus like he was the college minstrel. Of course, I thought of when he gave me a penny whistle and how thrilled I was at the thought of having an instrument of my own.

The next picture was of him in his hippie days, being chased by cops at a protest. In the background, the White House, the Washington Monument, and the American flag all stood. They were uncolored like the clouds of tear gas that surrounded him. He ran strong with determination, and his hands were fists cutting through the air, while his long hair blew in the wind. I remembered when he'd told me about a Protest he'd gone to in DC during his college years.

"They sprayed us with tear gas, Donna. But that didn't stop us," he'd said, his eyes filled with the spirit of revolution.

I turned the page to find what may have been my favorite. He was dressed in all black, playing a fiddle beneath a smiling crescent moon with a bottle of Jack Daniels at his feet. I could hear him calling himself a fiddler, making clear the distinction between a fiddler and a violin player. I could hear him playing in the kitchen of my old home as Mom kept beat while cooking. I could see his fingers dancing effortlessly on the fretboard. I could feel the joy he had from making music—a joy that could never be taken from him.

On the following page, he was putting a tray of doughnuts into a big vat with grease flying upwards in little waves. He was wearing a red shirt, a white apron, and a big, goofy closed-lip smile that made me remember how happy he was as a baker. The summer after my junior year in college, I'd stop by the bakery he'd worked at almost every day on my way home from my summer waitressing job.

"Yo, Donna," he'd said. "I just made a tray of baguettes. Wanna take one home?"

"Sure," I'd said, eyeing the delicious-looking pies in the shop. He'd known that lemon meringue was my favorite, so he'd brought one home whenever he could.

He was playing the dulcimer in the next drawing. It was uncolored like the one of him playing the bass. He sat on a stool with the instrument resting on his lap while singing with his mouth wide open. I thought of the time he'd played the dulcimer when he was home from college and how, at the time, the instrument was foreign to me. I could still hear its delicate sound, simple and complex at once like the person Vincent was.

I turned the page to see him painting a house. He was young, and his hair was going in all directions, like a palm trees' branches, but still not as wild as the big old head of hair he had in life. He was painting an invisible house, and his smile matched the one in his baker picture, but it was even bigger, reaching halfway up the profile of his face. I remembered driving around with him once as he'd pointed out all the houses he'd painted.

"We did that one too," he'd said, pointing at a pale green two-story house.

"That's beautiful," I'd said, smiling at the house that had once been an ugly shade of gray, like dirt-stained white.

The next picture was of him in the priesthood with a face that spoke of sadness and pain. His hair was short, and he was dressed in black with a white collar. He was looking out like he knew he didn't belong there and would have rather been anywhere else. As in all the drawings, I marveled at how he could create such feeling and complex emotions in his face with a few strokes of a marker. In the background, was a nun dressed in white beside a faceless old woman in a wheelchair. I thought of how much that experience, although not so pleasant, really helped him by showing him a life he didn't want and making him grateful for the life he had.

The next one was so much happier. He was wearing an orange and yellow striped T-shirt, playing the guitar, singing into a standing microphone. I thought of all the times he played guitar for me—Christmas carols, Beatles songs, old English ballads, and many more tunes with melodies that traveled pleasantly through me like flower petals floating on a stream. I could never stop hearing him say, "I've been practicing."

I turned the page to see him sitting at an office desk in a security uniform pressing keys on a keyboard that were attached to the surveillance system that surrounded him. He had a microphone before him and a bunch of video screens stood on both sides of him. A typewriter and a filing cabinet sat behind him. He looked serious but like he was having a good time and getting a kick out of feeling official. Once, I'd surprised him and popped in on him while he was working. He'd shown me the back office and proudly went around introducing me to his co-workers.

In the next one, he played the harp, and he was older than he was in any of the previous pictures. He was as old as he got in his life, with a beard, mustache, and bushy gray hair. He sat in a chair behind a harp, dressed in black, his long, thin fingers plucking the strings. I thought about how the harp was the last instrument he learned to play in his life and how appropriate that seemed, it being such a divine instrument.

He was a frail old man in the next sketch. He had a long beard and was dressed in an orange sweater and matching cap that looked like something a garden gnome would wear. He was looking at a bird that was in a tree as if wondering about the meaning of life or as he would have said, "What it's all about." I wondered if it was how he envisioned his future self as an old philosopher-type or if it was the old philosopher who always lived inside of him.

The final picture was him as a little boy holding Mom's hand. It was Mom in her twenties with a shapely dress, poufy hair, and a big purse. He was dressed in green overalls and smiling as big as any little boy could smile, and I thought of how happy he must have been to finally be with Mom again. I recalled him telling me how Mom was his best friend, and since he told me that, I hoped to hear one of my own children tell me that I was his or her best friend one day.

At first glance, it didn't make any sense to me that this last picture was one of him as a child, when the previous pictures had been in some sort of loose chronological order. Then, I heard him talking to me about how linear time was only a construct and how there was no beginning and no end to life just like the kaleidoscope painting that hung on his bedroom wall in our old home. The placement of the pictures was telling of how he lived his life—not at all like a straight line from start to finish but more of a never-ending circle.

I looked through all the pictures again quickly to see how varied and brightly colored they were, and I realized how free he was, how he didn't live by anyone else's rules—those contrived rules that trap us in. He was his own person. He was someone who defied all labels and categories, a true nonconformist. He wasn't that way to be pretentious either because he was the most down-to-earth person I knew. He wasn't trying to be so unique. He just was, and what a wonderful thing to be in this world of sameness.

Something else popped out at me as I flipped through the drawings—all the smiles. I realized that maybe he was happy all along and that my belief in his unhappiness was just that—a belief or as it turned out, a misperception that was a product of living in a world that dictates those things necessitated for happiness, none of which Vincent had. I could hear him telling me about how our physical perceptions could be inaccurate and potentially fool us.

So, could it be that I just imagined hearing the crack in his voice that day when he told me that he was happy? Half of me told myself that this crack in his voice was something that only I could hear and that I was projecting sadness upon him based on my own faulty beliefs, while the other half of me wasn't sure. Before I knew what was happening, I was picking up the phone in Vincent's apartment to call Dad's office, so I could ask Carmen what he thought about that time Vincent said he was happy. The secretary answered and said that he and Dad were just on their way out, and I asked her to grab him for me.

"What's up?" Carmen said into the phone, his voice, weak with pain.

"Do you remember the time we all went over to Vincent's apartment after Mom died, and we were all talking, and he said that he was happy?"

"I can't remember. Maybe later. My brain's too rusty now."

"No, Carmen! I'm sorry, but I need you to think back on it right now. Please. I'll explain later. Please!"

"All right, give me a minute." There was a silence for a few seconds, during which I was holding on to the hope of his memory coming through for me like I was hanging on to the ledge of a mountain cliff that rose thousands of feet above the ground. Finally, he said, "All right. What do you want to know?"

"I heard a crack in his voice when he said that thing about being happy, like he was trying to convince us and himself that it was true." I could hear desperation coming through my voice.

"I don't remember hearing a crack in his voice," he said. "I'm sure you were just imagining things."

"How do you know?"

"Well, I don't know for sure because I wasn't living inside his head. I can only tell from how he appeared in life, which was happy, for the most part. He wasn't like everybody else. Most people wouldn't like living outside on a porch, but he did."

"Oh yeah, I'm sorry. It's just that…"

"What?"

"I always felt bad for him for being alone without kids and not having much money and not having a good job. So, I thought because he didn't have any of that stuff, he must have been unhappy and that if he was happier, he would still be here."

"It's easy to think that way. That's how most people think. Hey, I got news for you. The CEO of my company had a wife—a really pretty one too—and kids and lots of money, and he just committed suicide." I thought of all the other people who appeared to have it all and were miserable or in extreme pain. I heard Vincent telling me about the high rollers in the casino and how no money in the world would ever be enough for them. Of course, it wouldn't. Nothing on the outside could ever be enough for anyone. Real wealth, like the kind Vincent had, resided inside.

"Thanks, Carmen," I said.

"Okay, I got to go. Dad's waiting. We have to go to the funeral home. Are you coming or what?"

"Yeah. I'll meet you there."

I hung up and slid down along the wall near the phone and sat on the floor in the dark small space that was the hallway of the apartment. I looked around at Vincent's place, and it looked bigger than it ever looked in the past. Much bigger. I got up, picked up the sketchbook, and walked outside to the endless sky and the trees covered with brilliant yellow leaves. I held Vincent's pictorial autobiography in my arms like I was holding something fragile and delicate as a baby but strong and wise as a sage. I unknowingly went on a treasure hunt and found the ultimate pile of gold—the story of my brother, a guidebook on how to live, my final gift from Vincent.

CHAPTER ELEVEN: 2004

"They got an all-white jury on top of everything," Frank said about the case he just lost. "The poor guy never had a chance." He sat across from me at the dinner table with Vince and Silvia on either side of us. His voice was dry and despairing, and he looked worn as an old sponge, eyes red and swollen, his forehead resting on his hand, strands of hair falling into his face. The bowl of white bean and escarole soup before him grew cold. Of course, if he could have ever let us turn the heat over sixty, it might have been warm or at least room temperature. He was drinking beer and said he was giving up every other sort of alcohol in what seemed like a sad attempt at sobriety.

"You did everything you could, Frank," I said in a positive tone. "You even got him a suit at Goodwill, so he wouldn't have to go to trial in an orange jumpsuit." We all stared at him hoping for a change, but he stayed huddled over in his same position like a sick dog.

"Yeah." He took a sip of beer that was about half of the can. "But whatever I do isn't good enough. There's no justice in this world." He used to say that he believed in a law of divine retribution, but I hadn't heard him espouse this belief in years. Vince and Silvia were sullen as they looked towards their father, and I feared that his negativity would leave a lasting effect on them. But I guess Frank being a pessimist should have been the least of my worries. He was still a raging alcoholic, although his rages were much less frequent and for that, I was grateful, especially because I no longer had the energy to deal with his crap. Vincent's death changed me.

It'd simultaneously weakened and strengthened me, zapping my energy, while forcing me to live in the world without him. I didn't realize, until he was gone, how much I leaned on him—not that I ever asked him for advice or support. It was just knowing that he was right up the street, and I could go see him any time. I not only lost him; I also lost my place of refuge and with it, the small part of myself that could let loose and be free.

The year that followed his death, a dark cloud loomed over me and every time I'd smile or laugh, I'd be hit with a surge of guilt, and I'd say to myself, "How can you smile when he's gone?" And then I'd answer back, "You know how he'd want you to be happy," and I'd go on fighting with myself and trying to convince myself that being happy was all right, but it was no use as long as that black cloud was around.

When I was raw and broken, I'd lose time staring at whatever was in front of me while nothingness filled my mind—not the kind of nothingness that Buddhist monks aspire to; more like an off-pitch humming sound, colorless and without any texture. I'd felt like I was stuck between two worlds— that of the living and another one that was between here and the afterlife. I'd have recurrent dreams that he was alive, but I could never connect with him despite my tireless efforts. I'd wake feeling so heavy with grief hanging in the air like noxious gas. I'd see his face in everything: other men's faces, a puddle of water, reflections on the wall. I'd envisioned him in his new life, somehow being able to play music and paint at the same time, and this thought made me smile inside, but still, the grief was glued to me, and I'd remained in that strange nowhere place.

Then one day, my worlds converged, and I'd rejoined the land of the living, at first feeling the pointlessness of everyday life, then seeing its occasional worthiness and finally, immersing in it fully, grateful for everything that came my way, especially the small things—a weed growing between the cracks of a city sidewalk, the center part of a Philadelphia pretzel, a drawing of a horse Silvia had made that hung on our refrigerator. But my deepest joy came from feeling Vincent with me. He was living on, not just within my memories or through me or my kids, who each held a part of him, but in the world—every time I saw a fiddler playing on the city street or had my daily cup of tea, he was there.

The summer that followed my new life, I met the nicest woman at the community pool named Ann. She played flute in a nearby orchestra and said she could give me lessons. So, I started learning the flute! I'd practice every night, and when I did, I could hear Vincent's voice resounding in my head with his favorite line, "I've been practicing."

"Mom, can you make tots sometime?" Silvia said, turning to me. Only one of her big, brown eyes was showing. Her other one was blocked by her hair that was parted off to the far side of her head. At fifteen, she looked more like ten or eleven, and I knew she couldn't stand that, but I also knew that in no time at all, she'd love having such young looks. In the meantime, she did whatever she could to make herself look older. I supposed this thing with having her hair parted so far over to one side that she looked lopsided was one of those things.

"Yeah, tots like in *Napoleon Dynamite!*" Vince said, smiling with his hands waving in the air. His cheeks were still red from playing in the cold February air earlier that day. He just got a haircut, and the hairdresser really went to town on him, making his bangs so short that they almost looked gone. I was glad he was too young to care.

"Oh, you mean tater tots?" I said. "Sure thing. One of these days soon." The smile on my face faded as I glanced in Frank's direction to see him still leaned over the table, even more despondent than he looked a few minutes ago. He finished his can of beer, went to the refrigerator for another, and walked in the direction of the den.

"Do you want me to bring you some ice cream, Frank?" I said as he walked out.

"Maybe later," he said. "Not now." That wasn't like him at all. He was always like a little boy at the Mr. Softy truck when it came to ice cream. Once, I'd seen him cut in front of some poor, little boy at the custard stand in town. He did it innocently as if the boy were invisible only to him, but I was sure he knew what he was doing.

He was so apathetic that he even passed by the broken drawer without messing with it as he normally did every night. He just walked out with his defeated-by-life limp. With his departure, a calm settled over the kitchen like a gentle, warm breeze, and the kids sat back in their chairs and loosened up like balls of yarn unwinding. Silvia asked me what his client was charged with, and I told her armed robbery.

"Yikes," she said, reminding me of Vincent.

"Does that mean he had a gun?" Vince asked.

"Or some kind of weapon," I said to him. "Probably a gun."

"I hate guns," Vince said firmly. He was only ten, but he already knew that guns stunk. Both Silvia and I said "Me too" at the same time, and then we crossed our pinkies together and made a wish reciting the line, "Blue blue, make it true! White white, make it bright!" It was one of Mom's superstitions—whenever any of us Tucci kids would say something at the same time, we'd do this little wish ritual. I wondered what Silvia wished for, but I'd never ask such a thing. I adhered to Mom's superstitions and knew that once a wish wasn't a secret, it had no power.

I wished what I always wished for any time I had an opportunity for a wish—that Frank would stop drinking. The smarter part of me knew that I was wasting my wish on something that would never happen, but there was still that tiny flame that burned inside of me despite all the times he blew it out. It kept coming back, re-igniting like one of those trick birthday-candles.

"We should call Cosmo tonight," I said to Vince and Silvia. He went away to college and was majoring in astronomy and physics at the University of Pennsylvania. I was so glad he stayed close and proud beyond words that he went to such a prestigious school. He talked about going away to study in Tucson, Arizona because they had a really great astronomy program out there, but in the end, he decided to go to school in Philadelphia instead. I think his decision was made when Frank told him he'd pay his tuition if he went to Penn. I was pretty sure Frank made the offer mostly so that he could brag that his son went to an Ivy League school.

"There're only five Ivy League colleges in the whole country," I could hear him boasting to the other lawyers. There were actually eight, but like Dad, he exaggerated whenever he had the chance.

"I just talked to him yesterday," Silvia said. "He went on and on about the Mars Rover thing." She sighed like she couldn't care less about it.

"We learned about it in science," Vince said, chin up and eyes glinting with pride.

"You want to talk to your big brother about it?" I said to him.

"Yeah," he said excitedly.

"And then we'll give Angie a call," I said. She was in her last year at Rutgers where she studied theater arts. She was a triple threat with movie star looks but lacked any interest in trying for Broadway. I thought her wise for not wanting to drown in that sea of competitive craze. I expected she'd probably marry rich and stay at home, which would suit her just fine.

Without Cosmo and Angie, the house felt empty, and I couldn't even imagine what it would feel like when Vince and Silvia were also gone. I secretly hoped that Angie and Cosmo would move back home then for lack of money but felt so guilty for having this fantasy. I should have wanted nothing but success for them, and I did, but I just couldn't imagine living alone with Frank. I saw myself in the chair in the living room looking out at the flowering dogwood with dull, despairing eyes. The tree would appear dead to me as if

I were colorblind to its pink flowers. The room would feel cold and sterile as a hospital and would smell like one too—no aroma of any food cooking, just an antiseptic, sick smell.

Elation lit up inside of me as I walked out of the building where all of my classes took place and headed to my car. I had plans to meet Randi downtown and with light still lingering in the sky at five o'clock, I was reminded that spring was on the way. I started driving, and as I approached downtown, my jubilant feeling faded because my car was moving slower than the people walking. I stared at them with envy, wishing I could be free of this steel enclosure, walking tall instead of sitting, leaned over a steering wheel, bursting with frustration.

I was grateful for finding parking pretty easily as I got really good at the whole city-parking thing. I walked to the restaurant against a tide of people in their Friday-night frenzy. The stink of city streets filled the air—a pungent stench composed of everything that ever dropped on the cement, melted and refrozen several times over several decades, and topped with exhaust fumes from an endless parade of cars and buses. As I approached the restaurant, the smell changed markedly to the aroma of steaks and fried fish.

We were meeting in an upscale British pub and inside, it was bright and airy, brimming with charm. It had white eyelet curtains and chairs with embroidered cushions. The high ceilings and hard-wood floors made the place loud, but once I saw Randi, the loudness faded into almost-pleasant background noise. She was sitting at a table by a window, wearing a bright red sweater with matching lipstick, looking fresh and vibrant. She saw me and waved with a smile. I went towards the table, and she got up to hug me. Her hair was in a short French bob that made her look about ten years younger. My hair still hung past my shoulders and dragged me down and got in my way, but I lacked the courage to cut it off.

"You look great as always," I said.

"You too, Donna," she said. I knew she was just being nice. I looked as tired as I felt, like I just lost a war that I never intended to fight. I always felt like that, especially at the end of my week or after sleeping like crap, like I did the night before with Frank tossing, turning, snoring, and getting up like every hour, once to go in the bathroom and throw up, undoubtedly the two six packs he had earlier.

"You weren't waiting long I hope," I said.

"No, not at all."

The waiter came to take our drink order, and Randi ordered a glass of white wine. I debated about whether or not to have one also because I was so turned off to drinking because of Frank. Also, I became such a lightweight from rarely drinking and feared driving home after having even one glass of wine.

When I told this to Randi, she said, "Oh c'mon. You can have some coffee afterwards, or if you want, you can stay overnight with us!" She seemed so thrilled about this prospect, and there was nothing I'd love more than being away from Frank for the night, but I couldn't stand being away from the kids.

"Thanks, but I have to get home," I said.

"Two glasses of your house white," Randi said to the waiter, and then she turned to me and said, "I'll drink whatever you can't." When the waiter left, she said, "Clarence would love to see you, you know. He's always asking about you." Clarence was her husband, whom she met in her last year of college. He played basketball for our school, and they met at some big victory party. Frank and I would double date in the City with them all the time when we were young, but Frank hadn't stepped foot in the City in years. He called it a toilet and said he wouldn't go in it even if it was right around the corner. I thought that offending Philadelphia was just another way he could put down my job, which had become one of his favorite pastimes.

"Well, I'd love to see him too. I wish I could get Frank to come in to meet us, and all four of us could go out like the old times." After I said this, I imagined what that would look like, and I saw myself being uncomfortable, anxious and guarded with Frank drinking the whole time, either being awkwardly outgoing or silently grumpy. "Actually, I take that back. I'm glad it's just me and you."

The wine came, and we toasted to our friendship. We both ordered fish and chips and chatted about work and our families. Then, she turned serious and asked me how things were going with Frank.

"Things are all right," I said putting my hand over half of my face as if to hide from her. She looked unconvinced, and I was relieved when the waiter showed up with our food. But I was only able to indulge in one delicious bite when she stared right into my eyes like she was trying to read my mind and said, "Last time we talked, you said how you wanted to leave him."

Sometimes I wished she was one of those friends who just listened and agreed with everything I said, even when my story was always changing like a new narrator was continually being drafted in to tell it.

"Things got better." I stared out the window to the street at the people walking by, hoping her stare would leave me, but when I turned my head back in her direction, it was still there, strong and unrelenting, piercing me for the truth. Still, I went on with my sorry attempt at deception, "I can't explain it. But maybe he's mellowing out with age like my dad did." She just kept on with her silent interrogation, so I just kept talking to keep myself from feeling awkward, but the more I talked, the more uncomfortable I felt. I was digging myself into a deeper and deeper hole—one that would eventually hit the center of the hard-rock earth. So finally, I said, "What am I going to do anyway, Randi, even if I wanted to leave?!"

"What are you going to do?" she said rhetorically. "Why are you suddenly so fucking helpless?!"

"So, I'm just supposed to move out with the kids and have us all live on my part-time salary?" I held my hands out with fingers splayed.

"Why do you think you wouldn't get the house?" She leaned in with anxious eyes. "And what about child support and alimony?"

"You forget I'm married to a lawyer and a very well-networked one to boot." I slouched over in a surrendering posture.

She looked down at the floor like she was searching herself for solutions. That's what she did. She always tried to solve problems, even when the scope of the problem was out of her reach. I thought she couldn't possibly understand how messy divorce could get with kids because she didn't have any. She was happily married without kids. Her life was free and uncomplicated, and if I didn't love her so much, I would have envied her. But then again, my children were the greatest thing that ever happened to me. I loved them beyond words, so I would have never traded them for all the uncomplicated freedom in the world. Besides, a divorce didn't make sense because I still thought there was hope for Frank. If he could just stop drinking, things would become good again. I still believed that he could too. When I told this to Randi, she just looked at me with her best duck face and said, "Really?"

"Why is that such an outlandish notion?" I said.

She said nothing as if my question wasn't even worthy of a response. I took a break to shovel as much of my meal in, trying desperately to enjoy the fried food that I so rarely allowed myself.

"You've been talking about him quitting for years now, Don," she said. "If he wanted to quit drinking, he would have by now. You know that."

"But he does try, you know. I know it's not much, but lately he only drinks beer. That's something." I was smiling as I talked as if I knew well that this was comical, and suddenly, my smile broke into laughter. She started laughing with me, and it felt so good to be on the same side again. I poured malt vinegar on my remaining fish and took a bite. As I was chewing, she looked me right in the eye and said, "You can't change someone. He has to want to change."

As soon as I pulled in the driveway, I felt Frank's crazed energy stirring in the house like a dust storm in the desert. All the lights were on, and I was pretty sure he was the only one home because Vince and Silvia always went out on Friday nights. Frank never liked being alone too much, and as he aged, he liked it even less. Being alone made him more anxious than he was already. It made him run around and turn things on—lights, the radio, the TV.

I walked into an explosion of light and sound in the kitchen, and his eyes popped out at me, blacker than black, with anger ripping its way through his skin. I thought I'd jinxed myself by thinking he was starting to mellow out as his rage had seemingly resurrected, refueled with a whole new purpose.

"Hi, Frank," I said, like I was asking a question.

"Where were you?!" he said, as if I were gone for weeks without contacting him as to my whereabouts.

"I stopped at the mall," I lied. Hearing I went out for a social engagement would just make his anger grow. "Is everything all right?" I knew this was a stupid question.

"No, as a matter of fact everything's not all right. I work my ass off all week and come home to an empty house! Those kids never say two words to me unless they want something, and you're always off with your job and whatever else you do!" He was making a vodka and tonic, marking the apparent end of his hard booze fast. A few years earlier, I would have been coming back at him with arguments and pep talks. I'd tell him that he'd feel better if he didn't drink so much. I'd tell him that when he drank, he acted up and drove all of us away. I'd tell him he had so much to be happy for and so much to offer and that that cheap, fleeting buzz he so prodigiously sought wasn't worth it.

But I stopped wasting my time and my breath. Instead, I just stood there and listened and let him diffuse like an over-inflated balloon, and eventually he did. That was Mom's big trick. Dad would be going off like a maniac, and she'd just be standing there with this deadpan look. It wasn't an easy behavior to cultivate, and because I was out of practice, I had to keep biting my tongue, but I managed, even though he tried his best to engage me.

"What did you go shopping for at the mall anyway? You know, I got college tuitions to pay. You don't make anything at your little college job. What do you do there all day anyway?" It was killing me not to tell him to go fuck himself, but I kept reminding myself that that was just what he wanted. Finally, he waved his hand in the air in disgust and walked out.

I went into the bathroom to wash my face, and as soon as the water came out of the faucet, tears started streaming from my eyes. I told myself that it was the wine that was making me emotional—the wine, and Randi's words repeating in my head, "You can't change someone. He has to want to change." I dried my face and looked in the mirror to see these helpless eyes staring back at me, pleading with me to do something, to get myself out of this life.

When I got down like this, I thought of poor Angie and the suicide attempt she had a couple years ago. It was a hot, still night, and her screams bolted through the air like jagged lightning rods. We'd rushed her to the hospital with me and Frank sitting in the ambulance, my body comatose with fright. She'd had her stomach pumped. When it was over, we'd found out that she had been on antidepressants and had decided to go off them without a doctor's supervision.

"I felt a pain so deep and endless," she'd said to us, laying in her bed, salt-white face with all of the life drained out of it. "I wasn't even thinking when I opened the medicine cabinet in your bathroom and found a bottle of your sleeping pills." She'd directed this to me as it was my bottle of pills. I'd never wanted anything as bad as I'd wanted her to make it. I'd prayed so hard to Mom and Vincent in hysterics in the ambulance and said prayers of thanks as soon as the doctor had saved her.

We'd slept over at the hospital and had taken her home the next morning. I'd stayed by her side all summer and even slept in the same bed. Silvia had stayed by her too, drawing and painting as Angie laid in bed, reading. Frank had taken her to court with him and out for banana split sundaes. Vince was too young to have known the full extent of what had happened but knew that something was wrong, and he entertained his big sister by playing his board games with her. Even Cosmo was nice to her. He'd come home for visits and spend the night watching TV with her—a truly rare and wonderful sight to see them sitting together peacefully.

"Promise me that you'll never do anything like this on your own again," I'd said to her one night as I laid beside her. And then I went on without giving her a chance to answer, "That you'll always talk to me about everything for now on—I mean everything. And if you're ever feeling down, you'll talk to me about it right away, honey. You don't have to run to a doctor."

"I just—" she'd started.

"I'm just trying to say that I'm always here for you, Ang," I'd started to cry tears of love and of remorse. I thought that I should have never started grad school so soon after she was born and blamed our lack of bonding on my premature return to school.

At that moment, I was feeling a drop of what she must have been feeling. It's not that I wanted out of my life. I just wanted out of what it had become with Frank destroying himself and trying really hard to take me down with him. I felt like he was constantly cutting me down, and I was constantly forcing myself to rise up, struggling all along like a plant that had to emerge from the ground through soil made of lava rock.

Those helpless eyes still stared back at me, and then out of nowhere, I heard Mom telling me to toughen up the way she did when she dropped me off at college. My inner voice hardened like stone and said, "So fucking what if I don't have a perfect marriage? I have my wonderful children, a job I love, a nice house, and good friends. I have a really great life, and so what, if one thing isn't right?" I thought of all the people in the city living on the streets, eating dirt, freezing, begging for loose change. I needed to be happy for all that I had and to stop focusing on the one thing in my life that wasn't right.

"Mom, did you get any raspberry doughnuts?" Silvia called out to me as I walked in from the car. It was

Saturday morning, and I was just returning from the bakery. The cold air hit me in the face, with a wind that blew so hard that I had to hold the bakery box close to me, so it wouldn't blow away.

"Yes, I got you raspberry and cinnamon-glazed for Vince," I said. "And a lemon cream for me and a salted caramel one for Dad." Some new yuppie doughnut place moved into town with lots of fancy, complicated flavors.

Silvia smiled gratefully and opened the door for me. Vince came into the kitchen, looking like he just woke up, hair pushed against his tired face. He was always a night owl and a late riser, and he reminded me of myself when I was a kid.

Poor Mom would have to turn the lights on and take all the covers off of me in an attempt to get me out of bed, and then I'd be clinging to the bed posts. Sometimes, she'd even have to tell me that the truancy officer had come for me. I'd peek out the front window to see a guy in a truck and even back then, I'd figured it was probably just one of Dad's friends she'd called on to do her a favor. But still, I'd gone with it and got ready for school, feeling that all her supreme efforts deserved some kind of reward. Vince wasn't as bad as I was, but he still didn't like to wake up early.

Cosmo always got right up, automatic and reliable as a machine, just like his Dad. His car was out when I got home, and I wondered what trouble he was up to that morning. But then I thought he might be on good behavior to make up for the night before.

"Have you seen Dad, Silvie?" I asked her.

"Yeah, he went to his office," she said, closing her eyes as she ate. I wouldn't dare interrupt her doughnut-nirvana, so I turned my attention to Vince.

"What are you up to today?" I said to him.

"I'm going over to Chris's house after I finish up some of my homework," he said. Chris was his friend from school who lived down the street. I was glad that I didn't have to worry about him playing video games all day as he was never all that enthralled with them, and I could trust that he and Chris would probably spend most of their time playing outside, riding their skateboards or bikes or whatever. Cosmo lived on video games, and I was constantly having to bargain with him. I could still hear myself saying to him, "If you only spend an hour gaming, you can have two Reese's Cups instead of one."

"Sounds good," I said to Vince, cutting my doughnut in half and putting the other half back in the box.

"How come you don't eat the whole thing?" Vince asked me.

"Because I get a sugar crash if I eat too much sugar," I said.

"What's that?" he asked.

"I get really tired and..." I tried to think of how to explain the feeling to him so he could understand, but nothing good came to mind, so I just used one of Vincent's favorite words, which I did whenever I got the chance. "I just feel really lousy."

"Yeah, I try not to eat too much sugar," Silvia said, who was health conscious at an early age. "Just for special things like doughnuts. But not just any doughnuts either. They have to be really good ones like these."

"That's good, Silvie," I said. "You always knew how to eat healthy."

"Thanks," she said, proud and smiling.

The sound of Frank's car coming up the driveway descended upon the kitchen, and the kids both looked up with anxious eyes. They then gobbled the remains of their doughnuts, put their dishes in the sink, and flew off to their rooms, reminding me of how us Tucci kids all used to run off when Dad would come home, like cockroaches that scurry in the new light. I wished I could also run off to my room and hide from him, but I couldn't, so I just got up and cleared the table and started unloading the dishwasher.

He was walking inside carrying a bunch of apology flowers in one hand and his briefcase in the other. He looked so pathetic with the grey sky casting a shadow over tired face, dreary eyes, and wrinkles like skid marks. Even the flowers, which were yellow and orange, didn't brighten him up.

"Hi, Donna," he said as he came through the door. He wore a forest green jacket and the weakest smile I ever saw on anyone.

"Hello," I said, standoffish, exploiting my having the upper hand to the fullest.

"Well, I'm sorry for last night, but I came home to an empty house after working hard all week and you know."

"The kids always go out on Friday nights, and I told you I was going to the mall after work," I said, continuing to take dishes out of the dishwasher.

"I forgot," he said, still holding the flowers in front of him as though they were somehow defending him. "Jesus Christ! I'm only human you know." He sure got a lot of mileage out of that only-human excuse.

"Well, so am I, Frank." I stopped what I was doing and looked him right in the eyes. "And I'm tired of being your punching bag." He looked down at the floor with forlorn eyes. The big scary monster became as small and powerless as a lost kitten. I wanted to tell him how that day would have been a great time to try to quit drinking and how if he really wanted to make things up to me, that would be the way. But I kept hearing Randi's voice saying that he had to want to quit on his own terms.

"I got you these flowers," he finally said, throwing the flowers on the table like they were garbage he found in the street. They were mostly mums, and I thought of the time he gave chrysanthemums to Mom.

"Thank you," I said, taking them and getting a vase out of the cabinet.

"I got some big news too," he said.

"What is it?" I said, putting the flowers in a vase with water.

"Well," he said, sitting down at the table. "I've been asked if I want to be a judge at the local courthouse, and I accepted. I think, if nothing else, I might have a little more control over things at least."

"Wow," I said, sitting down across from him, my mind blank for lack of knowing what to think. "That is big news." I imagined him sitting up high in front of a courtroom, dressed in one of those black robes with a gavel before him. I didn't feel anything because I wasn't sure what to feel. I thought it could be the best thing that ever happened to him—the thing that could make him sober up and fly straight. It could also be a really bad thing, worsening the stress he already had with the disturbed energy of someone scratching at a mosquito bite.

Usually, I had some notion of how things would play out, but that time, I wasn't at all sure. Still, I leaned towards being unhopeful, and his becoming a judge reminded me of when Vincent joined the priesthood, not just because both vocations required one to wear black, but because it was that same kind of searching for something he'd most likely never find. Unlike Vincent though, Frank never quit anything. He'd rather die struggling at some impossible feat than quit.

"Congratulations," I said in the most solemn tone that that particular word had probably ever been spoken.

"Thanks," he said with his eyes half-filled with hope and a strained smile that broke quickly and disappeared.

CHAPTER TWELVE: 2007

"C'mon, Uncle Carmen," Vince said, gesturing to Carmen as he headed into the ocean. He wore cut-offs that hung on his slender but muscular body, and his sandy brown hair fell down around his face with his eyes squinting cheerfully back at his uncle.

Carmen was dressed in green swimming trunks and a matching visor. He turned around after a few feet and said, "You sure you don't want to come in?" to me and Silvia. We sat on a flowered quilt on top of the sand, near dunes with tall grass that swayed rhythmically in the damp wind like a silent song.

"No," I shouted out, speaking for both of us. "Maybe later."

Silvia was wearing a mod straw hat that curved off to one side and a red and white polka dot bikini that showed off her cute, little figure. She was drawing the beach scene before her—umbrellas and sunbathers on sand that reached out to the sea. She was going into her second year of art school this fall at the University of the Arts in Philly. I went to war with Frank over it, and I triumphed, in part because she got scholarship money at my encouragement.

She was near Cosmo, who settled in the western part of the City near where he started college. He dropped out after a couple of years, sadly. I say sadly because astronomy was his passion. I wanted to push him to go back, but the wiser part of me stopped myself. I learned something from all those years of coaxing Vincent to do what I thought was best for him.

I sat, staring at the ocean as the continual music of waves drowned out the sound of nearby conversations and a radio blaring pop music. Seagulls squawked in the sky, and the ring of the ice cream truck sounded. Silvia said that she wanted to get some, so I gave her money and asked her to get ice cream sandwiches for me, Carmen, and Vince. I was junking out that day with an ice cream sandwich for lunch and planning on boardwalk pizza and movie theater popcorn for dinner. We were going to see *Harry Potter and the Order of the Phoenix* that night, and I may have been even more excited to see it than the kids.

I closed my eyes, listened to the waves, and remembered being a kid on the beach. Half of us would be gathered around Mom and Dad under the umbrella, eating cold eggplant Parmesan sandwiches while the other half were off playing in the sand and the sea. I can see Mom running over to the water's edge whenever she'd thought one of us too far away from the view of the lifeguard, waving her big arms in the air as she'd shouted our names. We'd get so embarrassed.

I was smiling in sweet remembrance when Silvia came back holding three ice cream sandwiches in one hand and eating a strawberry shortcake pop in the other. She stood looking at the dunes with that priceless look in her eyes, like all the beauty in the world was meant for her to recreate with paint and canvas. Carmen and Vince were coming back from the ocean, soaked and energized by the water that was too cold for me.

"Ice cream sandwiches!" Carmen said with popping eyes like he was five years old. We all laughed. Silvia held her hand out with the sandwiches, and we each took one. I knew I was eating pure crap, but it was so good. After we finished them, Silvia and Vince went for a walk by the ocean, and Carmen sat down in the chair next to me.

"So how are things at the old homestead?" he said, meaning *how are things with Frank.*

"Not bad," I said, and then quickly added, "I mean, it could always be better. The other night, he came home stinking of whiskey, zigzagged across the floor, collapsed two feet away from the bed, and kept waking every few minutes from the sound of his own snoring. But didn't bother to get up from the floor. I told him a couple times to come to bed, and he mumbled 'all right' but never made it."

"No big fireworks though?" Carmen said.

"I wouldn't quite say that. He still acts up every now and then but not like he used to."

"Well, that's good at least," he said.

"Yeah, it is."

"Good ole Frankie," he said with a mouth full of ice cream.

"When he first became a judge, he was better, almost like a different person. And then he went back to his old self again. I think he thought he was going to have all this control over things, and then he realized he didn't. He's trying to fix a broken system, that's what it is."

"That's too bad. Poor guy."

"I feel bad for him. I go between feeling sorry for him and being angry at him. There's never any good feeling towards him, though." I took a big sigh like I just released a small but savage monster from my stomach. I knew I could comfortably spill all this to Carmen because he wouldn't come at me with *that* dreaded question: "Why don't you just leave him?" like suggesting I get rid of a broken washing machine.

"Jeez, I'm sorry," he said, sympathy in his voice. He crumbled the wrapper from his ice cream sandwich. "Well, me and Karen are taking Jessica to New Hope next Saturday for a street-fair. Want to come? It'd be a lot of fun for the kids."

"I'd love to, but we're all going to see Angie Saturday." She just got married to a nice guy named Doug. Frank was really happy because his new son-in-law was a stock broker and made a lot of money, and I was happy because she was happy.

"Why don't you go to Angie's Sunday instead?" Carmen said. "The kids would love this thing. There'll be all kinds of craft booths and clowns and all that fun fair stuff."

"Great idea," I said. "I'll call her and ask her if that's all right. Maybe we can pick Cosmo up on the way too." I looked out on the gray green sea and the white sky with an even whiter sun, a bright ball that slipped in and out of the clouds. "Hey, do you think Vincent can hear us talking right now?"

"Sure," Carmen said. "Why not?" He wasn't into all that mystical stuff like Vincent was, so I knew this was the best response I could get, and I took it happily.

When we got home that night, Frank was out of the house. The kids went right to sleep, and I lay awake until I heard his car rolling up the driveway around midnight. He came in, trying to be quiet, and I pretended to be asleep.

"Donna," he said in his softest voice to see if I was awake. I didn't respond. He undressed and got in bed and in no time was happily snoring. I just lied there silently, thinking of all the times I couldn't wait to lay next to him in bed and how much I'd loved his smell and how he used to turn me on. Those days were long gone and my excitement at lying next to him had transformed into a sad hope that he'd just sleep on the couch, so I didn't have to be awakened by him every five seconds, snoring or getting up to throw up in the bathroom or flopping back and forth like a dying fish. He woke suddenly and said "hi" in a grumbly voice. I could hear in his tone that he was in one of his rare semi-peaceful moods.

"Hey," I said in a flat voice. I got a flash of a memory of when he and I used to talk and laugh in bed about our days or the kids or a memory we'd shared when we were young together, and before I knew it, a tear was coming down my cheek. I was turned away from him, so he couldn't see me, but still, he must have sensed something was wrong because he asked me if I was all right.

"Yeah," I said, trying to sound stoic.

He reached over and touched my arm with his rough, dry hand. I felt nothing. I dried the tear from my face and turned around to look at him in hopes of feeling something, but when I did, I saw his eyes—drab, empty and lifeless—and continued to feel nothing. He hit me not long ago with a sudden slap in the face that I think had cleared out all the remaining love I had for him. Vince and Silvia were home. That may have been the worst part. I was about Vince's age the time I saw Dad knock Mom against the refrigerator, and the awful vision of her sitting on the floor never left me. I could still see the look in her eyes with the strain and helplessness of a bug struggling to get out of a flushing toilet.

Frank felt terrible afterwards and said he'd never do it again, but I knew that that was an empty promise. That's what they all say, right? I knew that unless he stopped drinking, the violence would recur. It was the alcohol that made punches fly, that made him say terrible things, and that turned him into someone else—someone hateful. Just like with Dad.

I said goodnight and turned around.

"I love you," he said in a desperate voice as if wishing I'd reciprocate.

"You too." This was all I could say when he'd tell me he loved me. I didn't think I could ever say those three words to him again.

I woke the next morning, feeling like a deflated balloon, groggy from bad sleep and a disturbing dream that remained fresh in my mind. It was the dream I'd get recurrently right after Vincent died—the one with him being alive and me trying so hard to connect with him but never making it. I opened my eyes to feel a millisecond of relief at it being only a dream, and then the black cloud that had loomed over me right after his death made its return, darker and gloomier than ever.

I was grateful that it was summer, so I didn't have to worry about work and could take it easy. Vince and Silvia were with their friends, and Frank was out doing something. I made some coffee in a French press, which I recently got and was very excited about. That's what my life had come to—exuberance over a new way to make coffee. I poured the coffee in a mug with some half and half, got a blueberry muffin that Silvia made a couple days ago, sat down in the living room, and gazed out of the front window.

I was sitting in the same chair I sat in when I was waiting for Carmen to come over right after he told me of Vincent's death. The feeling of the sad dream I had washed over me, making me feel like I showered with dirty water. I got up and sat in another chair, but the feeling followed me like a depressed bathrobe I couldn't take off.

I needed to connect with Vincent in some way, so I went into my bedroom and got the sketchbook that I kept safely preserved and hidden in my top dresser drawer. I went back into the living room, sat down, and began looking through the pictures. As I was going through them, I started to think of what pictures I'd have of myself by the end of my life. I closed my eyes to visualize the pictures, expecting variety and color, but all I saw was a single black and white drawing of me sitting behind a window, trapped inside the house I always wanted, the marriage I always wanted, the life I'd always wanted. I opened my eyes and looked outside at the front yard that I once thought beautiful and full of life, but it looked drab and lifeless as a retired junkyard.

I knew my marriage was less than perfect and that most if not all of the love had drained out of it, but I had my great children and so many other people I loved in my life. I had a job I enjoyed and was even passionate about. I closed my eyes again with a strained focus on the positive things in my life in an effort to see some better pictures, but still, I only saw that same woman who looked lost and sad, like the drawing of Vincent in the priesthood. She looked as if she didn't know quite how she arrived where she was. How could she have ended up in this shitty place when she had such a perfect plan? Completely colorless, like Vincent's unfinished drawings, this poor woman was confined inside a prison of her own false beliefs, looking out at the world with a struggling hope that it just might give her something that would make everything all right.

I couldn't fool myself anymore. I knew, in that moment, that I had to leave Frank.

The next day, Randi and I met up at a café that was midway between my house and the City, where she lived, and I told her my latest realization.

"I've been waiting to hear you say that for about fifteen years now," she said, taking a sip of her cappuccino. "Why now?" Her hair was cut in a pixie for summer, and she wore a white cotton dress and turquoise beads around her neck. She still had all the light in her face that she had in college. I imagined that I had a tiny speck of light in my own face, about the size of a flea. It made its debut the day before when I decided to leave Frank, and I knew it would be growing to eventually cover the whole of my face.

"I was looking through Vincent's sketchbook— the one I told you about that I found after he died, and I started thinking about what pictures I'd have of myself by the end of my life, and all I saw was this poor, old lady sitting behind a window looking out and feeling totally trapped. And I realized that I just couldn't do it anymore."

"That's great, Don, just wondering why it took you so long."

"I think I may have had the same epiphany shortly after he died, but it didn't have the same impact. I was too heavy with grief. And besides, you know how it is with those epiphanies. I got the insight, it went away, it came back. I thought I could do it, but I got scared. It's tough to break down a lifetime of beliefs. I just really always thought I needed to live a certain way to be happy. I can still hear my dad telling me to be sure to marry rich. You know it's funny the voices that get stuck inside your head—even when you know they're wrong. But yesterday, it all just hit me. I have all the things I thought I always wanted, and I'm fucking miserable. All I need is myself to be happy, but I don't have that as long as I'm lying to myself."

"Wow!" she said. "That's a whole hell of a lot of insight."

"I just hope I don't lose it again."

"I don't think you will, and anyway, I won't let you!"

"You're the best, Rand. I love you."

"Love you too," she said matter-of-fact. "So now what?"

"Well, I'd love to leave him tomorrow, but it's not that easy." I said through a sigh, wondering where to begin. "You know he's a judge now and more well connected than ever, and the other night, I was at this party with him, and we're standing around with this lawyer friend of his who's a real shark, and he does a lot of divorce cases. So, he was bragging about a divorce case he did for some guy, and his client ended up getting custody of the kids."

"Maybe the wife was really messed up or something. That's not going to happen to you."

"Maybe she's not, and she just didn't make as much money as him, and somehow, this guy proved her incompetent."

"That's crazy, Don, it's not going to happen to you."

"I know it probably is crazy, and maybe I'm just being paranoid, but I can't take any chances. I'm going to wait until Vince goes to college or at least until he's ready to graduate high school. It's only five years. I waited this long."

"Yeah, that's true," she said, nodding in agreement.

"Besides, I don't need any more drama in my life. I can't take the stress. I'll start smoking again. I'm finally feeling healthy and like I might live to see sixty." My hands flew everywhere as I spoke.

"You'd think he'd be happy to get rid of you, the way he treats you."

"You'd think," I said. "But Frank is a strange bird. He still loves me, and even more than that, he needs me. I can tell. I know him better than he knows himself."

"I believe it."

"So, in the meantime, it won't be so bad. I have my kids and my job and my flute lessons. And more than anything, I'll have myself and the knowledge that I'll be leaving, and that's enough for now. I can start thinking about where I want to live, so when it comes time for the move, I'll be ready." Excitement ran through me like electricity. I saw a picture of me in a tiny apartment, maybe in the City, crammed with books and CDs, a music stand where I would practice my flute, and a small kitchen off to the side. Silvia's and Vincent's art would hang on my walls. I wasn't sure about the view outside. Maybe there would be a tree, and maybe there would just be a brick wall. It didn't matter, because I'd have everything I need inside.

CHAPTER THIRTEEN: 2012

It was one in the afternoon, and Randi would be arriving soon. All my bags were packed along with the few bits of small furniture I was taking with me to my new apartment. I sat in my living room looking out the front window of my house, which was soon to be my old house. I was finally leaving Frank and should have felt nothing but exuberance and relief, but in truth, I was a mixed-up jumble of nerves and emotions, with a new one coming along every five seconds like a wind current that was constantly changing direction.

The hardest thing was having to say goodbye to my old self—the person who fell in love with Frank, who spent her days dreaming of their future together, hoping things would get better when they started to sour, trying to fix him and our marriage, and make it something it wasn't meant to be. I was just glad to not be one of those people who viewed divorce as a failure. Besides having had wonderful kids with him, we had some really good times, and we were in love for a while, and as Alfred Lord Tennyson wrote, "Tis better to have loved and lost than never to have loved at all."

I'd waited until the last possible minute to tell him, which was right after Christmas. I'd made it an extra special holiday, doing the Seven Fishes dinner on Christmas Eve in Mom's honor. When I told him, he changed before my eyes, forcing the façade of a loving, caring husband on himself, like he was using cheap camera tricks to pull off his phony transformation.

"Donna, what are you saying?" he'd said, with his mouth hung open and mystified eyes.

"Just that I think it's time we go our own ways," I'd said, staying strong, reciting the list I'd made in my head of all the awful things he'd ever done: calling Cosmo a failure, hitting me, going on a rampage so bad that we'd be forced to stay in a motel overnight, and many more. It was a long and dynamic list that I was continually updating.

At first, he was in shock. Then, he pleaded with me. Then, he got angry and then sad. He went through all the stages of grief in about two days, and after that, he remained sweet and pitiful for the duration of my time living with him, bringing me flowers every day and doing everything he could have possibly done without admitting to all his fuck-ups and telling me that he'd quit drinking if I would stay.

Vince would be graduating high school soon and going to college in the fall. I would have waited until he was completely out of the house, but a place I really liked and could afford became available, and I had to jump on it, because I knew there wouldn't be another one like it.

Just as I was thinking of Vince, I saw him walking up the driveway. He walked just like me—fast and forward-leaning like he had to cram as much life as he could into each day. He saw me sitting in the window, and I got up to open the front door. Outside, the sky was a gray backdrop, and the air was cold and damp, but I was too tense to let it cut through me as it usually did. Though I was glad to see Vince, I didn't like that he left school early to come home.

"Vince, you know you shouldn't cut school. I don't care that you're a senior either." I knew he wouldn't take me seriously because I was smiling as I spoke.

"I just wanted to help you move, Mom," he said as he stepped up on the porch. He wore jeans, a blue ski jacket, and a black cap nearly covering his eyes, which glowed with senioritis, simultaneously jaded and excited.

"I hope you didn't miss anything important." I put my arm around him, and we walked back in the house.

"Only study hall and gym with Mr. Testa, screaming his head off the whole time. It's like Dad if he was a gym teacher." I laughed. "Oh yeah, I did miss my English class, but Jacob said he'll give me the notes."

"English of all things." I tried, unsuccessfully, to sound serious.

"Sorry, Mom. You're more important. Besides, what kind of a jerk would I be if I didn't help my best friend move?" I wanted to cry the happiest tears in the world at hearing him speak these words, but couldn't afford to be any more emotional than I was already, especially with the big day I had ahead of me. So, I just told him how much I loved him and thanked him for being such a great son.

I heard a car coming up the driveway and looked outside to see it was Randi, zooming up in her yellow Mini Cooper like the superhero of my life she had become. I could see her smiling face from where I stood. She was so happy that I'd be moving into the same area of the City where she lived. She said, "It'll be like we were back in college again." For me, it really would be too. My apartment wasn't all that much bigger than our dorm room. Vince and I went out to greet her.

"Hi, Aunt Randi," Vince said as she walked over to us.

"Vince!" she said, smiling big and holding her arms out. They hugged, and Vince patted her on the back a couple times, which was his signature hug.

"You know we can't take too much time," I said to Randi, looking at her snidely. She knew that I planned the move that morning when Frank was in court, but I told her that there was always a chance he could get out early.

"No problem," she said, her bright eyes popping. "I had a triple shot of espresso this morning, so I'm ready for anything."

The three of us began moving my stuff out to the van I rented that was parked in the driveway right next to Randi's car. Besides the several boxes consisting mostly of clothes and books, I was bringing a few items of furniture, my flute, a bunch of CDs, DVDs, albums, and art—most of which belonged to Vincent—and of course, the sketch book that I packed as if it were an original painting by a famous artist.

"I feel like I'm going back to college," I said to Randi as we moved stuff out.

"You're really going to feel like we're back in college, because I'm staying over with you tonight," she said as she put one of the boxes into the van.

"Randi, that's crazy," I said, even though I was so glad to hear that she would be staying over. "We're going to be sleeping on the floor, you know."

"No, we're not," she said. "I have an air mattress in my car. You can use it until you get a bed or a sofa bed or whatever you're going to sleep on." I smiled gratefully, and she said, "I can't let you stay alone your first night. We want to set you up for success after all."

"I'm so lucky to have you in my life." I looked at her with eyes near tearing, and again, I had to shake myself out of getting lured into an emotional state. I had to be steady and grounded to do what I had to do.

We all talked while we moved my stuff out to the van. Randi talked about her plans for us, which included a little party that Clarence and she would be throwing next week with a few of their close friends. She said it would be a good opportunity for me to meet some nice people who also lived in the City.

"That sounds great, Mom," Vince said.

"Yes, it does. Thank you so much, Randi. You're the best!"

"Oh, and guess what else I forgot to tell you?!" she said, too elated to regard my thank you. "Clarence and I are going to England this summer! I'm finally going to see Stonehenge. Remember how we used to talk about going all the time?"

"You are?!" I was so excited that I almost dropped the box I was carrying. "That's fantastic! I'm so happy for you."

"Hope you got places to stay," Vince said. "It's supposed to be crazy with the Olympics in London this summer?" He walked behind us carrying two boxes stacked on top of each other.

"I know," she said. I was sure she was well aware of this as she never let anything get past her. "We're going before the games."

"That's good," Vince and I both said at the same time.

"Oh, and guess what else?" Randi said.

"What?" I said.

"There might be another apartment available in my building. It's a little more, but it's all updated with new granite countertops and everything."

"That's nice," I said. "But not so sure I give a shit about countertops." Randi and Vince laughed.

Loading up the car seemed to have happened even faster than when Frank and I moved my stuff out of my dorm and into his apartment. The van was full, and we were ready to go, and I knew I should have been relieved that we'd finished it before Frank got home, but I wasn't. In fact, I wished he would have come home as we stood in the driveway, kicking me out in a massive rage so that I could feel more positive about going. So, I stalled. I told Vince and Randi that I wanted to go back in the house and make sure I didn't forget anything. That was such bullshit. I checked the place a million times already.

I walked through the back door and stood inside my kitchen and realized this would be the last time I'd be standing here and thought about all the great meals I made here and all the good times I spent in this room. I could walk around and visit the other rooms in the house, but they didn't matter to me like the kitchen did. The kitchen was the center of everything just like it was in the house I grew up in. Sunday dinners that seemed to last all day, my kids as babies learning to eat, all of us eating ice cream out of the carton on hot summer nights. When I tried to remember the bad stuff that had happened in this room—which had been plentiful—my mind went blank. The only pictures in my mind were those of smiles and laughter and eating delicious food. No fights or rampages or ruined dinners. I started crying. My tears came out without warning, and I even started sobbing. I heard the door open behind me and turned to see Randi coming inside.

"Hey, Don," she said. "You know you're doing the right thing." I told her I knew and that it was just really hard. She said that if we did it faster, it would be easier, like taking a Band-Aid off. I knew she was right, so I walked outside with her, not giving my kitchen—I mean my old kitchen—a second look. In the cold air, my tears dried almost instantly. I walked through my old backyard for the last time, and I could feel Mom pushing me forward into my new life and hear Vincent's voice saying to me, 'It's time to hit the road.'

I was living in my studio apartment for a few months when I finally got used to its smallness. When I first moved in, I kept thinking I was going to open my closet door to find a whole other room behind it, not just a closet that fit five pairs of shoes and the few hanging clothes I took with me.

The whole place was one room with a tiny bathroom off to the side that I was so happy to say, had a bathtub. It could have been a bathtub for a hobbit, but it was a bathtub nonetheless, and I could fit comfortably in it as long as I was sitting up. My bed was in the center of the place—a mustard-colored fold-out couch that I bought at IKEA and that was surprisingly comfortable. There was a desk that sat in front of a window that looked out to the branches of a skinny tree, which appeared as if it might get knocked down by the next strong wind. But still, it was a tree, and I felt lucky to have one outside the window of my city apartment. My little kitchen consisted of a small sink, a fridge that was something between a full-size and a mini, and a countertop that I used for drying dishes, chopping vegetables, and eating. I was glad to have a gas stove, and after cooking on it for only a short while, I couldn't have imagined ever going back to electric.

I had a bookshelf crammed with literary classics, and on my walls, Vincent's drawings and Silvia's paintings hung, including one she'd completed recently titled *The Golden Garden Bird of Peace,* devoted of course to her uncle for being the primary inspiration behind her art. It was a white dove surrounded with flowers, painted in bright colors with bold lines in the unique, folksy style that was all Silvia's.

But the best part of my apartment was the cat I got only after about a month of moving in. I named her Gilda (with a soft *G* of course). With sparkling blue eyes, white-grey long hair, and a bushy fox tail, she may have been the prettiest cat in the world, with a sweetness that blended perfectly with her beauty. She rolled on the floor as I rubbed her tummy, which put her in a state of cat-bliss that would make any human envious.

A friend from work suggested that I get a cat, and right after I got my landlord's permission, I was out shopping at all the local animal rescues. As soon as I saw Gilda, I knew I had to take her home. At first, I couldn't understand why such a little beauty hadn't been snatched up, but then I just figured that it was because I was supposed to have her.

Gilda lay on the floor in front of a small, white, wooden end table with a candle, a bunch of Vincent's old crystals, a stack of books, and a little notebook that I started writing poetry in. I got up, grabbed my laptop off the floor, and sat back down on the couch with her hopping up right behind me like a very small shadow. She curled up as close as she could possibly get to me while purring and kneading on the sofa.

I started grading papers and did so into the late afternoon, when the remains of the daylight came in my apartment in a shy blaze of light. It was Friday, and I didn't have classes on Fridays, so I usually did my work at home. It was four-thirty, and I was starving because all I ate all day was a fried egg and a slice of toast. I allowed myself one night a week to go out to dinner and that happened to be one of those nights. I put on my blue suede clogs (that I still had) and my denim jacket, locked up, walked down the hallway, and down the two flights of stairs.

My apartment was in an orange brick building with blue trim and sat on top of a pizza parlor with a bright neon sign and a delightful aroma that drifted up to my place on weekend nights. It was on a narrow, quaint street where the city noise sounded muffled and distant despite being in the middle of everything, only a few blocks from Rittenhouse Square—close to all the major bus lines, restaurants, a grocery store, and a big performing arts center where the symphony performed. I went to see them a little over a week ago. They played Haydn and Beethoven, and it was divine.

I walked down my street passing row home after row home, my favorite being one that appeared to be from the 1700s with snow-white bricks that had seen so much history unfold that they possessed a sort of wisdom. When I got off my street, occasional storefronts popped up here and there, while the continual murmur of noise played, punctuated by car horns and sirens. The balmy spring air settled over the buildings in a haze, and the potpourri of city smells hung thick in the air.

I ducked inside a Mexican restaurant that was only a few blocks away from home. Outside, the place looked like nothing special, but inside, it was a warm-lit room with white table cloths, an ornate chandelier, and deep brown, wooden archways with intricately carved flourishes. It was happy hour, and most of the people sat by the bar, which was lined with glass shelves of colorful bottles. I adored this place and really loved that it was within my budget.

I also loved going out to eat alone. When I first moved here, I'd never eat out alone. In fact, I had a tough time doing anything at all—alone or with people—when I first moved here. I felt like a visitor rather than a resident and like I was never where I was supposed to be. I felt more alone than I ever did in my life, even with Cosmo, Silvia, and Randi close by. It was partly because I wasn't used to living alone and because I missed living with Vince, but it was mostly because a part of myself was missing, as if half of me had decided to stay put in my old house.

But after about a couple months of feeling disconnected, my other half came to visit and decided to stay, at first a reluctant guest and then a proud resident who'd grown used to city life like it was a second nature she'd never get bored of. Also, Vince started visiting every weekend. Last weekend, he dragged me and Cosmo to an Occupy Protest. It was really something—people in droves, some camped out in tents, big anti-corporation signs everywhere. I'd felt Vincent's young Vietnam-War-protest energy. I'd also met someone there who told me about opportunities to help the homeless, and I'd decided to start volunteering in a local soup kitchen.

I grabbed a seat by a window and ordered a glass of white wine and three tilapia tacos. I got my work out and started grading papers. Soon after my food arrived, I got a text from Vince. We usually talked every night, but that night he said he wasn't up for talking because he was under the weather. That wasn't really like him, and I was a little worried because the other night when we'd talked, he sounded depressed. Fortunately, Silvia was living there with him.

After moving around the country for a couple of years after graduating art school, she moved back home. She was living in the City with a bunch of roommates, but her job had tanked, and she couldn't afford to stay. I wished my place was bigger, so I could have had her live with me. I gave her a call once I finished eating.

"Hi, Silvie," I said.

"Hey, Mom," she said, sounding glum as a tired donkey forced to carry people and their belongings over great distances. Living in the same house with Frank could do that to a person. I heard her moving around and imagined her in her old bedroom—the same room she shared with Angie for so long. I thought she'd be doing what she could to make it her own, hanging her art up, maybe even taking her clothing out of the orange crates that she always kept them in. Or at least, that was what I hoped.

"How are you, honey?" I tried to make my voice cheerful in hopes of raising her spirits.

"I'm all right, Mom." She didn't sound all right at all, and I wanted to ask her if Frank was getting to her, but I didn't, because I already knew the answer, and I didn't want to remind her of the fact that she was stuck living with her crazy dad. Oh, how I wished my place was bigger.

"You never called me back yesterday. Are you sure everything is all right?"

"No, I got fired."

I didn't know what to say, partly because I thought she deserved better than waiting tables in some little Turkish joint and partly because she couldn't seem to keep a job for longer than a few months. Still, I managed to come up with something, saying she'd find something else, something better. She said she didn't want to talk about it, so I asked her about Vince.

"He seems all right," she said with indifference.

"He sounded down last time I talked to him," I said.

"Mm, he hasn't said anything to me," she said.

We talked for a little, and as she was telling me about how she was going to start looking for a new job the next day, a great idea came to me—something that I was sure would help both her and Vince. I thought of having a little party to commemorate Vince's high school graduation, something simple like a family dinner at a nice restaurant. When I told Silvia my idea, she didn't say anything. Maybe she was slightly horrified by the thought of our not-so-harmonious family being gathered all together for the first time in years.

Still, I continued on about how nice it would be to have this little celebration and how it could be something she and I could do together. I knew I was drafting her into helping me and that she wasn't too excited about it, but I also knew it would be good for her once she got into it. I knew that having such a gathering would force me to see Frank, but a part of me wanted to see him, so I could show him how well I was doing without him. I thought he probably thought I was falling apart and wanting to get back with him.

"All right, I guess I can help you out, Mom," Silvia said reluctantly.

"Thank you, Silvia. I love you so much. You're still meeting me for dinner on Wednesday, right?"

"Sure, I'll see you at the Ethiopian place we met at last time."

It was Wednesday early evening, and I was waiting for Silvia in the Ethiopian restaurant—a narrow, dark place with hard-wood floors and olive-green walls. I wasn't crazy about Ethiopian food because the bread that they served with everything tasted like a soggy tortilla, but Silvia loved it and being a vegetarian restricted her from going just anywhere.

She came through the door dressed in vintage, sixties clothes with a bright, floral skirt and high, white boots. Her hair was straightened, hanging in glossy waves around her face. She smiled and held her head high, in stark contrast to the last time I saw her, with hair falling into her face, casting doomed shadows upon it. I thought that my idea to organize a party for her brother had something to do with her apparent metamorphosis.

We hugged, and as soon as she sat down, the waitress came over to take our order. I let Silvia make the choices for the dishes that we'd be sharing, and she ordered three entrees: one with yellow split peas, one with pumpkin, and one with collard greens. When the waitress left, I told her how good she looked.

"Thanks, Mom," she said. "You too."

I thanked her for the compliment that I felt justified in accepting for the first time in a long time. Since I left Frank and grown used to my new life, I felt like I was aging backwards.

"I have two big news stories," she said, taking a sip of her water.

"Let's hear them," I said.

"You're not going to believe this, but I got Dad to an AA meeting."

"Wow." I tried to sound happy, but my voice spilled over with confusion and the slightest bit of disappointment. My brain scrambled in questions: How come I could never get him to go to an AA meeting? Was he changing or healing since I left him, and if that was the case, was I the thing all along driving him to drink? And the scariest question of all, would he now become something great and either find someone else great or want me back, causing me to reverse all the progress I made since deciding to leave him?

"You don't sound too thrilled," she said, peering into my eyes. I should have been proud of myself for having raised such a perceptive, young woman, but the shame I felt for my true feelings about her getting Frank to a meeting while I couldn't, overpowered any kind of pride that might have come through like a giant wrestling an infant.

"Oh no, honey," I said. "I think that's great, and I'm really happy for him and proud of you." Again, I made my voice as positive as possible, but again, I wasn't fooling her as her skeptic expression indicated, so I decided to be honest. "All right, I'm sorry, Silvie. I am super proud of you, but I'm just disappointed in myself, because I always tried to get him to go to a meeting or therapy or take medication or something, and he never listened to me."

"Well, don't beat yourself up, Mom." She leaned into the table. "It wasn't so easy for me either, but I caught him in one of his good moods and told him that we had to go and that I would drive. He sat there smiling with a drink in his hand and said 'Okay, just wait till I finish this drink.' I think he didn't think I'd take him up on it because going to an AA meeting after a drink just seemed wrong, but I did."

I started laughing, and Silvia joined me with her rich, deep laugh that she inherited from her grandma. She was right. I shouldn't have been beating myself up. I did the best I could, and she was tenacious like her dad—a tenacity that was way beyond me.

"How'd he do there?" I asked.

"He sat there acting like he didn't belong," she said. That figured. I thought of all the times he told me that his drinking wasn't a problem for him, but one for me. Randi's words about him only changing if he wanted to change played in my head.

"That's just like your dad."

The waitress came with several plates of very colorful food, and we started eating. The yellow split peas were delicious and even made me change my opinion about Ethiopian food.

"What's your other big news, Silvie?"

"I got a new job," she said as she dipped bread in the lentil dish.

"That's great! What is it?"

"I'm a manager at a candy store in the mall."

I tried to keep the smile on my face, but I felt it quickly fading. It wasn't because I was expecting something better as she'd been working jobs, like retail and food service, that didn't have anything to do with her art degree and that didn't allow her to use her great talents. It was just that I expected something different. I couldn't see Silvia working at a mall. I thought she hated malls.

"I thought you'd be happy about that." She sat perfectly still with a bland expression as if she was posing for a serious portrait, seemingly without plans to continue eating.

"I am. I just thought you didn't like shopping malls, so I'm a little surprised."

"Well, I don't, but I needed a job, and as long as I'm living with Dad, it was either the mall or the casinos, and I chose the former."

"And you chose well. I just...I don't know."

"Well, it's better than nude modeling in the art schools, you know."

"Yes, I'm sure it is."

"And I need to make money, so I can move out of the house." It pleased me to hear that she was driven to move out.

"What's your plan then, honey, after you move out of your dad's?"

"I'm moving to Portland, Oregon." I wanted to cry at hearing this, not just because it would be so far away, but because she couldn't stop moving. It was hard not to blame myself for her unrelenting restlessness. If I would have left Frank sooner, she wouldn't have had to make all those middle-of-the-night escapes when her father would be on a rampage. I could still see her as a little girl sitting in the backseat of the car as I drove to a nearby hotel for us to stay in overnight. I could see her drawing in her sketchbook in the hotel room, doing whatever she'd needed to do to escape the lousy reality that our household had become. When she got old enough, she started escaping on her own by moving from place to place, like an escaped convict on the run, even though there was no longer anything to run from.

When I stayed silent for too long, she asked me what was wrong. "I'm just afraid that you're chasing rainbows, Silvie. If you go to this next place, it'll be great when you first get there, and then reality will sink in, and you'll have to get a job, and I'm afraid that you know..." She said nothing. She just looked at me prompting me to explain. "I'm afraid that you'll get depressed and come home and have to start all over again and—"

"I know it looks like that Mom because that's what I've been doing, but this place will be different. I just know it will be."

"How will it be different than Tucson or Chicago or Brooklyn or Philadelphia?" These were the last four places she lived in a timeframe of less than two years.

"Tucson was hot as hell. Chicago was crazy cold, and Brooklyn was getting too expensive, and Philadelphia is...well Philadelphia." She sounded like she had this answer prepared for some time now and would have spoken more harshly of Philadelphia if I hadn't just moved there. I bit my tongue; it was too easy for me to tell her what to do. She needed to find her own way.

"I'm sorry, Mom, but I'm doing the best I can." At hearing her speak Vincent's words, I got that lump in my throat that precedes tears and forcibly fought them off.

"I know, honey," I said encouragingly. "And you're doing great. I for one think it's so awesome that you're able to move so easily and so readily on your own and to far-away places too. You're courageous and strong and adaptable and well, just amazing. Just that I feel like you're never going to be happy if you can't stay put in one place long enough to build something. I don't know what that something is. Only you do. I just think you should start thinking about it. I just think that where you live wouldn't matter so much if you liked what you were doing more." She stared blankly at me, and I went on with an idea I thought of for her a little while ago. "What about teaching art in a school? I could really see you doing something like that." She listened intently, and her face began to brighten. After about five minutes, she was back to her old self, and she started eating again like she just got off a week-long fast.

A few days later, I visited Cosmo at a café by his apartment, a sweet little place that was tucked into the side of an old red Victorian house. College students sat outside on black, cast iron tables beneath umbrellas like they were in Europe. The sun moved in and out of the clouds like a restless ball of light, and the spring-time trees that lined the sidewalks went between being dull and shiny. I opened the door to the aroma of coffee brewing and a light, airy room with stained glass windows along the tops of the walls.

Cosmo was sitting in a corner table, staring down at his phone, dressed in his usual hoodie and baseball cap. I walked towards him and gave him a hug, and he asked me what I wanted to drink. I told him any kind of breakfast tea with milk and tried to give him some money, but he didn't take it. He came back with two china cups, one filled with coffee, and the other with my tea and said he'd be right back. He then came back with a couple of currant scones on two small plates.

"Thanks, Cos," I said.

"You like currants right, Mom?"

"Sure do. They look great." They tasted great too—buttery without being overbearingly sweet. Definitely homemade.

"So, how's it going?" I said, taking a sip of my tea.

"It's all right," he said, taking a Vincent-sized bite of his scone. He was hunched over, looking down at the table as if there was little point in looking up, and when he did occasionally look up, he did so with dull, tired eyes that seemed strained to stay open. He'd been working the same job since he dropped out of Penn a few years back—a desk job in the information technology department of some company, and I knew that he found it about as stimulating as Vincent found the cookie factory to be. He never played the guitar anymore or even looked through of his telescope. I knew this because I'd been to his apartment where both objects sat in remote corners, dust-covered and forgotten.

"Have you seen Silvia since she moved back in with Dad?"

"Yeah, she was here visiting a couple days ago, and she got mad at me because I said something about her moving again. She wants to move to Portland now."

"I know. Poor thing, she just can't stay still."

"She's a real piece of work sometimes." He grinned and rolled his eyes. The two of them were close enough to speak this way of each other, and they'd even do so in person. But even with their closeness, they were worlds apart when it came to how they lived their lives with her not being able to stay still and him not being able to get moving. My dream for him was that he'd go back to school to study astronomy, and as much as I tried to live and let live as Mom did with Vincent when he went to work at the bakery, my true feelings seeped out every now and then.

"Do you ever think of going out West?" I said. "Remember you used to talk about going to school in Tucson to study astronomy?"

He made one of those subtle, helpless laughs as if to say such a thing would be as impossible as building a mountain, but I didn't give in to his defeatism. I steadied my eyes on him and said, "Will you just think about it, Cos? Or at least, pick up your telescope and look through it again?" He remained apathetic, so I raised my voice in an attempt to get him to liven up. "Maybe we can all take a trip to the shore and sit out on the beach at night with the telescope. What do you say?"

"That does sound nice," he said, looking up with the energy of a turtle peeking its head out of its shell. I talked about how Silvia could drive, and Vince could come along. "Maybe we could go to Cape May and stay over. It's still off-season, so the rates won't be too terrible." He slowly became more animated as I talked like a cartoon character coming to life.

About a week later, I woke in the middle of the night from a dream about Frank. It wasn't the abusive drunk he'd become, but the sweet Frank of my youth who I fell in love with. For days, the dream stuck in my head and eventually, started to infiltrate my waking life. I was in the middle of teaching a class one day when I got an image of the two of us laughing in bed together. I was taking the bus home from work when I saw him kissing my neck while telling me I was the most beautiful woman in the world. One night, as I ate my lonely dinner on the stool in my apartment, I saw myself having dinner out with him on one of our first dates. I tried forcefully to supplant these loving images with bad ones, but it was no use. I took out my *Frank is a Jerk List,* but it read as meaningless and dry as a car manual, just words on a page.

I wondered how he changed since I left. In the days before my departure, he showed me more love and kindness than he did in the past twenty years of our marriage. He realized then how much he really loved and needed me because he knew he wouldn't have me much longer. I was like someone in his life who died or was nearing death in that he didn't fully appreciate me until that point. He took for granted that I'd always be there until I wasn't. I thought that since we'd been completely apart, his appreciation for me must have grown tremendously, maybe enough for him to quit drinking.

I started to think about the family gathering for Vince with ulterior motives. I thought about what I would wear, down to the shade of lipstick. This other half of me, in an image that was Randi, kept saying stuff like, "He'll only change if he wants to change." But this was easy to counter, because I reasoned that he finally *did* want to change. So, the thoughts and the fighting with myself continued until one night when I had one too many glasses of wine.

I was in my apartment, and with that rational part of myself out of commission, I went to my closet to get a box of photographs so that I could look at pictures of me and him in the old days. I was reaching for the box when Vincent's sketchbook flew down and hit me over the head. It dropped to the floor, and I picked it up, opened it, and started going through the drawings that I hadn't looked at in well over a year—the pictures that gave me sight after I was blind for so long.

I flipped through the pages, and I was back in that day of Vincent's death when I first saw them with my eyes opening to what a rich life my brother lived. Then, I was back in the day that I looked at the sketchbook years later and had tried to imagine the pictures that would be at the end of my life, but the only one I could see was one of some poor, sad, trapped, colorless woman. That feeling I had of wanting to create the great pictures that I knew lived within me resurrected, and I knew, as immediate as a tiger jumping, that I could never walk backwards. I looked up and said thank you to Vincent for hitting me over the head, both literally and figuratively, and waking me up, once again.

Randi must have somehow sensed that I was secretly contemplating getting back with Frank because only a few days after Vincent's sketchbook fell on my head, she introduced me to someone she worked with. We chatted on the phone and through email for a while before making a date. I hadn't been on a date with anyone new since Frank and I went to see *Carrie*. Where did the time go? Four decades of my life flew by in the blink of an eyelash. I could hear Vincent talking about how time was just a construct created so that we could all exist in this crazy world.

The City was a bunch of shades of gray on that day, so I walked through the park to see some green and got a much-needed break from the tall buildings that blocked the sky. In the park, there were artists painting with some selling their work, people reading, dog walkers, and an occasional stroller. I passed by big square patches filled with red tulips, Philadelphia lamp posts, and a square stone pool with a statue of a girl carrying a duck. People sat along the sides of the pool like birds perched on the top of a telephone pole. I got to my favorite statue in the City and stopped, as I always did, to take it in. It was a giant frog sitting on a rock, and it reminded me of the drawings in Vincent's sketchbook because it was so simple and yet so evocative. With its clean simple lines and balls for eyes, I could feel the frog's sense of contentment.

My phone rang, and I looked at it to see it was Randi calling. "Hi, Ran," I said as I continued on my walk. "I'm headed there now." I answered the question

I knew she'd be asking before she had a chance to speak.

"He's so excited to meet you, Don," she said. I could hear things banging around in the background and imagined her putting dishes away in her kitchen.

"Well, I am too." I looked to my right to see an old, gray, stone church with red, wooden doors and scrolling florets. "I'm not nervous either. I guess I'm too old to be getting nervous over dates, huh?!"

"Yeah right," she shouted above the background clamor. "Where are you guys meeting?"

"Some little café right near my place."

"Oh fun." She abruptly added, "Oh, Don, I got to go and get this call. Call me when you're done."

"Will do. Bye."

He was named Daniel, and when Randi told me that he taught philosophy at our old college, I knew I had to meet him even though it did feel too soon to be going on a date. When I got to the café, I got jittery, and as much as I told myself that I was too old to get date nerves, my stomach still fluttered like it used to in softball when that very rare ball would come out to me in right field.

He was sitting at a table off to the side of the cafe. I recognized him from the photo he sent me. He was tall and thin and gray and dressed in jeans and a button-down shirt. As I got closer, I saw his eyes, which were as deep and dark as mine. He held his hand out for me to shake.

"Nice to meet you, Donna," he said, shaking my hand, firm but gentle.

"Nice to meet you, Daniel," I said, shaking his hand while looking up at him.

"Can I get you a cup of coffee?"

"Thanks. That sounds great, or maybe I'll have tea instead. Earl gray with milk."

"Sure thing," he said, going to the counter. I watched him talking to the barista. He was reserved and soft spoken with a nice, calm manner—the kind of person Frank would have called boring, mocking him as "Mr. Personality" or saying something like, "That guy says two words a year" because he wasn't some gregarious, big mouth like himself.

The walls of the place were covered with brightly colored, abstract paintings, and the tables and chairs were tile mosaic—brightly colored with paisley shapes, leaves, and flowers. He returned with two cups of tea, and I felt a little emotional, thinking of having tea with Vincent.

"You're a tea drinker too then?" I said as he sat down.

"I drink both coffee and tea," he said, stirring sugar into his tea. His hands were big and expressive with skinny, long fingers.

"I have coffee in the morning on work days, but I only have tea on the weekends," I said, thinking I should switch to a topic more interesting than my daily caffeine intake. "So, you're a philosophy professor, Randi says, and at my old alma mater."

"Yeah, it's a good gig." He hunched over and laughed gently. "And you're an English literature professor?"

"Well, I never think of myself as a professor because I teach at a community college, but I guess I am." He nodded. "I really love my job because I get to teach what I studied in college and what I love."

"That's great that you love your job," he said.

"I do, but I still have some moments that aren't so great," I said. "Like the other day when one of the students let out one of these really obnoxious sighs, intended to let me know how bored he was. And last week, some girl was texting all during one of my lectures."

"Oh yeah," he said. "I sometimes think that future generations are going to be walking around with giant thumbs from their continuous texting and bumps on their necks from looking down at their phones all the time."

"That would make a great science fiction story. I should write it down."

"Do you write?" he said, "I mean, creatively."

"As a matter of fact, I've been writing poetry lately, just something I started for fun." I loved that he asked me this. "I also play the flute."

"That's great," he said, sipping his tea. "Everybody should have at least one creative outlet. It's our way of playing God."

"That's beautiful. I never thought of it that way. What do you do?" It was so nice to be asking what he did creatively and not referring to what he did for a job.

"I make ceramics, and I do woodworking."

"Oh, that's awesome. My brother, Vincent was into woodworking."

"Was?"

"He passed away years ago." I looked down. "A heart attack."

"I'm so sorry." He looked at me, his eyes filled with empathy.

"Thank you." I sipped my tea and sighed gently. "Actually, it's funny, he was also a philosophy major in college, and I wanted, so badly for him, to become a professor and that's why when Randi told me that you were one, I just knew I had to meet you." I smiled and felt young for a quick second.

"Well, I'm so glad you did." He said. "Did Vincent not want to teach philosophy then?"

"I don't think so. He said he studied philosophy because he wanted to find out what it's all about. Life that is."

"Did he ever find out?" he said, smiling.

"I actually think he already knew." His face lit up, and he prompted me to tell him more. "He didn't care so much about what society said about how you should live your life. He didn't look to the outside for happiness. He lived from the inside. He was a painter, a scholar, and a musician. His paintings never hung in any galleries. His name isn't in any scholarly publications, and he never performed for any audiences. He didn't have to. He knew the real joy and richness that came from learning and creating, and that was enough for him."

"A real Renaissance man."

"Yes, he was a real Renaissance man. I used to tell him that he should play music at Renaissance fairs. He was into all that stuff. It's funny because his name was Vincent Tucci, and he was one of the most Italian-looking people I knew, but he loved to play Irish music." We both laughed, and then he told me that he loved Irish music.

"You do?! So do I, but I haven't heard it in so long—not since Vincent used to play it for me."

"Hey, there're tons of Irish pubs in the City where they have live music. We should go sometime."

"I would love that." We smiled at each other, and I felt a light glowing inside of me, warm and bright.

After my date, I was off to a free chamber music concert at a school in South Philly. The bus arrived soon after I got to the stop, and I hopped on and got a seat by the window. I always got a seat by the window and took turns looking outside and reading whatever book I had. That day it was Melville's *Bartleby the Scrivener* for one of my classes. I became really good at ignoring all the unpleasantries on the bus like the toddler who was screeching in the front and the guy sitting next to me, who didn't know about the existence of deodorant.

We passed by historic row homes with boldly painted wooden doors topped with little archways divided up like half of a pie cut into slices. Quickly, the scenery changed to modern urban, and then back to row homes, and then back to modern urban. Then, the streets widened substantially, and a bunch of worn-down old warehouses took over.

I got a text message from Angie with a photograph of Isabella, her two-year-old daughter and my first grandchild. She was wearing a little pair of overalls with her light brown hair in two ponytails. Her skin glowed like her mom's, and her eyes were big and bright and beautiful like the rest of her. I went to visit them for a long weekend about a month ago. I'd taken the bus into New York, and we'd gone out to some fancy place for dinner, then back to their place in North Jersey. I'd brought my flute, so Angie and I could play music together.

We'd sat in her sleek and modern living room— a large white room with high ceilings, black leather furniture, and a black, baby grand piano, reminiscent of the piano in my childhood home. Doug was on the couch watching Isabella as she ran around making her little toddler sounds. Angie was at the piano banging out the tunes and singing while I played along. We'd played "Scarborough Fair" three times before it came out perfect, and then Doug had made a recording of it and emailed me a copy. I listened to it all the time, and when I did, I could see Vincent nodding his head and smiling so proud of me and his niece who, because of him, played the piano.

I tried to read, but it was tough to focus because my mind was occupied with the date I just went on. He seemed great, but who knew what the future held for me? I used to think I knew. I had it all planned out. What a happy accident that my plans went awry. Suddenly, I felt Vincent sitting beside me. I saw him making that big smile that took over his whole face and knew that the smile was for me, for the gift he gave me had been so well-received.

EPILOGUE

I'm outside in Angie's backyard, sipping rosé wine and eating smoked salmon rillettes from a silver tray. The air is warm and still, and the yard looks like an English garden with precision-trimmed hedges and multicolored flowers interspersed between full green bushes. We're all gathered to celebrate Angie's newest child's third birthday. With dark brown eyes and olive skin, he's the most Italian-looking of all her three children, and his name is Oliver. Crazy, huh?

"He's always smiling," Angie says about Oliver who sits contentedly in my arms. She's wearing a floral sundress that looks like it costs as much as one month's rent for my apartment. (I'm still in my little hobbit hole in the City.) Her dark hair is cut so that it frames her face and with sunglasses on, she looks like Jackie Onassis.

"You have happy kids, Ang," I say as Isabella comes over to us smiling big and bright. She's wearing her hair in a bun and a pale blue dress, and she's with another little girl who looks to be her same age, which is ten years old.

"Mommy," she says, looking up at Angie. "Can we eat some popsicles?"

"There's all this good food, and you want popsicles?" Angie says.

"We'll just get one and share it," Isabella says.

"She drives a tough bargain," I say to Angie, making her laugh.

"All right," Angie says. "Just one." She then turns to me and says, "I think she inherited my sweet tooth."

"And you inherited yours from your dad," I say. Just as I'm speaking of Frank, he comes over to join us. He's dressed in a purple button-down shirt with a red blazer without the slightest recognition of how badly those two colors clash. He never could get it together with his wardrobe. He came with his lady friend, Susan. She's tall with black hair and skin that's almost reptilian from years of sunbathing. I like her and think that she's a perfect match for him—she's tough and sturdy as a tree trunk and doesn't put up with any of his crap.

"Hey, Donna," she says in her deep, loud voice. "Love your haircut." My hair is cut in a pixie, and it feels so liberating.

"Hey, Susan, Frank," I say as I rock Oliver back and forth. I look down at him and say in my baby-talk voice, "Say hi to Grandpa, Oliver."

"Hi, Oliver," Frank says. He smiles and waves to the baby, who starts crying. I can see Frank is really trying, but he never had a way with babies, except for Angie, of course. I hold Oliver closer so that his little head is over my shoulder and calm him by rocking some more.

"Leave it to Frank to make the kid cry," Susan says, patting Frank on the back, hard like a man. She has no kids of her own, which is probably for the best, as she's the most non-maternal woman I know.

"Are you all headed back to the shore?" I say to Susan. Frank sold the house we shared a couple years ago, probably because there were too many memories for him there. He then bought a house in Ventnor that's not far from where Vincent used to live. He does seem to have mellowed out with age. This time I'm sure of it!

"I actually talked him into going to New York for the night," Susan says. "I figure as long as we're up here, we may as well go to New York, right?" Then she whispers in my ear, "Of course, I'm paying for the room." But even when she whispers, she's loud, and

Frank, hearing this says, "Well, I don't know why we get to have such an expensive room."

"Three hundred dollars a night for New York is cheap, Frank," she says to him in a joking, condescending tone.

"What was wrong with that other place? It was a hundred and fifty." Both of his arms are up in the air.

"It was right near JFK," she says, turning to me. "Like I really want to stay near an airport."

"Frank," I say. "Live a little, why don't you. You only go around once."

Frank looks down as if he's been defeated by us, and Angie chimes in to make him feel better, "You'll have a good time, Dad. I have a great restaurant recommendation. I just have to get the name from Doug." Doug is sitting under a weeping willow tree with Francis, named after Frank. She's Angie's second child and is wearing a lavender jumper, her blond hair in braids, and the usual happy and somewhat mischievous look in her big brown eyes, like she's up to something. Angie's headed in Doug's direction when Frank stops her.

"No please," Frank says quickly. "Don't worry about it, honey." Susan and I look at each other as if we both know that he doesn't want the recommendation for fear of the restaurant being too expensive.

"What about you, Donna?" Susan says.

"I'm headed back to Philly with Silvia. She's staying with me in my little place for a few days."

"And then she's staying with me," Frank says right away.

"You better be sure to bring her out to some nice meals," Susan says to him. I'm imagining the lunch special at the local pizza parlor.

A waiter comes around serving red wine and Frank has a glass, and Susan says to him, "That's your fifth glass of wine, Frank. That's it after this." He looks down as though defeated again and walks away to sit with Silvia, Vince, and Cosmo.

"That's amazing how you have such control over him," I say to Susan. "He never listened to me."

"He's something else," she says, and we share a laugh. "And he really mops up on whatever free food and drink there is to be had." We look at him now to see him taking a big bunch of hors d'oeuvres from a tray, and we laugh some more.

The rest of the day is lovely with eating, drinking, playing with the grandchildren, singing happy birthday to Oliver, and taking lots of pictures. After Frank leaves, and Angie settles the kids down, I tell my four children that I want to show them something, and we go into Angie's living room. I sit on the black leather couch, they all gather around me, and I take Vincent's sketchbook out of my bag.

"This belonged to Uncle Vincent. I found it in his apartment right after he died. I've been wanting to share it with you all for a while now." I put it down on the table and place it so we'll all be able to see the pictures.

"You had it all this time, Mom?" Angie says. "How come you never showed us before?"

"Oh, I know it's crazy, but either I was busy, or I'd just forget about it, and when I'd remember, we weren't all together."

"Open it, Mom," Silvia says, her eyes glowing with exhilaration.

"Yeah," Vince says, tucking his shoulder-length hair behind one of his ears.

I open to the first picture of Vincent as a boy reading a Thor comic book with albums and a big Tolkien book to the side of him.

"Oh, how cool!" Cosmo exclaims, his bushy hair puffed out like a raccoon's tail. I look at Silvia to see her staring at the picture as only another true artist would, with captivated and curious eyes, her face luminous.

As I go through the pictures, one by one, I pay attention to their facial expressions. When I get to the one of Vincent studying astronomy, Cosmo's face lights up in amazement.

"I want a copy of this one, Mom!" he says. I tell him I'll make him a copy tomorrow.

When I get to the picture of Vincent protesting, I look at Vince to see his jaw drop, and then he says, "Wow! I didn't know Uncle Vincent was so cool. I mean, I knew he was cool but not that cool. Can I get a copy of that one, Mom?" I tell him sure.

Silvia just sits marveling at each and every picture, and when we get to the one of Vincent with Mom, she says, "Grandma Tucci!" I see her eyes fill up, and she looks like she's about to cry. I tell her that I'll make a copy for her when I make the other two, and she says thanks.

"I love how he captured such expression and feeling just with using regular old markers," Angie says.

"That's what really amazed me too, Ang," I say.

"How come he never went to art school, Mom?" Silvia says. "He was great. He should have."

"He wanted to go, but your grandparents didn't think it was such a great idea at the time and..." I stop talking suddenly, wondering whether I should tell them that I also didn't think it was a good idea at the time.

"And what?" Silvia says.

"At the time, I didn't either. Grandma told me something about him becoming a starving artist, and I just thought that that would have been terrible." I pause again, taking a deep breath, and then the whole story comes out in a Cliff Notes version. "So, I started trying to convince him to listen to our parents and to take himself real seriously and go for all that stuff that I thought was necessary for him to be happy, like a good career and a family, a house, a nice car, the whole nine yards." My voice starts breaking up, and Vince, who's sitting beside me, pats me on the back. "And then, I found this sketchbook, and I realized that he was happy without all those things, and the big irony was that I had all those things, but I was unhappy." Then I quickly say, "Not unhappy with all of you. You're the best things that ever happened to me. What I mean is that I had all the things people say you need to be happy. I had it all, and I was miserable."

"Was that when you decided to leave Dad?" Cosmo says, smirking.

"Yeah," I say. "One day, I tried to imagine what pictures I'd have of myself by the end of my life, and all I could see was this one of this sad, trapped woman who believed that she could find happiness outside of herself and that there was only one way to live. I believed everything people told me I was supposed to believe, and then I learned it was all wrong. Before my big realization, I was always trying to form my life in a certain way. And Vincent's life too. But he refused to conform. He lived free, and that's how he was able to create all these bright and colorful pictures of his life."

"What a great thing to learn, Mom," Angie says. "Makes me think that I should start thinking of my own pictures. Right now, I'm not seeing many either." She laughs.

"You'll get there," Cosmo says to her.

"You all will," I say to them. "You're already making a bunch of great pictures." They're all looking back at me, eyes glimmering, and I can just tell that they're seeing the pictures of their lives so far and possibly imagining the pictures of all their tomorrows. No more words are needed. I say a silent thank you to

Vincent for showing us all the way, and I join my kids in imagining the pictures I'll have by the end of my life.

I can still see the colorless one of myself feeling trapped in my old house with sad eyes and frowning lips. But now, it's only one of many because it's no longer the endpoint of my life. I see one of me sitting in Vincent's old room with him and Carmen as we listen to albums. I see one of Mom and I cooking together in the kitchen of my childhood home. I see one of all of us Tucci kids with Mom and Dad in Canada. There's one of Randi and me in our dorm room, while I'm writing a paper, and she's studying for an economics exam. I see Frank, Vincent and me playing music together with a bottle of Bailey's in the corner of the drawing. I see Frank and me at the Atlantic City Pier. In one picture, I'm in a lecture in grad school, and in another, I'm teaching college students. I see me walking Vince in the stroller, driving Silvia up to college, shopping for wedding gowns with Angie, and sitting outside with a young Cosmo at night as he gazes at stars through his telescope. There are drawings of me playing the flute and writing poetry, and one where I'm sitting with my grandchildren around me, their brand-new eyes gazing out at the world, soon to be creating pictures of their own lives.

The pictures of my future are less clear because they haven't happened yet, but I can see one of me visiting Stonehenge and one of myself writing stories. I would love to write Vincent's story. The world sure needs to hear it. I see a picture of me playing another instrument besides the flute. Maybe a stringed one like all the ones Vincent played. Maybe the mandolin.

THE END

ACKNOWLEDGEMENTS

I'm so grateful for the support, help, and feedback from Alicia Young, Ruth Amernick, Linda Watson, James "Gaddy" Gadbois, Yvonne Gill, Lydia Brown, Tricia Callahan, Jessie Wiley, and my cat, *Cosmo, who sat on my lap as I wrote this book.*

More Books by Grace Mattioli

Olive Branches Don't Grow On Trees (2012): Silvia Greco's journey to unite her feuding family while finding direction in her own life.

Discovery of an Eagle (2014): A spirited road story in which Cosmo Greco acknowledges the fragility of life and learns how to live fully.

The Brightness Index (2016): A colorful collection of short stories that take place in Arizona.